Deadly Derailment at Honeychurch Hall

Hannah Dennison

CONSTABLE

CONSTABLE

First published in Great Britain in 2026 by Constable

Copyright © Hannah Dennison, 2026

1 3 5 7 9 10 8 6 4 2

The moral right of the author has been asserted.

All characters and events in this publication, other than those clearly in the public domain, are fictitious and any resemblance to real persons, living or dead, is purely coincidental.

All rights reserved.
No part of this publication may be reproduced, stored in a retrieval system, or transmitted, in any form, or by any means, without the prior permission in writing of the publisher, nor be otherwise circulated in any form of binding or cover other than that in which it is published and without a similar condition including this condition being imposed on the subsequent purchaser.

A CIP catalogue record for this book
is available from the British Library.

ISBN: 978-1-4087-2068-4

Typeset in Janson Text LT by SX Composing DTP, Rayleigh, Essex
Printed and bound in Great Britain by Clays Ltd, Elcograf S.p.A.

Papers used by Constable are from well-managed forests and
other responsible sources.

Constable
An imprint of
Little, Brown Book Group
Carmelite House
50 Victoria Embankment
London EC4Y 0DZ

The authorised representative
in the EEA is
Hachette Ireland
8 Castlecourt Centre
Dublin 15, D15 XTP3, Ireland
(email: info@hbgi.ie)

An Hachette UK Company
www.hachette.co.uk

www.littlebrown.co.uk

Hannah Dennison was born in Britain and originally moved to Los Angeles to pursue screenwriting. She has been an obituary reporter, antiques dealer, private-jet flight attendant and Hollywood story analyst. After twenty-five years living on the West Coast, Hannah returned to the UK, where she shares her life with Draco, her high-spirited Vizsla (no relation to Draco Malfoy) in the West Country.

Hannah writes the Honeychurch Hall Mysteries and the Vicky Hill Mysteries, both set in Devon, as well as the Island Sisters Mysteries, set on the fictional island of Tregarrick in the Isles of Scilly.

www.hannahdennison.com
www.facebook.com/hannahdennisonbooks
www.instagram.com/hannahdennisonbooks

Also by Hannah Dennison

Murder at Honeychurch Hall
Deadly Desires at Honeychurch Hall
A Killer Ball at Honeychurch Hall
Murderous Mayhem at Honeychurch Hall
Dangerous Deception at Honeychurch Hall
Tidings of Death at Honeychurch Hall
Death of a Diva at Honeychurch Hall
Murder in Miniature at Honeychurch Hall
A Killer Christmas at Honeychurch Hall
Dagger of Death at Honeychurch Hall
A Fatal Feast at Honeychurch Hall

The Island Sisters Mystery series
Death at High Tide
Danger at the Cove

The Vicky Hill Mystery series
Exclusive!
Scoop!
Exposé!
Thieves!
Accused!
Trapped!

*To my lovely friend, Lizzie Sirett –
and to Florian, at last immortalised in print.*

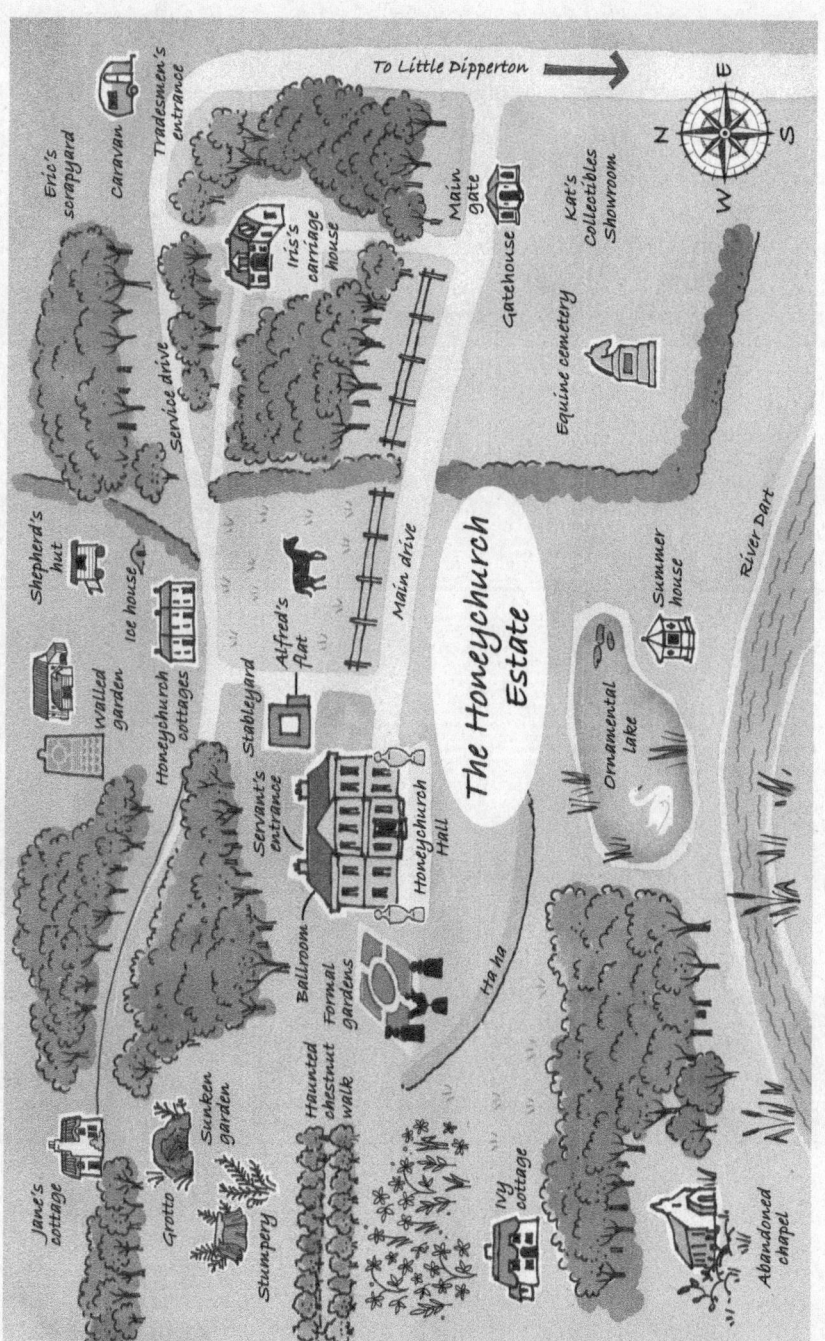

Earl of Grenville
Created by Henry V in 1414, the title of Earl of Grenville has been passed down the male Honeychurch line and still exists today.

8TH EARL OF GRENVILLE
Rupert James
Honeychurch
B: 1800 D: 1880

EARL of GRENVILLE

9TH EARL OF GRENVILLE
Edward Rupert
B: 1835 D: 1899
Fought in Crimean War (1853–6). Decorated soldier, brought back mummified hawk.

Gerald James
B: 1840 D: 1912
Married American heiress—moved to New York. *Died in 1912 in the Arctic. He was a Polar explorer.

Elizabeth Edith
B: 1864 D: 1895
Never married. No children. *Fell from horse and broke her neck out hunting.

10TH EARL OF GRENVILLE
Harold Rupert
B: 1865 D: 1912
Fought in the Boer War (1899–1902). *Died on *Titanic*.

James Rupert
B: 1873 D: 1950
Married showgirl. Ran a Turkish harem in London, fond of Burlesque & ran with Edward VII set.

Cassandra Mary
B: 1872 D: 1965
Never married. Lived in desert with a sheik, drove ambulances in WWI, war office WW2.

11TH EARL OF GRENVILLE
Max James
B: 1887 D: 1916
No children. *Fighter pilot shot down over France in WWI.

12TH EARL OF GRENVILLE
Harold Edward
Edith's father.
B: 1900 D: 1940
*Died in London Blitz with wife.

Gerald Rupert
B: 1903 D: 1932
Lived in New York. Lost everything in the Wall Street Crash and committed suicide.

Rose Anne
B: 1907 D: 1988
Married German POW at end of war, moved to Germany. Huge scandal! Had 3 children.

13TH EARL OF GRENVILLE
Rupert James
B: 1921 D: 1959
Spitfire pilot WW2. *Died in duel with Edith's lover Walter Stark.

Dowager Countess
Edith Rose
B: 1927
Married Cousin Edward in 1959 to keep hold of title.

14TH EARL OF GRENVILLE
Cousin Edward
B: 1931 D: 1990
Returned from New York to inherit the title and marry Edith.

15TH EARL OF GRENVILLE
Rupert Max
B: 1963
1st wife: Kelly Jones
2nd wife: Lavinia Carew

Harold Rupert Max
B: 2005

Cast of Characters

The Honeychurch Hall Estate
Kat Stanford (40), antique dealer and our heroine
Iris Stanford (70), widow and novelist, aka Krystalle Storm
Earl of Grenville, Lord Rupert Honeychurch (50s)
Lady Lavinia (mid 30s), Rupert's second wife
Harry Honeychurch (11), son and heir
The dowager countess, Edith Honeychurch (90s)

Tenants
Eric Pugsley (40s), handyman, operates a scrapyard on the estate
Delia Evans (60s), head of house
June Barker (50s), newcomer

The police
Detective Inspector Greg Mallory (40s), current village police officer
Chief Superintendent Stella Greenleigh (40s), Mallory's ex in more ways than one

Detective Inspector Shawn Cropper (40s), former village police officer
Desk Sergeant Malcolm (50s), cameo
PC Quinn (20s), Stella's driver and assistant

Returning minor characters
David Wynn (40s), international art and antiques investigator, Kat's former fiancé
Ginny Riley (30s), cut-throat journalist
Troy Barnes (40s), cameraman

And introducing (in alphabetical order)
Alison Fisher (early 50s), manager of Sunny Hill Lodge
Bradley and Leigh (20s), Alison's sons
Connie Hicks (50s), daughter of Stan Holden, signalman
Elena (30s), carer at Sunny Hill Lodge
Felicity Oxley (40s), wife of Giles Oxley
Giles Oxley (50s), prototypical model railway builder
Gloria Weaver (50s), interim head of planning and environmental strategy
Ian Hicks (50s), Connie's husband
Keith Fisher (60s), builder
Tony and Donald Draycott (80s), brothers
Marcus Draycott (50s), Tony's son

Chapter One

The turning was so narrow I almost missed it – just a gap in the hedge, no signpost to say where it led. I eased my Golf in, wincing as random brambles scraped the paintwork, slowly making my way along the lane strewn with water-filled potholes. I was used to Devon country lanes with their trademark high hedgebanks, but this was a whole new experience.

The lane was supposed to end at what was left of Honeychurch Halt, a tiny rural railway station where trains once stopped only on request.

As it happened, the Halt had been attracting a good deal of publicity, thanks to *Crime on the Line*, an exhibition by Giles Oxley, the renowned prototypical model railway builder, at Dartmouth Antique Emporium. Among his five dioramas – each depicting a notorious crime – Honeychurch Halt featured in a re-creation of a botched heist in 1974.

So when I received a text – peppered with capital letters – from a Connie Hicks from Shropshire, asking me to meet her at Railway Cottage to value her father's 'RARE model railway collection' from his days working on the old line, I was naturally intrigued, and cautiously optimistic.

I say 'cautiously' because between *Antiques Roadshow*, *Fakes & Treasures* – which I still missed hosting – *Bargain Hunt* and *Cash in the Attic*, it often felt like the whole country fancied itself an expert in what was more often than not just bric-a-brac.

But you never know!

Railway Cottage appeared suddenly, crouched next to a stone viaduct. It was two-up, two-down, built in the late-Victorian style – plain red brick with a steep slate roof, narrow chimney stacks and tall sash windows. It looked half derelict. A builder's hoarding lined the exterior, and a silver Kia was parked alongside.

I continued on to the Halt, where, just moments later, the lane widened into a muddy turning space.

So this was it.

Curious, I got out, struck by the pungent metallic smell of wet iron and a faint tang of soot.

Only the vague outline of the crumbling brick foundation of the platform remained. Corroded signal posts marked the points along the sunken track bed, now choked with grass and weeds. The signal box, fractured water tower and coal stack were somehow still standing. Across the way, half hidden in overgrown trees, was the carcass of a camping coach – a relic of the days when old rolling stock was converted into static holiday accommodation. A small lamp hut stood nearby, surprisingly intact. Beyond it, the track bed forked and sank into a mossy cutting, then rose onto an embankment and disappeared into a wooded glade.

At the edge of the site, a second run of hoarding fenced off the land. A planning notice, dated only ten days ago, announced that Bradleigh & Sons had applied for a 'change of use to commercial development'.

Yet another piece of British heritage gone. Why was I even surprised? Connie's father had only just died, and already the developer had snapped up the cottage and land.

I headed back to my car, turned around and parked nose-to-nose with the silver Kia.

'Don't park there,' a cane-wielding woman bellowed from the doorway. 'You've blocked me in!'

I hadn't. There was plenty of room for her to get out, but I didn't argue.

Bracing myself for what lay ahead, I plastered on a smile and went to meet her.

'Mrs Hicks?' I offered my hand. 'Kat Stanford.'

She eyed me with suspicion. 'What were you doing up at the Halt? Are you from the council? Because if it's about that planning notice, it's nothing to do with me. They couldn't wait, could they? Lifetime tenancy. Once Dad was out, they were in. Vultures.'

I hoped I looked sympathetic. 'We spoke on the phone – well, texted really,' I said. 'I'm here about your father's model railway collection. Remember?'

'Oh. Right.' She let out a faint wheeze. 'Sorry. I'm overdue for my jab. I suppose you'd better come in.'

She stepped aside to let me by, leaning heavily on her cane. She had the brassy locks of bottle dye and wore pink leggings and a matching oversized sweatshirt. I guessed she was younger than she looked – maybe fifties – but her health was poor. There was a greyish cast to her skin, and her breath was shallow.

'Sorry about the state of the place,' she muttered. 'Never knew he lived like this.'

The house was – quite frankly – uninhabitable. It looked like it had been ransacked.

Open boxes lay scattered on the thin carpet, worn down to the boards. Bulging black bin bags were shoved against the skirting. A sofa sagged under broken springs, its cushions tossed onto the floor. A bookcase and a cracked glass-fronted display cupboard stood empty. The only form of heating came from a three-bar electric fire. A handful of cheap prints clung to the walls, and propped on the mantelpiece stood a single framed certificate, oddly formal against the rest of the room.

In the corner, a nylon sleeping bag lay rolled next to a pillow edged with lace ruffles – presumably Connie was sleeping here. I couldn't think of anything drearier.

'I don't know when the builders are pulling the place down,' she said. 'I've only got this weekend to clear everything out. Hubby's coming down by train tomorrow. With my leg, I can't get up to the attic.' She nodded to a dark room beyond. 'Stuff's in the kitchen.'

The kitchen was no better. A gas stove blackened with grease, a rusting fridge, and a sweep of filth pushed into the corner with a broom. On the quarry-tiled floor sat a line of neat boxes, filled to the brim with empty whisky bottles. The sight was depressing.

Connie saw my face. 'Yeah, I know. Dad always loved his drink. Pity you can't get money back on bottles these days – I'd make a fortune. Still, maybe it's not too late.' She cracked a smile. 'Before she died, Mum told me that Dad had left me one – a fortune, that is.'

'Stranger things have happened,' I said lightly.

'Yeah, isn't that the truth. He owes me for a rotten childhood.'

I wasn't sure what to say to that. 'You must miss him all the same.'

Connie gave a wry smile. 'Oh, he's not dead yet.'

'Ah . . .'

'But he's as good as,' she said with a sniff. 'Dementia. Alzheimer's. What's the difference?'

'I'm sorry.'

'Don't be,' Connie said. 'He was a miserable man. Mum and I got away the moment we could.'

'Where is he now?'

'Sunny Hill Lodge,' she said with a sudden burst of disbelief. 'Yeah, I know. Fancy, right?'

My jaw had dropped. 'Lucky man!' Sunny Hill Lodge had to be one of the most expensive residential nursing homes in Devon.

'Got the call from social services two weeks ago now. Someone found him wandering on the main road, stark naked. Turned out she ran Sunny Hill Lodge and she managed to get him in – some fund for retired workers on the railway is footing the bill.' She thought for a moment. 'Although following Dad's injury, he hadn't worked for donkey's years. But I'm not complaining. Nice woman, she was.'

I knew Margery Rooke, the manager of Sunny Hill Lodge, from the odd fundraiser and doing a valuation or two. It was just the sort of thing she would do.

I took in the squalid surroundings and felt a pang of sadness at the fate of so many elderly people living alone. Connie's father would definitely have a better life where he was now.

'Did he get many visitors?'

She thrust out her chin, defensive. 'I called him at Christmas and on his birthday. Why?'

'I just wondered if you had siblings nearby.'

'Brother died a few years back,' Connie said flatly. 'Mum when I was ten. My aunt brought us up. After Dad got shot, he was never the same. Then the railway closed and he took to drink.'

'Wait – got shot?' I repeated.

'Why else do you think I got in touch?' Connie seemed incredulous. 'The hold-up! The robbery! Dad was the signalman who got his kneecaps shattered. Bastards!'

'That was your father?' I was stunned.

'Got a certificate for it, too. It's on the mantelpiece. Framed, it is. You can see for yourself.' She nodded to the sitting room. Clearly I was to go and get it for her.

So I did.

'Go on,' she said. 'Read it.'

It was a commendation issued by the South Devon and West Moorland Railway.

> Presented to Stan Holden, signalman, in grateful recognition of his courage and steadfastness of duty during the incident of 13 October 1974, by which further loss was prevented and the interests of the railway were upheld at great personal risk.

'A hero he was,' Connie said, adding bitterly, 'Pity he was never a hero to me. Course, I was just four at the time. But Mum remembered it well.'

I stood holding the certificate as a silence stretched between us.

'Worth selling, d'you reckon?' Connie asked.

'Possibly,' I said carefully.

'My hubby reckons that with people going to see the exhibition, someone'd pay good money for Dad's things. Said someone once paid fifteen grand for Winston Churchill's false teeth.'

I gave a surprised little laugh.

'Though Dad didn't have false teeth. Unless he's wearing them. I wouldn't know.'

'Are you planning on going to the exhibition?'

'No. I hate crowds. That's why I thought you could sell the stuff on my behalf.'

'Sorry. The exhibition is more of a historical display – not really a place for buying and selling.'

'That's what you think.' Connie gave a secretive little smile. 'Dad always told Mum he had something valuable. He was adamant. I reckon it's his precious train set – or the diamonds.'

'Ah, *those*.' I smiled.

'Yeah,' Connie agreed. 'Mum swore that's what the thieves were really after.'

'It's my understanding nothing was ever stolen. That's what made it so tragic. Two men dead – and for what? Your father was a hero.'

'You think?' Her voice was laced with sarcasm. 'Maybe that was the official version, but not according to Mum – and she should know.'

'Why? Was she there when it happened?'

'No, we were up north visiting family.'

I was about to ask why her mother would know in that case, but decided against it. I'd heard the rumour about the diamonds. Everyone had. But since I'd been coordinating the exhibition with Oxley, I knew for a fact it was just that – a rumour, an urban legend.

'Do you want to show me what you have?'

Otherwise I'd be here all day.

'In the pantry. Under the pink bedspread.'

I set the certificate on the counter.

The pantry was lined with shelves of tins I didn't even want to touch, let alone check for expiry dates. There were Oxo cubes in faded cardboard, a tin of Golden Syrup with the lion logo almost rubbed away, and a stack of rusting biscuit tins with brands I vaguely remembered from childhood that had been phased out years ago. I bent to shift the grubby candlewick bedspread and my heart sank.

What I saw was a muddle of scratched and faded engines, mismatched carriages, rusting and broken pieces of track and random figurines. One box held an assortment of photographs and several hardback books, minus their dust jackets. Another a rusted hand signal lantern, a dented guard's van lamp, and a couple of metal lever plates with barely a trace of lettering left.

'Hubby says, "Sell what you can, Connie." I mean, that certificate thing must be worth a bomb. As you said, Dad was a hero.'

'I honestly can't give you a valuation just like that,' I said. 'I need proper light. I need to sort through everything. Do you know if there's an actual set in here?'

Connie shrugged.

'Do you have any of the original boxes?'

She shrugged again. 'Maybe they're in the attic.'

'It increases the value if you have them. What about a track plan showing the layout?'

'You must be joking.' She clutched the door jamb. Her face crumpled, and for an awful moment I thought she might cry. 'It's sad. That's what it is. A whole life reduced to just boxes of nothing.'

Embarrassed, I was relieved to find something of value — and not only that, something perfect for Harry, the future heir to Honeychurch Hall and, though I'd never tell him, one of my favourite people. He'd just broken up for the Easter holidays and turned eleven today. Most boys might expect footballs or gadgets, but with Harry's new obsession with the railways, I knew this old book would be treasured.

It was *The Working and Management of an English Railway*, written by George Findlay in 1891, with a gold steam train etched on the faded red boards. I flicked through the pages, crammed with neat drawings and black-and-white photos of steam engines as well as chapters bearing intriguing titles such as 'Shunting', 'The Working of Goods Stations', 'Signals and Interlocking', and 'Railways as a Means of Defence'. Harry would absolutely love it.

'I can buy this from you right now,' I said. 'How about twenty-five pounds?'

'Forty,' she said.

I put the book back in the box.

'OK. Thirty,' she said quickly. 'I'm on disability. Hubby hasn't worked for—'

'Thirty. Final offer.' I turned away, annoyed with myself. The book wasn't even worth twenty pounds. Still, I pulled out the cash and handed it over.

Connie nodded to the boxes. 'What about those? I'm telling you, you won't be sorry. If you can sell them for me, I'll make sure you get a good commission.'

I was about to refuse when her eyes met mine. 'Please,' she whispered. 'It would mean a lot. And yeah, I'm sorry if I get snappy.' She pulled up her sleeve to reveal a medical alert bracelet engraved with *Type 1 Diabetes – Insulin Dependent*. 'Plays havoc with my moods.'

I caved in. 'I think the best I can do is take them back to my showroom for a proper look. When do you head home?'

'Sunday. I'm back at work Monday.'

Back at work? She'd told me she was on disability. I let it go.

I picked up my tote. 'I'll need you to sign a receipt of transfer . . . Oh, wait.' I cursed inwardly. This was turning into a waste of time. 'Since these belong to your father, he'll have to sign it.'

Her jaw dropped. 'You're kidding! He wouldn't have a clue what he'd be signing!'

'Sorry.' I didn't have a good feeling about Connie. Part of me even wondered if she was who she claimed – there were enough horror stories about people scamming the elderly.

'Unless you can prove you've got power of attorney?'

'Oh, for Pete's sake!'

'You have my phone number,' I said. 'Get your father to sign it and call me.'

'No, wait!' Connie cried. 'We'll go and see him now.'

I suppressed a sigh. Sunny Hill Lodge *was* on my way home.

'I'm not coming back for the boxes,' I said bluntly. 'Let's load them into your car, and if we get your father's signature, we'll transfer them to mine.'

Needless to say, it was left to me to heft them out to the drive.

'I'll meet you there,' I said.

Chapter Two

I hadn't been to Sunny Hill Lodge for months. Once, it had been a beautiful Regency villa with tall sash windows, slender iron pillars and a delicate cast-iron veranda that wrapped around the front. Now a residential nursing home, it was – if you had the money – a warm, gentle place to spend your final years.

Turning through the imposing gates, I was startled by how much it had changed. To be fair, nowhere looks its best in late March. There were plenty of daffodils and primroses peeking through the long grass, but the verges hadn't been mown, and the once-crisp topiaries flanking the front door had lost their shapes.

I parked my car on the gravel forecourt. Connie had already said there was no reason for me to go in with her.

While I waited, I checked my phone – happy to see that Mallory had found a moment to text and tell me he missed me. Over the last ten days, we'd hardly seen each other. He'd been seconded to his old patch in Plymouth to work a cold case, and was being unusually secretive about it.

A knock on my window broke into my thoughts. I recognised the woman gesturing for me to lower it. I'd seen her quite a few times at the Emporium, hovering around Oxley's dioramas, taking photos on her phone.

In her early fifties, she wore distinctive oversized glasses bearing the Chanel logo, their rims accented with small diamonds. Her shoulder-length hair – stiff and unforgiving – was marked by blonde highlights several shades too bright. There was plenty of gold jewellery on show, and usually she carried a Birkin but this afternoon she wasn't even wearing a coat.

'Can I help you?' She shivered in her thin jersey dress in the cold wind.

'I'm waiting for someone,' I said. 'Her father's a resident – Stan Holden.'

'Ah.' She nodded. 'That'll be Connie Hicks.'

'Yes. That's right.'

'Do come inside where it's warm.'

'She'll be back in a moment, but I appreciate it.'

Recognition flickered across her face. 'You're Kat Stanford,' she exclaimed. 'I used to watch your show, but . . . Of course – the Emporium!' She slipped her hand through the open window to shake mine. I caught a glimpse of a Rolex on her wrist. 'Mrs Fisher. But do call me Alison. I'm the new manager here.'

I was both surprised and dismayed. 'Margery Rooke has left?'

Alison looked equally taken aback. 'You know Margery?'

'Not personally,' I said. 'In a business capacity.'

'We hoped she would have stayed on, but she decided to retire instead, which was such a shame. We took over just before Christmas . . . Oh!' She broke off as a black hearse sped towards us – and I mean *sped*. There was nothing dignified about its arrival. The horn gave a sharp beep, the driver – a young man sporting a handlebar moustache – waved, and the vehicle tore around the corner, flinging up gravel before vanishing from sight.

Alison seemed flustered, hastily adding, 'New company. I don't know what's happened to the world. No respect. The undertakers are getting younger . . .'

'Like policemen,' I offered, trying to ease her distress. 'If you want a recommendation, Hollis & Webb are very good. They've been around for ever.'

'Thank you, dear.'

'Got it!' Connie crowed as she joined us, waving the transfer receipt. 'Don't think Dad knew what he was signing, but oh well.'

'Hello, Mrs Hicks. I'm Alison Fisher,' Alison said warmly. 'We spoke on the phone.'

Connie blinked. 'Oh. So *you're* the lady who found him.'

'Poor man. I'm happy to say he's settling in very well.' Alison's gaze flicked to the paper in Connie's hand. 'I heard you mention signing?'

Connie stiffened. 'Did I?'

'You know,' Alison said pleasantly, 'if you ever need legal paperwork witnessed or certified, we can handle it right here. We like to make things easy for our residents and their families.'

'Thanks, but we're good,' said Connie. She turned to me. 'Let's shift the boxes, Kat.'

Alison, almost blue with cold, offered to help, but Connie waved her away. 'Kat's got it.'

'I've got it,' I muttered, and started loading the boxes into the back of my car.

'Goodness,' Alison exclaimed. 'What have we here? Are these Stan's? Perhaps he'd like them in his room.'

'No, he wouldn't,' Connie shot back. 'There's enough of his junk to clear out at the house as it is – I don't fancy having to come here and sort through more of it after he's gone.'

Alison blinked. 'Of course. Well, if there's anything I can—'

'There isn't,' Connie snapped, but then she seemed to soften. 'You've been kind enough already.'

With a polite nod, Alison headed back to the building.

'I don't trust her,' Connie said suddenly. 'You know what these places are like. You read about it all the time – staff nicking stuff from rooms and the like. If she got wind of what's in those boxes . . .' She gave a knowing nod before adding, almost as an afterthought, 'Did you see that Rolex she was wearing?'

She wasn't expecting a reply, so I didn't give one. 'Let me take a quick look at the transfer receipt before you go.'

Other than Stan Holden's signature – looking surprisingly legible – the receipt covered all the bases.

> I, Kat Stanford, hereby acknowledge receipt of three assorted boxes of vintage toy trains and miscellaneous items belonging to Stan Holden for the sole purpose of valuation. I confirm that these items will remain the property of Stan Holden until they are returned. No sale, transfer or other disposition of these items will occur without prior written consent.

We parted ways, with me promising to call her in the morning. At the end of the drive, she turned right, while I turned left and headed for home.

I paused to let a striking Mercedes G-Wagon turn in – matt black, blackout emblems, deep-dish rims, no number plates. Harry would have called it 'murdered out'. As it rolled slowly past, I caught a glimpse of the driver – late fifties, handsome in a rugged way, with charcoal hair streaked with silver. Beside him sat a much older man, gaunt, with receding iron-grey hair.

Margery had always managed to give Sunny Hill Lodge an elegant, old-world charm. Now, under Alison, it seemed to be attracting a very different sort of clientele.

Alison and her bling were soon forgotten when I passed through the towering granite pillars of Honeychurch Hall, each topped with a hawk, wings outstretched. I loved living on the estate.

I used one of the eighteenth-century gatehouses as a showroom and appointment venue for my business, Kat's Collectibles and Valuation Services, and the other as a storeroom for my stock. My home, Jane's Cottage, sat on a hill at the far edge of the property.

Unlike my mother, who owned the Carriage House outright, I rented all three buildings from the ailing dowager countess. While she was alive, I felt secure. But Rupert, the 15th and current earl, had made it increasingly clear that my future here was far from certain. I'd never truly warmed to him – and the more I saw of him, the less I wanted to.

Because of the remote location, I rarely got foot traffic unless there was an event at the Hall – an open garden, the annual English Civil War re-enactment or something similar.

The following weekend was Easter, and the Museum Room would be open, with a display on the eccentric Arctic explorer Gerald Honeychurch, brother of the 9th earl, alongside the grand launch of the Polar Tearoom. Just another of Delia Evans's tireless fundraising schemes to make Honeychurch Hall a popular stop on the country house map.

My mother's on-again-off-again best friend – and self-appointed head of house – had certainly turned the Honeychurch fortunes around. But she was like Marmite: people either loved her or couldn't stand her. I hovered somewhere in between.

I parked outside the showroom and disabled the burglar alarm, then ferried the boxes inside before making a quick cup of tea. After that, I took Findlay's railway management book out of my tote and wrapped it in tissue paper, usually reserved for shipping dolls or bears. I'd already bought

Harry a copy of *STEAMIMAGES9: The Year of the Tornado* by renowned photographer Peter Slater for his birthday – we were all due at the Hall at four for cake – but I thought he'd enjoy this little extra surprise.

Setting my tea down on the floor, I dropped to my knees, grabbed a pen and paper, and turned my attention to the first box.

My instincts had been right – not exactly junk, but close enough.

There was a handful of battered engines and carriages – mostly from the 1950s and 60s – with missing parts, chipped paint and wheels that didn't quite sit straight. A couple of tin wagons, various sections of track, crumbling model trees, and a tunnel made of warped cardboard. Dutifully I made a detailed list, thinking that since I would be paid a percentage of the valued objects, it wasn't exactly going to make me rich. Or even buy me lunch. Still, an agreement was an agreement.

I picked through the contents of the remaining boxes. The lantern, lamps and levers belonged on a scrap heap, but several of the framed photographs might hold some historical value for a railway enthusiast – especially now that the Halt was destined to become a business park.

I took out my loupe. Frankly, the figures could be anyone. The man in uniform was presumably Connie's father, but the others? Who knew, or cared!

Then my heart gave a jolt of excitement. Tucked at the bottom of the box was a vintage travel poster – linen-backed, the colours still sharp. Bold lettering announced

Camping Coach Holidays at Honeychurch Halt, with a stylised steam locomotive pulling a single carriage nestled beside a wild-flower-dotted platform. Dartmoor rose soft and blue in the distance. I grabbed my loupe again to check the signature: Tom Purvis, one of the great commercial poster artists from the Golden Age of Steam. A real find. Probably worth around £800, maybe more to the right collector. At least I'd have some good news for Connie.

The short peep of a car horn sounded outside – my mother. It was almost four, time to head to the Hall for Harry's birthday tea. We'd agreed to go together. I'd have to finish this later.

Mum had been low for months, avoiding people and rarely leaving the house, but she would never dream of disappointing Harry. I'd been trying to get her alone for weeks, yet she always claimed she was either buried in the latest *Star-Crossed Lovers* draft or noodling with a proposal for a new series that she *must* sell to keep the bills paid. The events of last autumn – the devastating betrayal by a man she'd trusted for decades – had aged her, and her usual 'get on with it' mentality had taken a hard knock.

I'd watched her cheerful energy ebb away under the weight of what she owed HMRC. The money embezzled in her name had wiped out her savings, and she'd only narrowly avoided prison, spared because she was the victim rather than the perpetrator. Her publisher's contract already tied her to three books a year, but she was desperate to write more, hoping a new series might keep her afloat. Unfortunately, every proposal had been rejected, and she'd slipped into a kind of inertia that frightened me more than I dared admit. She was even falling behind on her contracted books, and had stopped keeping to her daily schedule in her writing house – the little sanctuary that she loved even when she wasn't putting words on the page.

I collected Harry's gifts, locked up and went outside, plastering on a bright smile and remembering not to sound too cheerful, or come out with things like 'at least you've been published' or 'at least you didn't go to jail'. Mum called it 'silver-linining', and it drove her nuts.

I slid into the front seat of her Mini, relieved to see she'd made an effort – a dark green kilt, cream polo neck under a black padded gilet, and a dash of make-up.

'You look nice, Mum. Is the kilt new?'

'You've seen it before,' came the short reply. 'Did you know Delia's going to be on *West Country Round-Up* tonight – and she won't let anyone forget it.'

'What for?'

'What do you think?' Mum said wearily. 'Next weekend's Easter affair. I don't know how she manages to get all this free publicity. Lucky she does, as his lordship certainly can't afford any.'

'Oh well,' was all I said. 'What did you buy Harry for his birthday?'

'A book on knots.'

'Knots? Ah. I'm afraid he's into trains now.'

'Oh, for heaven's sake,' Mum groaned. 'I thought he wanted to sail single-handed around the world. Isn't he still with the Sea Scouts?'

'Don't worry about it,' I said quickly. 'I have two books for him on trains. You can give him one of those if you like. And it's already wrapped!'

'I just can't keep up,' she grumbled.

Nor could I. When I'd first met Harry, he was obsessed with Biggles, the fictional First World War fighter pilot. He even dressed like his hero, in goggles and a white scarf, and collected everything he could on him. Since then, he'd wanted to be an astronaut, captain a pirate ship, and sail around the world. Trains seemed to be the latest craze.

'I suppose I could keep the book on knots,' Mum said grimly. 'Just in case I want to hang myself.'

'Don't talk like that,' I said sharply. 'You should never joke about a thing like that.'

'I got another rejection this morning. I mean, how can I pay back HMRC if I don't have any income?'

'At least you're still getting royalties. I mean . . .' Too late. The two dreaded words had slipped out. 'I wonder if the sun will come out today.'

Mum scowled. 'Nice try.'

We didn't speak again until the soaring chimneys of the Palladian-fronted Hall rose into view. Where the drive divided, one way leading to the stable block and its neat sand arena, Mum took the left fork to the main entrance, where Rupert's new Range Rover – an Autobiography model in gunmetal grey – and a battered Fiat 500 bearing a decal of Earth with the slogan *There Is No Planet B* were parked in the turning circle. The fountain in the centre, with its rearing bronze horses, seemed more exuberant than usual, its high arcs of water reaching almost Bellagio-like heights.

The grounds looked immaculate under Delia's formidable management. Her rotating crew of day gardeners and 'day dailies', as she called them, was nothing like the army of staff the Hall had had in its heyday, but it was impressive enough. I still couldn't help wondering who was footing the bill. Delia always behaved as if she ran the show single-handed, but there was a new *je ne sais quoi* to things lately that made me suspect Rupert had come into some money.

A large skip sat beside the drive, brimming with rubble and broken concrete. Next to that was a Ford Transit flatbed truck with the faint outline of a logo – *Bradleigh & Sons*. It was strewn with planks, cement bags and coils of electrical wire, all secured with fraying ropes. On the dashboard was a sea of food wrappers and empty plastic bottles. The wing mirror was cracked and the rear bumper had half fallen off. A battered toy gorilla rode the front bumper.

Gesturing to the skip, I said, 'Wow. The builders are still here! The exhibition is next weekend. That's cutting it a bit fine.'

Mum parked. 'Her ladyship was adamant that the general public shouldn't traipse through the main house. Why else do you think they've put in a new entrance?'

'A new entrance?' I was genuinely surprised. 'Where?'

She pointed to a flagstone path that wound around the west wing. 'Through the Polar Tearoom and gift shop—'

'Gift shop!' I blurted out. 'Edith agreed to that?'

Mum shrugged. 'What do I know?'

We were halfway up the front steps when the door flew open and a woman in her early fifties – red-framed glasses, frizzy grey hair, long patchwork coat – brushed roughly past Mum.

Delia followed, wearing a look I could only describe as gloating. She was sporting a new chin-length wig in a gorgeous chocolate brown – she'd lost her hair to alopecia years ago, but never seemed self-conscious, wearing her wigs with the same brisk confidence she brought to everything else. Like my mother, she was a loyal Marks & Spencer fan, and today wore a neat navy dress with a Peter Pan collar.

The woman floored her little Fiat, spraying gravel as she sped away.

'You'll never guess what's happened,' Delia said with glee.

My mother bristled – she hated it when Delia had the upper hand. 'Go on. The suspense is killing us,' she said drily. 'Presumably it's to do with that very rude woman who nearly knocked me over.'

'Gloria Weaver. She's the interim head of planning and environmental strategy.'

'I know,' Mum sniffed, though I was quite sure she didn't.

Delia paused, positively bursting to deliver her news. 'The doors have got to come out. The bifolds!'

'What bifolds?' Mum looked utterly baffled, and I was none the wiser.

'The entrance to the Polar Tearoom.' Delia rolled her eyes. 'I warned his lordship, I said to him, you need to have planning permission. You can't just knock down walls willy-nilly.'

'I thought it was your idea,' Mum declared.

Delia turned pink. 'I only suggested it. Frankly, I didn't think he'd agree, but he made a deal with the builder.' She lowered her voice to a whisper. 'He came into some money. Probably won big on the Premium Bonds.'

'His sort don't do Premium Bonds,' Mum said with scorn.

'Wait a moment,' I said. 'I thought Giles Oxley was the planning officer.'

'Where have you both been?' Delia laughed. 'Oxley's been suspended pending an investigation into bribery and corruption. Pushing stuff through when he shouldn't have.'

'When did you find out?' I asked.

'About half an hour ago.'

Awkward didn't begin to cover it. Whatever this was had clearly been simmering under the surface for a while, and yet I struggled to take it in. Giles Oxley was so mild-mannered, almost shy. It was impossible to picture him at the heart of a scandal. Of course, I only knew him as a railway enthusiast, not in his day job as a planning officer.

'Oh,' said Mum. 'So not common knowledge *yet*.'

'I'm telling you – heads are going to roll. Ms Weaver is on the warpath. You don't want to mess with an environmentalist. They're a different breed.'

'Speaking of rolling,' Mum cut in, 'we need to get a move along or we'll be late for birthday cake.'

Delia spun around and set off, heels click-clacking over the black and white marble floor, a flash of red sole with each step. She moved with exaggerated poise, rather like a horse doing passage in dressage. Walking in high heels had never come naturally to her, and it showed.

'Wait – are those new shoes?' Mum said suddenly.

Delia threw her a smug glance. 'Yes.'

'Wait,' Mum said again. 'Are they . . . Louboutins?'

Delia just gave an airy wave and continued on her way.

Mum turned to me, incredulous. 'Louboutins! They must have cost a bomb.' She snorted and raised her voice. 'Someone's got money to burn.'

'If you must know, I have two pairs,' Delia tossed back. 'I'd let you borrow one, but your feet are so much wider than mine. I don't want them stretched.'

Mum baulked at the insult. Then, with mock sympathy, she said, 'Such a shame about the bifolds. I suppose you'll have to cancel the event. You'll never be ready now. I'm sure his lordship must be livid.'

'Cancel?' Delia stopped, spun around and laughed. 'Of course we can't cancel. What an extraordinary thing to say. I'm on *West Country Round-Up* tonight. Tickets have been sold, two hundred commemorative copies of *Tales from the Tundra: Adventures of an Arctic Explorer* have been printed, sponsors are in place – oh, and I meant to tell you, Iris, that we're going with Salcombe Gin. They're paying a fortune for product placement.'

I waited for Mum's reaction. She'd made a lot of her own gin specifically for this occasion.

'I'm sure Salcombe will be thrilled,' she muttered, before adding with a frown, 'But this book? I suppose writing is just another of your many talents.'

Delia laughed again. 'Who has time for writing? No, I just borrowed a few photos of Gerald from the Museum Room, sent them off to one of those new online publishing services – I forget the name – and they did the rest. Layout, captions, everything. Then I put the photos straight back.'

'So what was the point?' Mum demanded. 'If they were already in the Museum Room.'

Delia rolled her eyes. 'Because people will *pay* for the book, Iris, and that'll cover the cost of printing and make a nice little profit too.'

'It still sounds like a waste of money to me,' Mum retorted. 'And if the tearoom isn't finished, just be careful you don't end up with egg on your face.'

'Oh well, if I do, I do.' Delia shrugged. '*C'est la vie.*'

'*C'est la vie?*' Mum's eyebrows shot up. 'Are you feeling all right?'

I was amused. It was a valid comment. In normal circumstances, Delia would've had a full-blown crisis if she couldn't find her scalloped paper doilies.

Delia gave a secretive smile. 'Very much so. Oh yes. I couldn't be better.' She turned pink. 'I've been bursting to tell you, but . . .' She nodded at me and mouthed, 'Not in front of the children,' before adding brightly, 'Come, we mustn't be late for June's cake.'

I looked at Mum. 'Who is June?'

'One of Delia's day dailies,' said Mum.

'Not exactly, Iris.' Delia paused, in that annoying way she had, before blurting out, 'I'm training my replacement.'

Chapter Three

'Your replacement?' Mum's voice shot up an octave. 'You're leaving? But that's absurd! You've turned the Hall around – you love it here! You've worked miracles! Why on earth would you walk away now?'

'You'll be in excellent hands with June,' Delia said smoothly.

'I don't want June, whoever she is,' Mum cried. 'Kat, talk some sense into her.'

'Later, later,' Delia cut in airily. 'Right now, we're expected in the morning room. Yes, I know it's the afternoon. Her ladyship's orders.'

The morning room was unmistakably the dowager countess's domain. It was cluttered with silver-framed photographs of dogs and horses and littered with copies of *Horse & Hound*, *The Field* and *Sporting Life*. A side saddle straddled a love seat and a dismantled bridle lay in pieces across a coffee table next to an assortment of prescription bottles.

I was instantly struck by just how frail Edith had become. No one knew her exact age, or if they did it was a family secret, but I guessed she had to be the other side of ninety now. In normal circumstances she lived in her riding habit – in fact, she wore it like a uniform. But today she was seated in a wingback chair, swathed in a moth-eaten Newmarket horse blanket with a tartan nightdress peeking at her throat. Mr Chips, her faithful Jack Russell, lay at her feet.

A log fire roared in the grate. The room was stifling. The smell of horse, wet dog and bits of oiled tack was overpowering, but no one dared suggest opening a window.

Mum and I exchanged looks of concern. Why hadn't Delia warned us? Edith started to cough. It sounded like she was tumbling gravel.

Delia jumped forward. 'Water, milady?'

'I'm not dead yet,' Edith growled. 'Where is everyone? I thought we said four o'clock! Where's Harry? Where's the cake?'

'I'll go to the kitchen.' Delia scurried out.

Edith pointed at the footstool next to the fire. Dutifully, I sat.

'That woman,' she muttered. 'She's getting too big for her boots. Frightful mistake. All of it.'

'I know, milady,' Mum agreed, the traitor.

'All this nonsense. I told Rupert . . .' Edith started to cough again.

Mum swiftly poured a glass of water, which Edith gratefully accepted. She sank back against the cushions.

'Oh, milady,' Mum whispered. 'Is there anything we can do?'

Edith nodded. She beckoned me closer and lowered her voice. 'Lavinia is off with a chum on Sunday. Need your help. You can take Tinkerbell. Harry can ride Duchess.'

'Of course,' I said, but my heart sank. Although I loved Edith's temperamental chestnut mare, I didn't enjoy riding her. She was unpredictable, skittish and moody.

'I'd like you to ride the north-west boundary. The edge of the estate. Do you know where I mean?'

'I'm not sure,' I said.

'Up by Ivy Cottage and the abandoned chapel,' said Edith. 'I need to know what's going on, but you must only tell me. Do you understand?'

'Of course,' I said.

'Here we are,' Delia trilled, wheeling in a trolley adorned with half a dozen helium balloons that bobbed and bounced in her face.

The cake was a masterpiece – a two-tier tribute to Honeychurch Halt in its heyday. The base was moss-green buttercream, dotted with tiny fondant flowers. The top was sky blue, edged with silver tracks and dark chocolate sleepers that formed a miniature track. A fondant steam engine sat on the rails, puffing candyfloss smoke from its funnel, followed by a coal carriage brimming with chocolate-coated raisins. *Happy Birthday Harry: 11 Today!* was piped in elegant chocolate script.

Honeychurch Halt again. This time on a cake.

'I was there today, in fact,' I said. 'At Railway Cottage, doing a valuation. I would have liked to have seen the Halt in its heyday – it's a bit depressing now.'

'Ah, yes,' said Edith, with a faintly regal air. 'It used to be very busy in the summer. Naturally it belonged to the estate, but my great-grandfather was forced – forced, mind you – to sell it to the South Devon and West Moorland Railway sometime around the turn of the century. A compulsory purchase. Frightful for landowners. That would be the ninth earl—'

'Edward Rupert,' Delia jumped in. 'Older brother to our heroic explorer.'

'Yes.' Mum spoke sharply. As the self-appointed family historian, she hated anyone trespassing on her territory – especially Delia. 'Edward was born in 1835 and died in 1899. He brought the mummified hawk back from the Crimea.'

'But not the polar bear, Iris,' Delia said with smug triumph.

'The bear's name is Florian,' my mother declared. 'Gerald allegedly captured and slew the poor animal with his bare hands, dragging him across the ice for miles and—'

'Yes, yes, we know all that,' Delia interrupted before turning to Edith. 'Did you know, milady, that Gerald once rode a walrus?'

'Is that so?' Edith said drily.

'I don't know where you heard that,' Mum scoffed.

Delia beamed. 'Oh, it's all in the commemorative souvenir book, *Tales from the Tundra*. And of course, if you tune in to *West Country Round-Up* tonight at six—'

'Wow! How cool!' Harry burst into the morning room, followed by Lavinia, looking her usual dishevelled self in dirty jodhpurs and a brown sweater with a hole in the elbow. Her hair was scraped back into a lopsided ponytail. Harry, almost as tall as his mother now, wore horn-rimmed spectacles and had a mop of hair flopping over his forehead. Whatever his hobby, he approached it with a fanatical enthusiasm that I found endearing. 'A railway cake!' he gushed. 'And guess what? I'm doing a school project on old railways. I want to win the Headmaster's Cup.'

'You tell them, my pet,' Edith said, her fondness for her grandson more obvious than I'd ever seen.

'It's called *Hopping On and Off: A Brief History of Halts*,' said Harry. 'Halts were very important in the olden days because they helped people who lived in the countryside get to the towns. That's before cars were invented, although,' he frowned, 'they could have gone on horseback, I suppose.'

'But trains were faster than horses,' Edith said with a smile. 'Shall we cut the cake?'

For a few moments, pandemonium reigned. Plates were passed around, candles lit and blown out and the birthday song belted with great gusto – although Lavinia's voice was painfully off-key. Delia sliced the cake and handed out forks and paper serviettes decorated with little steam trains.

'I'll post on social media,' she said, snapping photos on her mobile. 'We're getting quite a following. After tonight's *West Country Round-Up*, I think the Honeychurch profile will really be elevated.'

'Elevated? Elevated?' Mum whispered in my ear. 'Who does she think she is, Meghan Markle?'

'How delicious,' Lavinia chirped, scattering crumbs that Mr Chips gobbled off the carpet. 'Well done, Mrs Evans.'

'Oh, the credit's all June Barker's,' Delia said. 'She's an excellent cook. I know you'll like her. She's busy working on the tearoom menus or she'd have joined us.'

Edith scowled. 'Ah, yes. That white elephant.'

'I think you mean white polar bear, milady,' Delia said, attempting a coy joke.

'No,' Edith replied coldly. 'I know exactly what I mean.'

Silence fell.

'Rupert's late,' Lavinia said, a little too brightly.

'He had that meeting with the planning officer,' Delia put in, 'although she left a good twenty minutes ago.'

'Planning?' Edith said sharply. 'What planning officer? *Here?*'

But before Delia could answer, Rupert strolled in mumbling his apologies.

I hated to admit it, but age suited him. In his fifties, slightly balding, with a military moustache, dressed as usual in corduroy trousers, a checked shirt and an olive-green Guernsey sweater, he carried an air of entitlement that seemed to intimidate most people – but no longer me.

Our relationship had been strained ever since the fiasco with Eric Pugsley, his tenant, handyman and fixer, whose noisy scrapyard was uncomfortably close to Mum's house. Rupert had demanded I vacate Jane's Cottage and the two gatehouses. I'd offered to buy them. He'd refused. I'd offered to pay higher rent. He'd refused that too. Only later did I discover why. He'd intended to hand them over to Eric and his future bride – an arrangement that was ultimately doomed – without consulting me, let alone Edith.

The injustice of it left a bitter taste. Edith had always treated me with kindness, and yet Rupert was ready to sweep me aside as if I were nothing more than a tenant to be dismissed when it suited him. It was a brutal reminder that once the dowager countess was gone, my entire domestic situation would fall into his hands.

With Edith's health clearly failing, I couldn't afford to be caught unprepared. Selling my Putney flat was the right decision. I had no intention of going back to London. Things were working out well with Mallory, but regardless of whether we had a future together, my life was here now.

Harry tore into his presents, whooping with excitement at Peter Slater's book – Mum gave me a grateful smile – but even more thrilled with Findlay's book on railway management.

'This is epic,' he grinned, leafing through the pages. 'This will bag me the cup!'

'I know you must have seen your father's Hornby collection,' said Edith, 'but what about the Honeychurch Kaiser Adler?'

'A Kaiser Adler?' I was gobsmacked. 'But . . . that's extraordinary! They're extremely rare.'

'A family heirloom,' Edith said. 'Where is it, Rupert?'

'Presumably somewhere in the attic,' said Rupert, sounding bored.

'Märkisch & Sohn only made twelve locomotives,' I said, still stunned at the coincidence. 'They're also incredibly valuable.'

'Wicked!' Harry clapped his hands in delight. 'And we have one! Can I see it?'

'Not today,' Rupert said firmly.

'Please, Father. It *is* my birthday.'

'It is his birthday,' Edith echoed.

'And I don't want to spend his birthday scrabbling about in the attic,' Rupert said crossly.

'How did a Kaiser Adler come into your possession?' I asked Edith.

'I was told it was a gift from King Edward VII to one of my ancestors.'

'Wait! What?' Delia squeaked. 'A royal gift from the king? To Gerald Honeychurch – *my* Gerald?'

'Wrong ancestor,' Mum muttered.

Edith seemed taken aback. '*Your* Gerald?'

'I'm sorry, milady,' Delia blustered. 'I could have included it in *Tales of the Tundra*.'

'Hardly suitable for the North Pole,' Edith said. 'And besides, as Iris pointed out, the wrong ancestor.'

Delia's face fell.

'And where are these commemorative books?' Edith continued. 'Why wasn't I informed?'

Delia reddened. She made a silent appeal to Rupert, who found something far more interesting on the cuff of his sweater.

'Why don't you tell us more about this very rare train, Kat?' said Edith.

'Of course.' I smiled. 'What makes a Kaiser Adler so valuable is that each was built by hand, with gold-plated fittings, real mahogany detailing and a fully functional miniature steam boiler.'

Harry pouted. 'I don't mind scrabbling about in the attic.'

'They weren't toys,' I went on. 'They were made for German aristocrats and senior railway executives. In 2021, a pristine Kaiser Adler went to auction in Munich and sold for ninety-eight thousand euros. That's about eighty grand.'

I glanced at Rupert, expecting to see delight. Instead, there was something else. Panic.

'As a matter of fact, the Emporium has an exhibition of Giles Oxley's dioramas,' I said. 'One of them features a Kaiser Adler. That's why I was so surprised when you said you had one too.'

Edith nodded. 'That is extraordinary indeed.'

'Giles Oxley is what's known as a prototypical model railway builder,' I said.

Harry frowned. 'What's a proto . . . proto . . .?'

'Someone who creates actual scenes from history,' I said. 'But Oxley goes one step further. He presents a challenge. There are five dioramas, and each has one a historical inaccuracy. If you can guess all five, you have a chance to win the grand prize.'

Harry's eyes were like saucers. 'I love prizes! What is it?'

'Two tickets for an all-inclusive round trip on the legendary Flying Scotsman, complete with a champagne welcome, silver-service dining and an overnight stay in Edinburgh at a five-star hotel. Worth about five hundred pounds apiece.'

Harry pulled a face. 'But I don't like champagne.'

Everyone laughed.

Then he frowned again. 'What's a diorama anyway?'

'It's different from a layout,' I explained. 'A layout is a whole working railway with trains running. A diorama is a frozen moment in time, like stepping into a photograph where every detail tells a story. Oxley's exhibition has a theme – crimes committed on the railways. He even found the original newspaper articles for each one.'

'Cool.' Harry nodded. 'So which diorama has the Kaiser Adler?'

'Cologne station in 1916 – there was a murder,' I said.

'And what are the others?'

'Stalin's Iron Train rumbling through war-torn Russia. The Palace on Wheels in 1923 – silk and scandal in the days of the Raj. A Wild West gold-rush hold-up. And last but by no means least, the disastrous Honeychurch Halt Heist of 1974.'

'But . . . that's near here!' Harry exclaimed, barely able to control his excitement. 'A real robbery!'

'No,' Edith said. 'Some small-time crooks tried to copy the Great Train Robbery of '63 and made a complete hash of it. Frightful tragedy. I was away on the Continent at the time, but a police officer and a guard were killed.'

'Now that school has broken up for the holidays, you should come to the exhibition tomorrow – a proper birthday treat,' I jumped in quickly. The last thing Harry needed was more fuel for his overactive imagination.

'Oh, Father, please! At least I can see someone else's Kaiser Adler.'

'We're already taking a ride on the West Somerset Heritage Railway,' Rupert said. 'The answer is no.'

'If you can drop him off, I'll show him around,' I said, knowing I was breaking the cardinal rule of parenting by interfering. 'Tomorrow is the last day.'

'How kind,' Edith put in. 'Harry will love it, won't you, darling?'

'The Raj,' Lavinia said slowly – she'd been very quiet up to now. 'Didn't one of your relatives run off with a maharaja, Edith?'

'It was a sheikh, milady,' Mum said, shooting Delia a look of superiority. 'You're probably thinking of Cassandra Mary Honeychurch. Born 1872, died 1965—'

'She was completely mad,' Edith cut in. 'A friend of Elinor Glyn, of course, who often came here to writhe about on our tiger skin. I believe Great-Aunt Cassie's steamer trunk is still in the attic, full of God knows what.'

Mum gave a cry of excitement. 'Her trunk is here?'

It was a light-bulb moment. A trunk. A sheikh. A Krystalle Storm novel waiting to happen – the kind that had made her an international bestselling romance writer. It had been a long time since I had seen her so animated.

'Would I be permitted to take a look?' she asked eagerly. 'Naturally, as the family historian . . .'

'I've no objection,' said Edith. 'And while you're up there, you might find that train tucked away somewhere.'

Harry's eyes widened. 'Can I come?'

'I've already told you. Not this weekend,' Rupert said, exasperated. 'For now, the Hornby collection will have to do.'

'While we're on the subject of collections,' Delia cut in brightly, 'thank you for allowing the Grenville Standard to be part of Gerald's exhibition. It's proving quite a draw.'

Mum frowned. 'What standard? I don't know anything about a standard.'

'It's a flag, Iris,' Delia smirked. 'A heraldic one, with the family crest.'

'I am perfectly aware of what a standard is,' Mum snapped.

'They flew it over the Hall when the family was in residence and carried it into battle too – Bosworth, Naseby, Flanders . . . possibly Dunkirk, for all I know.'

'Dunkirk?' Mum spluttered. 'Don't be ridiculous.'

'Oh, yes. I found it in one of the cupboards when I was clearing out the old nursery. Imagine my delight – an actual standard! Of course, I ran it past his lordship.' She gave Rupert a hopeful look, but he was back to fussing with his cuff.

'I've done my research,' Mum persisted, 'and I can assure you there is no such thing.'

Edith's lips twitched. She seemed about to speak, but thought better of it.

Delia jutted her chin. 'If you don't believe me, I'll show you.'

'Not today,' Mum declared. 'In fact, Kat and I really must be off – if you'll excuse us, your ladyship.'

Edith inclined her head graciously. 'When would you like to explore the attics?'

'Sunday would suit,' Mum said, surprising me – I'd expected her to jump at the chance immediately. She gave me a nod to follow, wished Harry a happy birthday once more and moved for the door just as Rupert did, seeming anxious to escape.

'Rupert,' Edith called. 'Not you. I'd like to know about this planning officer Mrs Evans mentioned, and why she was here.'

'Mrs Evans is misinformed,' said Rupert curtly.

Delia stiffened 'But that's—'

'And should remember her place.' His voice was icy. Silence fell. Delia looked as though he'd struck her.

'Steady on,' Lavinia began. 'Mrs Evans has a frightful lot on her plate at the moment. I think she's doing a tremendous job.'

'Thank you, milady,' Delia said, relief evident. 'I was—'

Rupert cleared his throat – deliberately.

'But of course you really should have mentioned this open-house idea to Edith ... and me.' Lavinia's voice was tentative. She shot a quick glance at Rupert, colour rising in her cheeks. He gave the smallest of nods, and she stumbled on. 'And ... and ... yes, well ... I suppose we were a little taken aback by all the fuss. The publicity. You know we're a very private family. Very private.' She hesitated, her hands twisting together. 'And now it all feels . . .' another glance at Rupert, 'yes, rather like a circus.'

Delia thrust out her chin. 'But his lordship told me—'

'That will be all. Take the trolley out, please.' Lavinia's voice was sharp now, though her face was scarlet. She turned away and bent over Harry's gifts with forced cheer.

Delia had been dismissed, so the three of us left.

Mum's hurry to go seemed to have faded. I could see she was worried about her friend.

'How rude!' she exclaimed, helping steer the trolley towards the kitchen. I trailed behind, listening in – naturally.

'She's not normally so mean,' Delia said. 'It's him. His lordship. She wouldn't have spoken to me like that if he hadn't been there. He's been in such a filthy mood these past few days. I can't do anything right.'

'Is that why you're leaving?' Mum demanded. 'Because of *him*?'

'Perhaps you shouldn't have mentioned the planning officer in front of Edith,' I suggested. 'It's a sensitive topic.'

Delia's eyes blazed. She was angry now. 'His lordship said he'd spoken to Lady Edith. He told me he had!'

'Well . . .' Mum hesitated. 'Did he say that exactly?'

Delia faltered. 'I don't quite remember – but I heard him arguing with Gloria Weaver! She said the bifold doors had to come out, and he shouted at her and said they were staying right where they were. I won't repeat the language.'

'Oh, do repeat it, Delia. Do.'

'I'd rather not,' she said hastily. 'My mother always said that if I used that word, my tongue would turn black.'

She drew herself up. 'I work my fingers to the bone for this family. I could quit right now, then they'd be sorry!'

Mum shot me an anguished look. I shrugged. Clearly worried, she tried to lighten the mood. 'Come on then – prove me wrong. Show me the Grenville Standard. Mind, we can't stay more than five minutes.'

Delia brightened instantly, her threat forgotten. 'And the Polar Tearoom. Just wait until you see it. You're going to be impressed.'

Chapter Four

'Where are we going?' Mum grumbled as we followed Delia along a narrow, low-ceilinged back passage that I'd not seen before. Discovering new areas at the Hall happened all the time. Once, I'd asked Edith how many square feet the house covered – basement, ground floor, first floor and attics – and wasn't surprised to learn that it was close to thirty-eight thousand square feet.

It wasn't the largest stately home in Devon, but in its heyday it would have taken twenty staff just to open the shutters. Now, much of it lay unexplored – whole wings shut off and forgotten – but slowly it was coming alive. And it was all due to Delia. Which was why her announcement that she was planning to leave came as a surprise.

Honeychurch Hall was her baby.

'You can't have visitors coming this way,' Mum went on. 'It's like a rabbit warren.'

'They won't,' said Delia. 'This is the shortcut for staff. Visitors will access the museum through the Polar Tearoom.'

'You mean, through the bifold doors that have to come out?' Mum said.

We rounded the corner, and she gave a little cry of alarm. A massive shape loomed in the gloom, blocking the end of the corridor.

'Wait!' she said, her voice catching. 'Is that . . . is that the polar bear?'

'Florian, yes. The Museum Room is just through there. We didn't want the builder snooping around. Florian is standing guard.'

To the right, a torn sheet of builder's polythene had been haphazardly taped over what looked like a makeshift doorway – presumably the newly created staff entrance to the Polar Tearoom. It billowed slightly in the draught, revealing glimpses of bare plaster and dangling wires.

'Of course, we'll be moving him into the tearoom once it's finished,' said Delia. 'Follow me.' She lifted a corner of the sheeting and we slipped inside. 'Now, I know it's not finished . . .'

Not finished was an understatement.

What had been a hexagonal anteroom – a highly unusual shape to begin with – linking the state rooms along the west wing had been altered with no regard to aesthetics. In addition to the new entrance we'd just stepped through, bifold doors now stretched across an entire wall. Worst of all was the gaping maw of a serving hatch, presumably leading to a kitchen for preparing refreshments. The remaining walls were still adorned with delicate frescoes of trailing ivy, wild roses and tiny sparrows, all rendered in faded greens and dusky pinks.

'I hope you're not going to paint over that,' I said, a little primly. 'This is a listed building.'

'We are,' Delia declared. 'I thought eggshell blue would be lovely – the theme is polar. I'm thinking snow. Ice. Penguins—'

'Penguins live at the South Pole,' Mum pointed out. 'Polar bears at the North.'

Delia waved this away. 'In the summer we'll have tables and chairs outside on the terrace. Planters filled with flowers. Bees—'

'Surely the new planning officer told you not to paint over it.' I was concerned. 'And this new entrance – isn't that a load-bearing wall?'

The ceiling was already sagging, held up by adjustable steel props. Frayed electrical wires dangled from torn plaster, and there was a faint smell of burnt insulation.

'Keith knows exactly what he's doing.' Delia paused, then squinted around with a dreamy expression. 'I can see it perfectly. I'm very pleased . . . Ah, here he is now.'

'I'm off then.' A burly man – sixties – in overalls and work boots and sporting a ferocious beard stepped through the bifolds.

'This is Keith the builder,' Delia said. 'Iris and Kat Stanford.'

He gave us a brief nod. A woman who could only be described as Amazonian – fifties, with closely cropped hair

– towered behind him. She was at least a head taller than Keith, dressed in dungarees and a checked shirt.

'And this is June,' said Delia.

As Keith stepped back through the bifolds to leave, June let her fingers brush his hand. He jerked away as though scalded. June didn't flinch – her gaze held steady, calculating. And this was the woman Delia was hoping would replace her?

June didn't look pleased. 'You've still got that polar bear.'

'How are the menus coming on?' Delia asked, breezing past the remark.

'The cake was incredible,' Mum said. 'Absolutely delicious.'

'Thank you. I studied at the West Country Baking Institute and hold an advanced certificate in patisserie and cake decoration.'

'Well, we were impressed,' said Mum. 'Weren't we, Kat?'

I nodded. We were. There was something imposing about June – maybe it was simply her height.

June did not seem to warm to our compliments. 'And I'm not supposed to do rough work, I'll have you know. I was hired to manage the tearoom and bake.'

'I'll be with you in a moment, June,' Delia said pleasantly. 'Why don't you pop into the kitchen and make yourself a cup of tea?'

'No thank you,' June said. 'What are you talking about?'

'We're busy,' said Delia. 'Go on. Off you go.'

June didn't budge.

'Now, June,' Delia said, more firmly.

With a scowl, June stomped off, ducking neatly through the bifold door.

'She didn't seem so tall on Zoom,' Delia muttered.

'Maybe June can move the polar bear,' Mum suggested. 'She could probably sling it over her shoulder with one hand.'

'I wish.' Delia grinned. 'Unfortunately, June's allergic to stuffed animals. Can't stand to be anywhere near them.'

'You mean she's got a phobia,' Mum declared.

'Whatever. I asked her to dust the Museum Room and she refused. As you know, we've got the ninth earl's *Fur, Feather and Folly* collection. He did all the work himself, you know.'

'And it shows.' Mum sniggered. 'The family cat – those whiskers were a good inch above the poor creature's eyes.'

'Have you ever tried stuffing a dead animal?' Delia shot back. 'It's harder than it looks!'

I wisely kept my thoughts to myself.

'Well, I've never heard of anything so silly,' Mum said with scorn. 'Afraid of stuffed animals? Whatever next – post-traumatic stress disorder from too much Winnie-the-Pooh?'

'You might think differently if *you'd* been shut in the National History Museum overnight on a school trip, Iris, and woken up crushed under a lion. Poor June.'

There was no comeback to that, so I didn't try.

'She's local then,' Mum said finally.

'Worked in a hotel over Bovey way,' said Delia. 'Used to live in, and with number two being empty, I threw in the accommodation for free.'

'Married? Single? Significant other? Don't you want to interview anyone else? I mean, how did you even find her, Delia? Seriously.'

'One of my dailies knew her from way back when. We're lucky to have her,' Delia said firmly. 'She got to the second round of *The Midnight Pantry* – did you ever watch it?'

'Never heard of it.'

'Wait,' I said. 'Is that the show where—'

'That's the one. The contestants only use whatever random half-finished ingredients callers say they've got in their cupboards.'

I tried to keep a straight face. I'd stumbled across it by accident – one contestant had whipped up a recipe out of powdered soup and tinned tuna. I had swiftly changed the channel. That was enough for me.

'She's done all sorts of things,' Delia burbled on. 'She's been a croupier on a cruise ship, delivered Land Rovers across Africa . . .'

'Pity she didn't learn how to tame that lion,' Mum muttered.

'She can turn her hand to anything,' Delia said with a hint of pride.

'Except stuffed animals.'

'Oh, for heaven's sake, Iris!' Delia snapped. 'Give her a chance.'

But my mother wasn't having any of it. 'She sounds . . . unstable. Won't it be a little dull for her here? Why has she had so many jobs?'

I wanted to ask the same question. June's history hardly inspired confidence.

'She likes a challenge. And it'll certainly be a challenge here. June's staying and that's final.'

'Well. It sounds like your mind's made up,' Mum said bitterly. 'When are you planning on leaving?'

'At the end of the summer.'

The two friends glared at each other.

'Um . . . do you want to show us the Standard?' I ventured, anxious to defuse the situation.

Delia shot me a look of relief. She crossed to the wall and pressed the centre of a painted pink rose. A concealed panel sprang open, revealing a narrow recess. She disappeared inside. I couldn't help wondering how she'd ever find it again once the walls were painted over in eggshell blue.

Moments later, she reappeared looking worried. 'That's strange. It was here yesterday.'

'Maybe June shinned up the flagpole and stuck it up there,' Mum suggested.

'No.' Delia shook her head. 'No one knows that cupboard exists.'

'Well, someone must. If you put it in, someone took it out.'

'Unless . . . unless I'm – you know – going senile.' Her voice cracked. 'I can't lose the Grenville Standard. I just can't!'

'You're not senile,' Mum said, but her tone was brisk rather than comforting. 'You're just disorganised. Look around you – this event, the tearoom.' She glanced pointedly at the surrounding chaos. 'No wonder things go missing.'

Delia gave a shaky laugh. 'No, you're right. I'm just spinning a lot of plates. And with Henri's demands . . .'

'Henri?' Mum exclaimed, her voice rising in dismay. 'Don't tell me *that's* why you're leaving. You've met a man!'

Delia went pink, suddenly bashful. She darted a look at me, the meaning plain. *Not in front of her*. Was this what she'd been hinting at earlier?

'I think you've got some explaining to do,' Mum said sharply.

'I've wanted to say something for ages, but you've been so bad-tempered. So distant. You've not answered the door. You've avoided my phone calls—'

'I'll leave you to it,' I cut in. 'But Mum, can you give me a lift home first?' It was a twenty-minute walk, and the sky – glimpsed through the bifold doors – looked ominously black.

'Put the kettle on,' Mum ordered Delia. 'I'll be back.'

Chapter Five

I could hardly keep up with my mother as she strode towards the car, muttering under her breath, 'A man! How? When? And as for June...'

'You see,' I said lightly. 'The world collapses when you hide away.'

'It certainly does,' she declared. 'Oh, for heaven's sake. Look at her. Trouble written all over her face.'

June was leaning into Keith's cab, one foot propped on the running board, an arm draped over the window. She tossed her head back, laughing at something he'd said.

The moment Keith spotted us, he started the engine. June staggered as the cab jolted forward, then righted herself and sauntered towards us as if nothing had happened.

'Where are you going?' she asked.

'I'm taking Kat home,' Mum said.

'Can I cadge a lift?'

'I'll squeeze in the back,' I offered.

June angled herself into the passenger seat, the top of her head brushing the ceiling, and we set off.

'It seems like you and Keith are getting along,' Mum remarked drily.

June gave a grunt. 'We are. Pity about the beard.'

'Do we know if he's free?' Mum said sweetly, catching my eye in the rear-view mirror.

'Do we care?' June retorted.

'Someone might.'

'It sounds like you've had a very interesting life, June,' I said quickly.

'I have.'

Flat. Final. That was the end of it. No one spoke again until we dropped her at her cottage. I climbed into the front passenger seat.

'What on earth is Delia thinking?' Mum moaned. 'I can't see June and me sharing a pot of tea and a friendly chat.'

'Oddly enough, it's not always about you,' I teased. 'Delia probably chose her because she seems the type of woman who will simply get the job done. Still, yes, she does come across as a bit blunt. Maybe she's just shy?'

'Shy?' Mum said with scorn. 'Did you see how she was flirting with Keith? Poor man looked terrified.'

'Speaking of men, who is this Henri person?' I demanded.

'Your guess is as good as mine,' said Mum. 'Why else do you think I'm going back for a cuppa? I won't be able to settle – or write – until I know who he is. Delia always swore she'd wait for Lenny to come out of prison. He'll go ballistic if she's changed her mind.'

'How long is his sentence?'

'He got fifteen years,' Mum said. 'And with good behaviour, he might be out in ten.'

The thought of Lenny Evans roaming free made me nauseous.

'I thought they were divorced.'

'Well, they're not,' said Mum. 'I don't want to talk about Delia any more, or Lenny – or June. I want to talk about me and my new idea.'

'Absolutely!' I said. 'The moment Edith mentioned her great-aunt and the steamer trunk, I just knew the muse had awoken.'

'Harem Historicals,' Mum beamed. 'That will be the title of the series. I'll take each nubile beauty and build a racy story around her life. Once I get home, you won't see me for dust.'

'What about the attic?' I reminded her. 'Surely that comes first?'

'It can wait,' she said. 'I need to get these ideas down before they vanish.'

I smiled. 'Well, I'm just happy to see my mother back again. I've been worried about you.'

Mum shot me a grin. 'So have I.'

She dropped me off at the gatehouse, executed a neat three-point turn and headed back to the Hall. I'd barely stepped inside when my phone pinged. A text.

URGENT. Want stuff back. Don't need valuation. Come NOW. Connie.

I hadn't even finished the valuation – though there wasn't much to value apart from the vintage poster. I'd spent time listing the inventory, which I obviously wasn't going to be paid for now. It wouldn't have amounted to much, but it was the principle. I'd have to chalk it up as a bad experience. Frankly, I was done with Connie.

Forget texting back; I called her. 'Since this is urgent and you need the boxes back now,' I said, emphasising 'urgent' and 'now', 'you can come and collect them yourself from my showroom. I'll be here for the next hour.'

Silence.

'Do you want my address and directions?'

Connie gave a heavy sigh. 'OK, I'll get there when I can.'

But an hour turned into two, and there was no sign of Connie. I called her mobile, but she didn't answer. I sent her a text – no response. Exasperated, I called again to say I'd drop the boxes over in the morning on my way to the Emporium. I put them back in my car and whizzed home, just in time to catch Delia's pre-recorded interview on *West Country Round-Up*.

The Grenville Standard filled the screen – a bold royal-blue shield edged in gold and flanked by two hawks. A scroll bore the Latin family motto, *Ad perseverate est ad triumphum*.

'Once carried into battle across the fields of Flanders by Gerald Honeychurch himself,' the voice-over claimed, 'a true local hero.'

Quite the miracle, considering Gerald had died in the Arctic in 1912, two years before the Great War even began.

'To persevere is to triumph, right, Bella?' said the host, all gleaming teeth and fierce eyebrows, to his companion on the red sofa. 'Do *you* have a family motto?'

Bella snorted. 'Just one, Alex. In laundry we trust. With two boys under the age of four, it's practically stitched on my soul.'

Delia, looking very polished in a new suit, hair coiffed, seemed unfazed by their sarcastic exchange, and when she boasted about resurrecting the village tradition of touching the golden fringe of the Grenville Standard for luck, Alex could barely control his mirth.

'Well, we hope you'll tune in and join us at the Polar Tearoom at Honeychurch Hall over the Easter weekend,' he said. 'Can't wait to touch that fringe.'

'Count me in,' Bella added. 'I've got a load of socks that need blessing.'

Despite not being Delia's biggest fan, I felt a pang of protectiveness. No one likes to see someone made a fool of, especially in public. I felt embarrassed for her. She was so earnest – so unaware of their snide remarks – and I knew from my own days in front of the camera how quickly things could turn cruel. Mercifully, the programme cut away to the final day of *Crime on the Line*, focusing on a different kind of treasure: a lingering close-up of the spectacular Kaiser Adler. It really was a magnificent piece of craftsmanship.

At 9.30, my mobile rang. It was an unfamiliar number. 'Is Connie with you?'

'Connie Hicks?' I said. 'No. Why? Who is this?'

'It's her husband, Ian,' he replied. 'I found your phone number online. You're valuing Stan's stuff, right? I can't get hold of her. I thought maybe she might be with you.'

'She was supposed to come and pick the boxes up, but she didn't,' I said.

'What time was that?' he asked sharply.

'Maybe six-ish? Is everything all right?'

'I don't know.' A silence followed. And then, 'Do you live far from her dad's place?'

I blinked. I could see where this was heading. 'Not really. Why?'

'Only . . . I wondered if you could just pop over and check on her.'

I was already in my pyjamas. I'd enjoyed two large glasses of wine. I didn't feel like going anywhere.

'I'm sorry, I really can't. I've been drinking. I don't want to risk being stopped by the police. Maybe there's someone else you could call who lives nearby?'

'Don't know anyone,' said Ian. 'Connie's not been back there since they left. Me, never.'

A silence. I felt a stab of guilt, but pushed it aside. I barely knew Connie, and I didn't know Ian at all.

'Maybe call the police for a welfare check,' I suggested. If Mallory hadn't been away, I suppose I could have asked him to swing by.

'It's just . . . with Connie's health,' Ian said. 'And we've only got one car. I can't get there until tomorrow.'

'I understand. Call the police,' I said gently. 'I'm sure she'll be fine.'

Later, though, climbing into bed, I couldn't shake a nagging sense of unease. I kept picturing Connie curled up in that sleeping bag in the damp, dreary front room.

She'd been so abrupt when I'd called, almost as if she couldn't get off the line fast enough. And why, after being so eager to have her father's memorabilia valued, had she suddenly changed her mind?

I switched off the light, telling myself I'd be seeing her in the morning.

But as I neared the Halt the next day, a police car blocked the entrance.

Something must have happened to Connie after all.

Something bad.

Chapter Six

The police officer in a high-vis vest stepped forward as I stopped my car and got out. Fortunately, it was Malcolm, the desk sergeant, bacon sandwich in hand. I'd never once seen him without something to eat. If anyone knew what had happened, it would be him.

'You can't come any further,' he said through a mouthful of crumbs. He gestured wildly behind me. 'Been a fatality.'

My stomach dropped. 'Is it Connie Hicks?'

Malcolm gawked. 'You knew her?'

Knew, not know!

Guilt didn't even begin to describe how I felt. Maybe she'd missed her jab. Ian had been worried enough to ask me to check, and I'd selfishly refused. If I'd driven over last night, would she still be alive? Yes, I'd drunk two glasses of wine, but I could have taken the back roads. I just hadn't wanted to go.

'Do you know if her husband – Ian – asked for someone to do a welfare check?'

'You know him, too?' Malcolm narrowed his eyes. 'Why?'

'It doesn't matter,' I said. 'I need to talk to whoever's in charge. Presumably, with Mallory away, someone else is handling . . . whatever this is.'

Malcolm leant in, lowering his voice. 'I figured something big was going down because . . .' he pushed his wire-rimmed spectacles up his nose, '*she's* here.'

'Well, let me talk to whoever she is,' I said. 'I have information that might help with the timeline of events.'

'Sorry, Kat. I can't let you pass.'

'Oh, for heaven's sake, Malcolm.' I darted through the gap between the bumper and the hedge and hurried up the lane. I heard a pathetic 'Stop. Police!' followed by two peeps on his whistle, but I carried on.

Up ahead, a white forensics van, emblazoned with blue and yellow chequered markings and the words *Crime Scene Investigation*, was parked outside Railway Cottage. Two more police cars were stationed further along the lane.

Something truly terrible must have happened to Connie to warrant this level of police activity. I hesitated, wishing Mallory were here – but he wasn't.

I had to find whoever was in charge.

Striding past the cottage, I caught a glimpse of a figure in white overalls standing in the doorway. They stepped aside to let someone pass, and I did a double-take. It was Mallory.

Surprise gave way to relief then quickly flipped to the familiar butterflies I always felt when I saw him. With his grey-green eyes, lantern jaw and chiselled features, physically Mallory looked every inch the hero in a romance novel. But it was his kindness, intelligence and dry humour that truly set him apart.

Yet the moment our eyes met, my delight turned to dismay. His expression said it all.

He wasn't pleased to see me.

'You can't be here, Kat,' he said, hurrying over. 'Where did you leave your car?' Before I could answer, he took my arm and steered me away from the cottage, phone still in his hand, eyes flicking nervously up the lane.

A young uniformed policewoman was already striding towards us.

'I knew Connie Hicks,' I said quickly as he bundled me away. 'I saw her yesterday. Her husband called me.'

'Called *you*?' He stopped short and released my arm. 'Why? What were you doing with Connie Hicks?'

A text pinged. He glanced down at his mobile and swiftly replied with a flurry of taps before turning his attention back to me.

'I'm returning the boxes of railway memorabilia she asked me to value yesterday,' I said. 'They belong to her father.'

'Stan Holden?'

'Connie called me last night wanting them back straight away, then her husband rang around nine thirty saying he couldn't reach her. I feel . . . I feel awful.'

He frowned. 'Why did he call?'

'He wanted me to check on her, and I'd had some wine and refused. Connie was insulin-dependent. Is that what happened? Although . . .' I looked around at the police activity, the crime-scene tape. Another white-suited figure was heading up to the Halt carrying a forensic case. 'What's going on?'

'Ma'am is waiting for you at the camping coach.' The policewoman who joined us couldn't have been more than twenty, with mousy brown hair scraped into a tidy bun, polished shoes and no make-up.

'Tell her I'll be right there, Quinn,' said Mallory.

PC Quinn stood her ground. 'She told me to wait.'

Mallory's jaw tightened. I knew him well enough to know he resented the request, and wondered why. 'Thank you, Ms Stanford. We'll be in touch.'

Ms Stanford?

As PC Quinn turned to leave, he said quietly, 'I'll come by tomorrow evening,' before going after her.

Thoroughly rattled, I walked back to my car to face Malcolm, who was tucking into a Kit Kat. He wasn't terribly bright – maybe I could get some information from him.

'Sorry I defied your order, Malcolm,' I said feigning regret. 'What's with the camping coach?'

'Yeah.' He nodded. 'We didn't find her until first thing this morning.'

'In the camping coach?' I was stunned. Apart from the fact that Connie wasn't exactly mobile, what on earth had she been doing up there in the dark? 'Didn't her husband call you last night to request a welfare check?'

'Bit of a cock-up, to be honest,' he said. 'I forwarded the request to the main station, but for some reason Plymouth picked it up – no idea why. Took them ages to find the place. Their defence was that they didn't think anyone lived there, and they never thought to look in the camping coach until this morning.'

'Oh,' I said. 'You mean Plymouth picked it up because Mallory's based there at the moment?' That made sense. Sort of.

'I suppose so.' Malcolm shrugged. 'MCU has it now.' Seeing my confusion, he added, 'Major Crime Unit.'

'Major Crime?' I thought of the police tape, the forensic van. 'So you're treating Connie's death as suspicious?'

'I'm not at liberty to say.' Malcolm trotted out the well-worn phrase. 'But Greenleigh's the SIO.'

Greenleigh. I knew that name.

Chief Superintendent Stella Greenleigh. Mallory's ex – in more ways than one.

A tight, sick feeling churned in my stomach.

A moment later, the wail of a siren galvanised Malcolm into action. He stuffed the rest of the Kit Kat into his mouth and, pointing at my car, made it clear I needed to move. I pulled away just as an ambulance, lights flashing, appeared in my rear-view mirror.

I still had Stan Holden's boxes in the boot of my car and found myself obsessing over what to do with them – anything to keep from thinking about what had happened to Connie.

The Major Crime Unit had been called in. Even if Totnes hadn't been first on the scene, why bring in Plymouth and not Exeter? Exeter was closer.

Which, inevitably, made me think of *my* ex, Detective Inspector Shawn Cropper, now based there. The incident was at Honeychurch Halt, his old patch. It stood to reason that he should be here.

I made myself switch back into work mode. It was the last day of Oxley's exhibition, and if Delia was right about his suspension, the fallout could be brutal. Thank God the news hadn't broken last night. With any luck it would hold until the event was over.

I'd coordinated the whole thing. I was the main point person. If the story leaked, the questions would come straight at me. How could I not have known?

With a heavy heart, I headed for Dartmouth.

Chapter Seven

With its narrow medieval streets and the naval college perched on the bluff overlooking the estuary, Dartmouth was steeped in over eight centuries of history. Once a fortified harbour town supplying ships to the Crown, it now thrived on its regattas, tall ships and year-round festivals.

The Dartmouth Antique Emporium was housed in a converted barn, with twenty-five spaces rented by a mix of dealers. Some, like mine, were small booths specialising in a single field; others spread into larger areas for furniture and display cases.

It was an emporium in the true sense of the word. Mahogany long-case clocks brushed shoulders with vintage gramophone players, old leather-bound books and maps. Oriental carpets and tapestries jostled with china figurines, model animals and ceramics. And I loved it there.

I'd initially rented a booth just for one summer, and discovered I thrived among kindred spirits. The showroom, with its rare trickle of foot traffic, was ideal for quiet work, but after years in London and the bustle of my former TV job hosting *Fakes & Treasures*, I often felt isolated. Splitting my time between the Emporium, auctions and mobile valuations turned out to be the perfect balance.

As expected, the car park was packed. Fiona and Reggie Reynolds, who owned the Emporium, had pulled out all the stops – trade magazines, local papers, social media and regular spots on the nightly news. The coverage had been impossible to miss, and the buzz had brought enthusiasts from all over the British Isles.

Although the Emporium had hosted other exhibitions and festivals – *BearFest* being my personal favourite – *Crime on the Line* was the first of its kind.

Giles Oxley was an odd little man, quiet and timid – until someone mentioned his pet subject. Then he'd light up. He'd been a keen trainspotter the moment he could walk, and could quote the boiler pressure of any engine built before 1960. By the age of ten, he was already building miniature railway stations out of cardboard. But his real obsession lay in re-creating historical events. His dioramas took years to complete, his attention to detail extending far beyond the static. He focused on movement and timing too – running trains simultaneously, never touching, rerouting them into sidings or onto branch lines with track changes calculated to the second.

It was an expensive hobby, and Oxley needed serious money to fund it. That was where his day job as senior planner for the council came in. I knew he was married, though Felicity Oxley hadn't even appeared at the opening reception held in his honour. There were rumours of 'trouble at home', which I made a point of ignoring. As my mother loves to say, 'stay in your own lane'; in other words, mind your own business! Not that anyone really does.

I parked my car and headed inside.

The exhibition had been set up under a vast Clearspan tent in the outdoor courtyard. Each of the five dioramas had its own generous space, screened by free-standing panels hung with overblown sepia photographs of the original stations and surrounded by planters overflowing with daffodils, tulips and evergreen shrubs. Gas-fired heat lamps took the edge off the spring chill.

Slowly I made my way through the crowds, stopping here and there to greet familiar faces.

A hand touched my shoulder. I turned to find Rupert with Harry in tow.

'Just dropping him off,' he said. 'I've business in town.'

'Don't you want to see the Kaiser Adler, Father?'

'Kat will show you,' he said. 'I'll come back in an hour.'

Harry seemed disappointed. So much for a birthday treat.

'Come with me,' I said warmly. 'Let's see if you can take the Oxley Challenge.'

The Clearspan was filled with excited chatter. A long table, stocked with paper and pencils, was manned by the ever-efficient Fiona. Behind her, a huge projection of the Flying Scotsman lit up the canvas wall.

As the local celebrity and coordinator, I'd be drawing the raffle and presenting the prize for the Oxley Challenge later that afternoon. All the correct answers would be folded and dropped into a hat, and the winner would be announced with much fanfare.

We stopped at the table so Harry could grab a pencil and paper. His eyes lit up seeing the projection of the Flying Scotsman.

'If I win,' he said, 'do I *have* to drink the champagne?'

I laughed.

What I loved about Oxley's dioramas was that he'd sourced original newspaper articles, proof that these events had actually happened. It was genius. He even listed train models and waybills for accuracy.

'Ready, Harry? Let's go to the prairie!'

> Deadwood Gold Rush Hold-Up, 4 September 1876
> *Black Hills Pioneer*: Gold Train Ambushed on
> the Prairie!

This one sat in a velvet-framed theatre box with a painted prairie sky fading into dusk. A Rogers 4-4-0 steam engine thundered across the foreground, frozen mid-motion – brass fittings, dusty cowcatcher and curling smoke. Tumbleweed scattered the dry earth. Telegraph poles leant crookedly. Five bandits galloped alongside, rifles raised. Four wore colourful bandanas. The leader had a nylon stocking over his face.

'What do you see, Harry?' I said.

'A Rogers 4-4-0! Four leading wheels, four giant drivers for speed, no trailing wheels behind the firebox.'

'You certainly know your trains.' I leant in to whisper in his ear. 'Take a look at the lead rider. What's he wearing on his head?'

Harry squinted. 'Tights!'

'Well done!' I grinned. 'Nylon wasn't invented until 1935.'

'Cool!' He jotted it down. 'What's next?'

> The Palace on Wheels, India, 21 April 1923
> *Calcutta Courier*: Royal Saloon Looted – Priceless Gems Gone!

A gleaming BESA 4-6-0 in deep green with gold trim sat beneath a saffron sunset. The maharaja's cutaway saloon revealed opulent details – low divans, a Persian rug, a miniature tiger skin. Inside, a uniformed Indian officer stood beside an overturned jewellery case. Next to him, oddly out of place, was another man in scarlet tunic, breeches and wide-brimmed hat.

Harry gasped. 'Isn't that a Canadian Mountie!'

I laughed. 'Correct again.'

'We did Canada in geography. Two out of two! Now where's the Kaiser Adler?'

'In a moment, but first – Stalin.'

> Sabotage of Stalin's Iron Train, 11 November 1940
> ПРАВДА ВОЙНЫ: ПОЕЗД ТОВАРИЩА СТАЛИНА УЦЕЛЕЛ (*War Truth*: Comrade Stalin's Train Survives)

All rusted steel and gloom, the FD-class locomotive sat like a fortress – barred windows, angled plating. The end carriage had been blown apart. A tiny American flag was stuck in the crater. Bodies lay scattered in the snow.

'Well?' I prompted.

Harry frowned.

'It's 1940. Look again.'

His eyes lit up. 'America didn't enter the Second World War until after Pearl Harbor in December 1941!'

'Bingo!' I grinned. 'Three out of five. Now we'll see your Kaiser Adler.'

> Murder at Cologne Hauptbahnhof, 2 May 1916
> *Rheinische Morgenpost*: Rote-Kreuz-Schwester Stirbt Unter Rätselhaften Umständen (*Rhenish Morning Post:* Red Cross Nurse Dies in Mystery)

The Kaiser Adler stood centre stage on polished rails, its black-and-gold paint gleaming beneath a stylised glass canopy. The craftsmanship – the rivets, the intricate piping, the tiny engraved plate bearing the Adler's name – was stunning. I took out my loupe and passed it to Harry.

'Take a look at the details,' I said. 'See if you can spot what's off.'

'And it's worth thousands and thousands!' Harry leant in to take a closer look. 'Maybe it's the engine?'

'Maybe,' I smiled.

He frowned in concentration. 'It looks like the front buffer beam is missing a rivet.'

I was surprised he'd noticed that tiny detail – although it wasn't the answer and I told him so. 'Look at the soldiers.'

German soldiers in field grey lined the platform in formation, bayonets gleaming, while the Kaiser – unmistakable in Pickelhaube and cape – extended a hand to his men. One soldier with his sleeve pushed up checked his watch. In the background, half obscured by a luggage cart, lay the figure of a Red Cross nurse, her white uniform splashed with blood.

'That's a hard one,' came a voice. It was Alison Fisher, looking immaculate in a navy cashmere coat. Over one arm was her gorgeous taupe Birkin, which must have cost a fortune. I'd have to take a closer look to be sure it wasn't a knock-off, but the saddle stitching looked hand-done and the tiny Hermès lock that dangled from the leather clochette seemed to be the right size. Sunny Hill Lodge must be doing well. She flashed a smile. 'Do *you* know the answer, Kat?'

'I do,' I said. 'Do you?'

'Yes.' She gave a little laugh. 'I've been here practically every day trying to work it out. The Kaiser Adler is just . . . well, a masterpiece. What I'd give to own it.'

'You're a collector?' This surprised me.

'I'm just an admirer of beautiful things.' She turned to Harry. 'Well, young man. Do you want me to give you a clue? Clues aren't cheating.'

Harry heaved a sigh. 'OK.'

'Cologne was a major rail hub in the German Empire at the start of the First World War,' said Alison. 'Look at that soldier.'

Harry leant in again, wedging the loupe in his eye. 'He's checking the time.'

'Regular soldiers carried pocket watches,' Alison went on. 'It was only later in the war that anyone wore a wristwatch, and that was mainly officers.'

Harry pulled a face.

'I'm impressed,' I said.

'Don't be.' She laughed. 'I've been eavesdropping all week. But the Honeychurch Halt Heist defeats me – any idea what the inaccuracy could be?'

'That's the one I can't work out either,' I admitted.

The three of us crossed to the final diorama to join a circle of admirers surrounding Oxley, who was discussing the botched robbery. He wore the same shapeless beige jacket over a limp, washed-out shirt that he'd been wearing for the past two weeks. There was something almost ghostly about him – pale complexion, grey eyes, long, thin fingers, perfect for the painstaking work required to glue a milk churn to a model platform.

> Honeychurch Halt Heist, 13 October 1974
> *West Country Gazette*: Botched Robbery –
> Two Men Shot Dead

The diorama was encased in a blackout curtain because the heist had taken place under the cover of darkness. Clever lighting illuminated the signage, the short platform, the wooden shelter, signal box and lamp hut. A bridge crossed the cutting. A carefully placed spotlight acted as a full moon.

A Hornby Class 37 S6734, headcode 6B47 – boxy, weathered and streaked with exhaust – stood idling on the track. The wagons were an authentic jumble – a ventilated van, one piled with coal sacks, and a crimson brake van with a tiny guard's lamp mounted to the end platform.

Crates of whisky and cartons of cigarettes were stacked on the siding. In the shadows beyond, a row of camping coaches loomed, their windows dark. Behind the lamp hut crouched a small figure beside a bicycle lying on its side.

At the centre stood a man with his arms raised in surrender, facing a masked figure aiming a gun. Another masked man lingered nearby. The signalman – clearly Stan Holden – was slumped against the wooden shelter, badly injured – blood everywhere. The uniformed guard sat bound and gagged, lashed to an iron railing.

Seeing the diorama made me uncomfortable. It felt different – personal. I'd met Stan's daughter and heard what the failed heist had done to her family. Before, I'd looked at it as just another piece of local history. Now, it felt voyeuristic, and I didn't like it.

Harry, of course, was fascinated. To him, it was still only a story.

'Is that the policeman who got killed?' he asked eagerly. 'But why isn't he wearing a uniform?'

'Very interesting diorama,' said a voice, sounding faintly amused.

The elder of two men had come up beside us to study the diorama, the younger trailing a step behind. Alison's eyes lit up, and she smiled warmly, her affection for him obvious.

'Ah, there you are,' she said. 'I wondered where you'd got to.'

She darted forward to kiss his cheek. He gave a gracious nod as he leant on his cane. I noticed that his knuckles were heavily tattooed, which seemed at odds with his Savile Row suit. The younger man wore a leather jacket and was scrolling through his phone. I remembered at once where I'd seen them before – turning into the drive of Sunny Hill Lodge in a murdered-out Mercedes G-Wagon.

'Allow me to introduce Kat Stanford,' said Alison. 'You might have seen her on TV.'

'Tony Draycott.' The older man smiled, giving me an eyeful of bad English dentistry. 'I thought you looked familiar. *Fakes & Treasures*?'

His name sounded familiar too, but I couldn't quite place where I'd heard it before.

'And our paths crossed yesterday,' I said. 'On the drive at Sunny Hill Lodge.'

'So they did.' He gave a low chuckle. 'Marcus is trying to get me incarcerated, but I said no thank you. I'm perfectly happy where I am. Do you have a loved one at the lodge?'

'No. I was there on business.'

'I'm sure there must be a demand for your valuation services,' he said. 'Wouldn't you agree, Alison?'

Alison, who had been hovering in the background, stepped forward. 'I was thinking the same thing, Uncle Tony. We need someone like Kat on board.'

So not only did they know each other, they were family. The other man seemed uninterested. He was still absorbed in his phone.

'Marcus?' Tony said sharply. 'Don't you think it's a good idea?'

'Sure,' he muttered, without looking up.

'Do you have a business card?' Alison asked, holding out her hand.

I always carried a few with me and gave her one.

Her eyes widened. 'The Honeychurch Hall estate?'

'My showroom is there,' I said. 'But most of the time you'll find me here.'

'How extraordinary.' She gave a tinkling laugh. 'And here we are, in front of Honeychurch Halt – and no one can spot the error.'

'The Halt was closed in 1975,' Harry chimed in. 'I'm doing a project on it for school.'

'Ah, is it about the robbery?'

He shook his head. 'No, it's called *Hopping On and Off: A Brief History of Halts*. I want to win the Headmaster's Cup.' He leant closer to the display, frowning. 'You know, we have to do a practical part, too. I wonder . . . would it be cheating if I copied this idea and made my own diorama?'

Tony smiled. 'Well, I won't tell if you don't – and you are . . . ?'

'Harold Rupert Max Honeychurch, sir,' Harry replied with a little bow.

Alison snapped her fingers. '*West Country Round-Up.* Isn't there some event next weekend at Honeychurch Hall? An Arctic explorer – an ancestor of yours, perhaps?'

'Yes!' Harry beamed. 'That's my great-great-great-great-uncle, the honourable Gerald James Honeychurch. He wasn't an earl, though, because the title always passes down the eldest son's line. I'll have a title when Father dies. I'll be the sixteenth earl of Grenville!'

Everyone laughed. Even Marcus.

I ruffled Harry's hair with affection. He was so adorable.

'You should all come,' Harry said suddenly. 'There's a real polar bear. We call him Florian. My great-great-great-great-uncle captured him and brought him back to England . . . and I suppose he killed and stuffed him.'

'Good heavens!' Alison chuckled.

'There'll be cake and everything.'

That brought more laughter.

'And I can show you my Kaiser Adler – well, it's a family heirloom really, but when I'm the earl, then I suppose it will be mine!' Harry grinned, clearly pleased with the attention.

'A Kaiser Adler? Really?' Alison rolled her eyes. 'Somehow I doubt it.'

'We have!' Harry shot back. 'Haven't we, Kat? They're very rare and worth thousands and thousands of pounds. Only twelve were made in the whole world. You can ask Father. He'll be back in a moment.'

'Why don't we go and find him?' I said quickly.

'I'm not lying.' Harry stood his ground, looking from face to face with solemn earnestness. 'We really have!'

'Harry, come on,' I urged.

But he wouldn't budge. His chin came up. 'We have,' he said again.

'I've seen Alison here, of course, but I don't think we've met.' Oxley broke away from his admirers and joined us, neatly defusing the situation. 'Gentlemen? And you are . . .?'

To my surprise, Marcus stopped scrolling, suddenly alert. He clasped Oxley's hand in a firm grip. 'This is my father, Anthony Draycott. I'm Marcus. Impressive work here, and from what I hear, historically accurate.'

Oxley went rigid. Colour surged into his pale cheeks. 'I'm sorry – what did you say your name was?'

But before Marcus could answer, a voice cut through the crowd.

'Giles Oxley – a word, please.'

Ginny Riley, investigative reporter and a former friend, was striding straight for us with Troy Barnes, her cameraman, in tow. Phone out recording, camera rolling, she barged into our group.

'Is it true you're under investigation for bribery?'

Chapter Eight

Oxley's face, once flushed, now turned ashen.

'Ginny Riley, *Devon Live*,' Ginny said crisply. 'Is it true you accepted bribes for planning approvals? Because I have the names of every developer and landowner who lined your pockets. Would you like to comment?'

A hush fell. A ripple of unease moved through the onlookers, and someone near me muttered, 'Bloody hell. So it's true.'

Oxley opened his mouth to speak, but no words came out.

Harry tensed. I began edging him towards the exit, though it was hard to resist watching Ginny go in for the kill. Dressed all in black, with her sleek bob, scarlet lipstick and matching nails, she was the epitome of a hard, ruthless journalist. And then there was Troy – older, designer stubble, leather jacket and faded jeans. If Ginny was the hunter, Troy was the hound at her heels, effortlessly filming the chaos she created. Together they made a formidable pair.

The silence grew.

Ginny scanned the sea of curious faces.

'OK,' she said finally. 'Let's read out those names.'

I thought of the shoddy workmanship in the Polar Tearoom and the illegally installed bifold doors. My heart sank – what if Rupert's name was on the list? Harry was old enough to understand. I needed to get him out of the building quickly, but we were hemmed in.

'That's quite an accusation, young lady,' Tony broke in quietly.

Ginny turned sharply. 'Not an accusation. A statement of fact.'

'I think Mr Oxley is perfectly well within his rights to ignore such a loaded question,' Tony said.

Ginny's eyes narrowed. 'Excuse me?'

'I'm sure your editor appreciates sensationalism, but this is not the place,' he continued. 'This is a community event.'

'You're defending him. Why?' Ginny wasn't backing down.

'I'm simply asking you not to make a scene.' Tony nodded towards Harry. 'There are children present. It's unprofessional.'

Ginny's grip on her phone tightened. The camera continued to roll. 'The public deserve answers.'

'From who?' Tony's eyebrow lifted, mocking. 'An elected councillor merely under investigation or a desperate reporter who'll twist anything for a story.'

Ginny turned white. I'd never seen her rattled before. A murmur spread through the crowd. Someone called out, 'Fake news!'

'Marcus?' Tony said quietly.

Marcus sprang forward and grabbed the camera, deliberately lowering it. Nothing was said, but the message was clear. Stop, and get out.

I glanced at Oxley, expecting relief, but instead, he looked terrified.

'Let me assure you,' Ginny said stiffly, though her voice wobbled, 'the truth always comes out.'

Just then, Reggie muscled through the crowd. He looked flustered. Any kind of conflict made him feel uncomfortable, and it showed.

'Excuse me, Miss Riley, I'm going to have to ask you to leave, or I'll be calling the police.'

Ginny muttered something derogatory under her breath, then nodded to Troy. The crowd parted in silence to let them through.

Harry pressed closer to my side, his small hand finding mine.

'Come on,' I whispered. 'Let's go and find your dad.'

Rupert was waiting outside the main entrance, texting on his phone. He shoved it hastily into his pocket as we joined him. A black Escalade peeled out of the car park with Troy at the wheel and Ginny riding shotgun.

'You didn't see the Kaiser Adler.' Harry sounded flat, but then he brightened. 'And you missed the fight.'

'Hardly a fight,' I said hastily.

'A fight?' Rupert frowned.

'The lady reporter and the cameraman,' Harry went on. 'Lining pockets – whatever that means. And having a special list.'

'A list? What kind of list?' Rupert asked sharply.

'Of names connected to Oxley,' I answered. 'In case you hadn't heard, he's been suspended pending an investigation into accusations of bribery and corruption.'

Rupert went very still. Then he briefly touched Harry's shoulder. 'Come on. Let's go.'

'Will you take photos of the Halt diorama?' Harry shouted to me as he was practically dragged away. 'For my project!'

They headed off. I turned to go back inside, almost colliding with Tony and Marcus on their way out.

'Unpleasant scene,' said Tony. 'I do hope young Harry wasn't too upset.'

'It was awkward,' I agreed. 'But Harry's fine. He's already forgotten about it.'

To my surprise, Alison was waiting in my booth. 'You've got some lovely things. I told you I admire beauty.'

'I've got more back at my showroom,' I said.

'I wasn't sure if you'd heard about Connie Hicks,' she said. 'Her husband called me. Someone's got to break the news to poor Stan, not that I think he'll really understand. Dementia is such a cruel disease.'

I hadn't thought much about Stan – maybe because Connie had been so dismissive of him. Or maybe because

I was still stuck on the feeling that I could have done something to save her. Then an idea struck.

'Would you happen to know what actually happened?'

'Ian said she suffered a hypoglycaemic episode.'

The surprise must have shown on my face. It might explain how Connie died, but not why the MCU were involved. I kept that thought to myself.

'I'm afraid Ian's going to have to decide what to do about Stan.'

'Oh?' I said. 'I thought some kind of railway fund covered his fees.'

Alison blinked, taken off guard. 'I don't know where you got that idea.' Her eyes narrowed. 'What did Connie tell you?'

'I must have misheard,' I said lightly. 'But I do need to sort out Stan's memorabilia. I suppose it all goes to Ian now.'

'I'm happy to take it off your hands,' Alison offered.

'That's kind,' I said. 'But given the circumstances, I'd rather return it to Stan directly.'

She hesitated, then said, 'Did you know that Connie's father was the signalman injured during the heist?'

'I didn't until yesterday,' I admitted. 'Connie showed me his award.'

Alison had edged closer, backing me into the corner. She stood near enough that I could smell coffee on her breath. Her skin bore the telltale greyish sheen of too much Botox.

'Such a tragedy,' she said. 'Two men shot dead for a few cases of whisky – unless the rumours were true and they'd expected to find something more.'

'Oh,' I smiled, 'the infamous diamonds. No, everything was accounted for.'

'*Tant pis*,' she said with a little shrug. 'I wondered if that might be the answer to the Oxley Challenge. A historical inaccuracy by omission.'

'I hadn't thought of that.'

'The diamonds were on the waybill, after all. I'll say this for Oxley, he's thorough. I suppose we'll have to wait for the prizegiving to know for sure.'

'I'd like to find out too,' I said, relieved when she finally stepped back.

'Oh, that reminds me – could you value a few paintings for me on Tuesday?'

'I'd have to check my diary. Perhaps I can call . . .'

'I'll wait while you do.'

Suppressing a sigh, I dug my paper diary out of my tote. She leant in, reading it upside down, and jabbed a finger at the page. 'There. Two o'clock. Perfect.'

The rest of the afternoon flew, and soon it was time for the raffle: a freight train ride in the brake van, a 'Drive a Train' footplate experience, and a dining trip for four on the South Devon Railway's murder mystery evening.

Then came the climax of the exhibition – the announcement of the Oxley Challenge winner.

But Oxley seemed oddly subdued. No one had spotted all the historical inaccuracies – least of all the one at Honeychurch Halt – and he flatly refused to reveal the answer.

I was stunned. There would be no winner. I was disappointed, too. The least Oxley could have done was to give us a few clues.

The crowd didn't take it well.

'Bit convenient, don't you think?' someone called out.

'How much do we have to pay you for the answers?' laughed another.

Then a sharper voice cut through, 'Yeah. Bet he'll take a bribe.'

Oxley went rigid. The mood was turning ugly.

Fiona appeared, red-faced, pushing through the crowd. 'All right, that's enough. This way, Giles.' She hustled him out of the tent, through a rear door and out of sight.

The crowd began to disperse, still grumbling. It was such a let-down, made worse by a few people demanding the answers from me, and insisting I must know them – which, of course, I didn't. A miserable end to what had been a successful exhibition.

Just then, a woman tapped me on the shoulder. I braced myself for another complaint.

'Do you have a moment to show me the Jumeau doll? I rang about it a few days ago.'

'Ah, of course.' I seized on the welcome distraction. 'Let's go to my booth. I set her aside yesterday.'

It must have been half an hour later, after my customer had left with her purchase, that Reggie sought me out.

'Kat, have you seen Oxley? We're closing up in a few minutes, but his car's still outside. I'd hate to lock him in.'

Inexplicably, I thought of June being stuck in the Natural History Museum overnight. 'I'll go and find him.'

I returned to the Clearspan tent, where Oxley was hunched over Cologne station, carefully lifting the Kaiser Adler from the tracks. A dark wooden case marked with the imperial eagle – *Märkisch & Sohn, Berlin, Germany* – sat on the floor. A long gouge cut across the eagle's wing on the lid of the crate.

A specialist team were scheduled to arrive first thing in the morning to dismantle the displays and crate everything for storage before returning it all to Oxley's home. I'd organised them myself, knowing better than to let volunteers loose on anything this valuable.

'I thought the displays were being taken down tomorrow,' I said. 'We're closing now.'

He didn't look up right away. When he did, his face was pale and damp with exertion.

'Just need to take this.'

'Let me help you.'

Together we settled the locomotive into the faded royal-blue silk padding. She fitted perfectly. Oxley replaced the lid.

'Are you selling it?' I asked, curious.

He didn't answer, and I didn't push it. My feelings were mixed. What should have been a triumphant end to the exhibition had turned sour, and I felt irrationally responsible.

'I'll help you carry it to your car.'

Outside, the car park was deserted except for my Golf, Oxley's dark green Bentley and Reggie and Fiona's BMW.

We loaded the case into the boot. He covered it with a tartan blanket, then, murmuring a thank you, climbed in and drove off without another word.

Why take the Kaiser Adler home tonight when everything else was being packed up tomorrow? I stood there watching the Bentley disappear though the gate, then turned back inside to let Reggie and Fiona know he was gone.

Chapter Nine

I'd missed the Friday-night rush hour and was anxious to get home. It had been a stressful day. I was desperate to speak to Mallory – not just about Connie's death, but about the scene Ginny had made at the exhibition. It was good to have a partner to confide in, someone I could simply talk through the day with. Mum would understand, of course, but I also knew her well enough by now to realise that once she was writing – or 'hunkered down', as she liked to call it – she wouldn't want to be disturbed.

But all that was forgotten as I rounded a bend and came to an abrupt stop. A *Road Closed* sign partially blocked the lane to Ashcombe Barton – my usual shortcut to Honeychurch Hall. A yellow diversion board pointed left, sending traffic off on a longer, winding route that would easily add fifteen minutes to my journey.

Two men in their late twenties wearing high-vis jackets were leaning against a white transit van parked on a grass verge. One, in a South Devon Rangers baseball cap, was scrolling through his phone. The other had a handlebar moustache and was smoking. It looked like they had finished for the day.

I hit the horn.

The baseball cap wandered over.

I smiled. 'What's the problem here? I took the road this morning. There was nothing wrong with it then.'

'Filling a pothole, love.'

'A pothole?' I frowned. 'Where exactly?'

He called over his shoulder. 'Hey, Brad, when can we open the road?'

Brad wandered over. 'She'll have to take the diversion.'

'But I live at Ashcombe Barton,' I lied.

The two men exchanged a look. 'I'll make a call,' Brad said, already turning away.

A call? Who to? On a Friday night?

The one in the baseball cap went back to scrolling.

That was enough for me.

I dropped the car into gear and drove straight around the *Road Closed* sign, darting down the narrow lane, confident I wouldn't meet any oncoming traffic. It was very much off the beaten track.

At the bottom of the hill lay Ashcombe Barton. The old farmhouse stood long abandoned, its windows and door boarded up. The cowsheds and corrugated-iron farm buildings were empty, surrounded by the usual detritus – rusting agricultural equipment, tangles of baler twine and scraps of black plastic.

And that was when I saw the dark green Bentley.

It was parked on the concrete apron outside what would have been a milking shed. I'd heard there were plans to build four executive homes here – no doubt Oxley had had a hand in that. Perhaps that was why he'd stopped. Interesting that he'd circumvented the *Road Closed* sign too.

I slowed to squeeze past and glanced at the car.

Oxley was sitting bolt upright, staring ahead, hands locked on the steering wheel. The events of the afternoon must have unsettled him more than I realised. He'd been very subdued when we parted ways. I just hoped he was all right.

I pulled up a few yards on and got out.

The Bentley's engine was still running. My heart began to hammer. I knew at once that something was wrong. He hadn't even noticed me. I rapped on the window. Nothing. I knocked again, harder. Still no response.

Gingerly I opened the door – and to my horror, he tumbled sideways, collapsing into my arms, unexpectedly heavy. I couldn't hold him. I sank to my knees, and he lay awkwardly across me, half in, half out of the car. I could feel that his body was still warm.

'Mr Oxley,' I said, insistent. 'Giles! Giles! Can you hear me?'

No reaction.

I eased myself out from under him. His lower half remained twisted in the seat, held by the belt.

I fumbled for his wrist, for a sign – anything.

No pulse.

I rushed to my car for my mobile and dialled 999.

'It's urgent,' I said, my voice cracking. 'I'm at Ashcombe Barton. A man has collapsed in his car. I . . . I don't know what happened. I just found him.'

'Help is on the way,' the operator said, calm and deliberate. 'Do you know if he has an ICE contact or medical ID on his mobile?'

I saw a magnetic holder on the dashboard, but no mobile. 'Hold on, please.'

I ran around to the passenger side and pulled open the door – reaching over to turn off the engine – then peered under the seat and into the footwell. I spotted a strange little plastic cap the size of a fingernail, but nothing else. The car was new and the carpets clean.

'I can't see it.'

'Try his pockets,' the operator urged.

I hesitated. The idea of rifling through Oxley's pockets felt intrusive, but I was desperate. No luck again.

'The ambulance will be with you soon,' the voice reassured me. 'Is there a blanket in the car? A coat? Something to keep him warm.'

'I think there's a blanket in the boot.'

But when I opened it, the tartan blanket had been shoved aside, revealing . . . nothing.

And then it hit me.

The case holding the Kaiser Adler was gone.

Oxley had been deliberately stopped. The road closure, the diversion – I'd already had my suspicions, but now I was certain. The two young men hadn't been road workers. This was planned.

'Hello? Are you still there?' the operator prompted.

'Yes . . . yes,' I said quickly. 'There's . . . there's been a theft. Please tell the police.'

'They've been notified,' said the operator smoothly. 'I'll stay on the line until they arrive.'

But I needed to talk to Mallory. I felt sick and shaken. I put the operator on hold, my fingers trembling. Thankfully, he answered on the first ring. It all tumbled out in a rush. For a moment, he was silent, then he said, 'I'm on my way.'

It couldn't have been more than ten minutes before I heard the sirens. A police vehicle arrived, then the ambulance. A second patrol car appeared from the opposite direction, boxing my car in.

I couldn't have left if I'd tried.

I scanned the police cars for Mallory, but he wasn't there.

The driver of the first car jumped out. It was PC Quinn, the officer I'd seen at Honeychurch Halt the day before. She hurried around to open the passenger door, and a woman stepped out, dressed in a trench coat and heels, self-assured and confident.

I knew at once who she was.

Chief Superintendent Stella Greenleigh.

Chapter Ten

I was taken aback by the sudden activity surrounding Oxley and his Bentley: the flashing lights, the ambulance, the police – and the Major Crime Unit. I hadn't even mentioned the name of the train to the dispatcher, let alone its value. So what were they all doing here?

Anxiously I watched from the shadows, unable to see what the Cruickshank twins – our local paramedics – were doing with him. Was he still alive? I just didn't know. Stella also disappeared from view. When she emerged minutes later, she was barking orders, efficient but urgent. Quinn kept close, constantly speaking into her shoulder mic.

The forensics team arrived in paper suits and gloves. One unfolded a collapsible screen while another laid out yellow evidence markers surrounding the Bentley.

I knew at once that Oxley was dead.

And still no sign of Mallory.

Stella looked up and spotted me. For a split second, she seemed startled, then the professional mask came down.

'Well, Ms Stanford,' she said drily, 'you do get around. Yesterday it was Honeychurch Halt, and today here you are again.'

She was so cold, so devoid of emotion. I just couldn't imagine her with my Mallory.

'Isn't Detective Inspector Mallory with you?' I asked.

Stella gave a slow, measured smile and glanced at the woman beside her.

'Did we stow him away in the boot, Quinn?'

'No, ma'am,' Quinn replied with a small smirk.

'Giles Oxley.' Stella already had her police notebook in hand and a Montblanc rollerball poised. 'You found him?'

'He's dead, isn't he?'

'Why don't you tell me what happened?'

I repeated everything I'd told Mallory. Stella bombarded me with questions – short, pointed and relentless. But when I mentioned that Oxley had fallen out of the car on top of me, her expression hardened.

'You mean you touched the body!' she exclaimed. 'And then you said you opened the passenger door?'

I blinked. 'I didn't know he was . . . he was dead. I thought he was unconscious.'

'So the body and the vehicle have been contaminated.' Her jaw tightened as she made a note.

'Contaminated?' My stomach dropped. 'I . . . I'm sorry. I was only trying to help. He was alive when—'

'Alive? How exactly do you know that?'

Under her cold stare, I faltered. 'His body . . . it was still warm. I thought maybe he'd had a heart attack.'

'Leave the diagnosis to the medical profession,' Stella said coolly. 'Dispatch mentioned there was a theft.'

'The Kaiser Adler,' I said, then added, 'It's a valuable model train.'

'A train?' she said sharply. 'How do you know about that?'

'Because I helped him load it into the car. There were plenty of people at the exhibition who saw it.'

'Exhibition?'

'*Crime on the Line*,' I said. 'It's been running at the Dartmouth Emporium for two weeks. Today was the last day.'

Stella frowned. She and PC Quinn exchanged puzzled looks before she was back to business. 'Why do you think it was stolen?'

'The last Kaiser Adler sold at auction for eighty thousand pounds. It's a collector's dream.'

'Is that so,' she said slowly. 'Interesting.' She didn't seem convinced.

'I'm sure it was deliberate,' I said. 'There was a diversion. You must have seen the *Road Closed* sign at the turn-off from the main road.'

'The road was open,' said Stella. 'I don't recall a diversion, do you, Quinn?'

'No, ma'am.'

'But that makes it all the more obvious!' I exclaimed. 'They must have cleared it away. Two young guys – not looking remotely like road workers, by the way.'

Stella cocked her head. 'Which route did you take if the road was supposedly closed?'

'I drove around the sign,' I admitted. 'And the Bentley's engine was still running when I found it. Maybe I interrupted the thief?'

I hadn't considered that before, but now it seemed perfectly logical. Still, whoever took the train would've needed a vehicle, and I hadn't passed anyone. They must have come from the other direction. With all the twisting lanes, it would have been easy to make a clean getaway.

'Maybe.' Again Stella didn't sound convinced.

'Perhaps the shock prompted a heart attack,' I suggested.

But her mind seemed to be somewhere else entirely. 'So not only did you touch the body and both the driver's and passenger-side doors, you also handled the car keys. What about his mobile phone? Did you happen to pick that up too? Pop it into your pocket, perhaps?'

I bristled. 'There was no mobile. The dispatcher asked me to look for it in case there was an emergency contact. I believe he's married.'

'Yes, we know.' Stella flicked through her notebook. 'And your role at the Emporium?'

The change of subject felt dismissive. Clearly Mallory hadn't told her much about me. I didn't know if that was a blessing or a curse.

'I have a booth there,' I said. 'I specialise in collectors' dolls and—'

'Did anything unusual happen at the exhibition that stands out in your mind?' she demanded.

I shrugged. 'Everything was fine until Ginny Riley turned up.'

'The reporter?' Stella's sour expression made her feelings clear.

I nodded. 'She breezed in with her cameraman demanding answers about the bribery and corruption investigation. I wasn't sure if—'

'Yes, we know about that.' Stella cut me off. 'Quinn, check the security cameras inside the Emporium and in the car park.' She glanced back at me. 'I assume they have them.'

I nodded.

Quinn was already speaking quietly into her shoulder mic.

Stella's gaze drifted past me to where the Cruickshank twins were preparing to load Oxley's covered body onto a gurney.

I felt sick. 'Could I have done anything to save him?'

Stella just looked at me. 'As I said, let's leave that to the medical profession. That will be all for the moment.'

'The Kaiser Adler could be out of the country by now,' I said. 'Thieves move quickly.'

'Yes, they do.' She snapped her notebook shut. 'As I said, you're free to go.'

'Free?' I raised an eyebrow, gesturing to my Golf, trapped between a patrol car and the ambulance.

'On it, ma'am,' Quinn murmured, speaking into her shoulder mic again.

A moment later, the patrol car reversed into a gateway, clearing my exit.

Stella's questions were unsettling, but not as much as her obvious hostility towards me. And where was Mallory? There had to be a good reason he hadn't shown up. I wasn't about to play the needy girlfriend and demand explanations. He knew Stella had taken charge; he'd find out soon enough that we'd spoken.

Yes, I was jealous. Stella Greenleigh was everything I wasn't. I couldn't picture them together – and by mutual agreement, Mallory and I never discussed our past relationships.

All I knew was that Stella had once been married. She and Mallory had had an affair. There were even rumours of a boxing match with her husband. Mallory had requested a transfer. Stella had got divorced – and now she was free.

Free to pursue Mallory again, perhaps?

I hated that insecurity was creeping in. I'd been through it before, with my ex-fiancé, David Wynn, who had never truly severed ties with his estranged tabloid-journalist wife. I'd ended it, and he'd eventually got divorced.

But Mallory wasn't David, or any of my ex-boyfriends.

I could feel myself spiralling. Maybe it was easier to fixate on my love life than dwell on Oxley. Or Connie. Could I have saved them both if I'd reached them sooner?

I needed to talk to someone. And the only person I knew who would always listen was my mother.

Chapter Eleven

I was so lost in my own thoughts on the drive to see Mum that I barely registered the turn. I slowed to take the tradesmen's entrance, only to have Keith come barrelling out at the same time.

It was dusk; my headlamps were on, but his weren't.

I swerved, cursing, as he shot past with a cheerful thumbs-up. Before I could catch my breath, June stepped straight into my path. I hit the brakes, tyres skidding.

She slammed both palms down on my bonnet – as if that would've stopped anything. Then, gesturing for me to lower my window, she stepped up alongside.

'I nearly hit you,' I exclaimed.

'Can I cadge a lift?' she said. And without waiting for an answer, she wrenched the passenger door open and folded herself into the front seat.

She flipped down the visor, the light flickering on, and leant in close to study her reflection in the mirror.

'Thought as much,' she grunted. 'Beard burn. Is it obvious? What do you think?'

She turned to face me. I glanced over. Even in the dim light, I could see her skin was inflamed and blotchy.

'It looks painful,' I remarked.

We set off.

'It's not an allergy exactly,' she said, rubbing her chin. 'More like . . . epidermal trauma due to aggressive follicular abrasion.'

'Oh dear.' I didn't know what else to say.

'Oh well.' She flipped the visor back up. 'I told Keith he'll have to shave that beard off or we're finished. But his wife likes it.'

'Oh, so he *is* married?'

'That's how I like them,' she said bluntly. 'I don't want to be tied down.'

There was nothing to say to that. So much for loyalty. Mum was right. It was highly unlikely she'd last long at the Hall.

So I asked her.

'My long-term plans?' She sounded incredulous. 'I'm here now, aren't I?'

There was nothing to say to that, either.

I pulled up outside Honeychurch Cottages. June opened the door as if to get out, then paused. 'Do you want to come in? There's sherry.'

'Sorry, I've got plans,' I said, which was true – and in any case, sherry wasn't a favourite of mine.

She cocked her head. 'What kind of plans?'

'I'm seeing my mother.'

'I'll come!'

I blinked. 'It's personal, really. Sorry.'

'I don't mind.' She settled back in the seat and shut the door again. 'I've been longing to take a nosy around her place. The Carriage House, right? Has she got sherry?'

After the day I'd had, I didn't have the energy to argue. I'd let Mum send June packing.

We pulled into the courtyard, setting off one of my mother's latest obsessions – motion-activated security lights. They flared up, blinding us. It was like driving onto a floodlit football pitch.

'Blimey,' June muttered. 'I feel like Rudolph with this chin.'

'It was his nose.'

We drove into the carriageway through the high arched double doors. More security lights burst into life in rapid succession.

I parked next to my mother's red Mini.

'She owns all this, does she? Nice skylights.'

I'd grown so used to seeing the Carriage House that I often forgot how impressive it truly was.

My mother had retained all the original fixtures and features of the carriageway. The floor was laid in cobbled herringbone. At one time, it would have housed four horse-drawn carriages.

A row of stalls lined either side, each accessed through red-brick arches engraved with the family crest and motto. Polished metal nameplates still marked where the horses had once resided – now resting peacefully in Edith's beloved equine cemetery in the park.

We got out just as Mum and Delia – embroiled in a serious conversation – emerged from the doorway leading to the old grooms' quarters, where my mother now lived. Both squinted into the sudden glare of the security light.

'Oh,' said June. 'Have we missed something?'

Mum and Delia exchanged a look that made it clear June was not welcome.

'I'm just leaving,' Delia said pointedly.

'Well all I can say is that I hope you find it,' said Mum.

'That flag still hasn't turned up?' June asked. 'You'll be in trouble if it doesn't.'

'It's not a flag. It's a standard,' Delia said with a sniff. 'And it's not missing. It's been mislaid.' Her eyes narrowed as she studied June's appearance. 'What have you done to your chin? It looks infected.'

'I could say the same to you,' June shot back. 'How d'you get that bruise? It wasn't there this morning. Or last night when you were on *West Country Round-Up*.'

'That was taped days ago,' Mum pointed out.

'So what happened to your face?' June asked again.

She was right; a dull flush, tinged with the first hints of purple, bloomed across Delia's cheekbone.

'She came off her new bicycle,' Mum said. 'What's *your* excuse?'

'Beard burn,' June said dismissively. 'I told you to be careful, Delia. I told you those things have a mind of their own! Electric, isn't it? Must have cost a bomb.'

That was when I noticed a shiny bright pink bicycle leaning against the rear wall. The electric motor was barely visible, discreetly tucked into the rear hub, but the fat tyres and oversized basket had all the subtlety of a carnival float.

'It was a gift,' Mum said. 'Wasn't it, Delia?'

Delia gave a coy smile.

Mum caught my eye. She must have sensed something was up and mouthed, 'Are you OK?' I shook my head.

'Well,' she said briskly. 'We'd all better get on. I'm sure June wants to talk to Delia about what she plans to do with Florian.'

June scowled. 'I need that polar bear out of sight or I'll be gone, mark my words.'

But Delia seemed more concerned with her bicycle, eyeing it with something close to fear. She swapped her Louboutins for flat pumps, carefully placing the designer shoes into the pannier.

'Why don't you make sure Delia gets home in one piece, June?' my mother suggested. 'I'm sure you can keep up with her. You've got a big stride.'

June nodded. 'Go on, Delia. Mount it.'

Delia straightened her shoulders, grabbed the handlebars and straddled the frame. June darted forward to help.

Delia twisted the throttle. Too much. The bike lurched forward, and she let out a startled squeak, feet scrabbling for the pedals. But it went nowhere, held firm by the strength of June's arms.

'I'm fine,' Delia shrieked. 'Let go. Let it go!'

Freed from June's grip, the motor kicked in and Delia shot out of the Carriage House. June set off after her at a steady jog.

Mum sniggered. 'What kind of man buys his girlfriend an electric bicycle? Designer shoes, yes. But that thing?'

I managed a half-hearted smile.

Mum frowned. 'What's wrong, darling?'

Now that we were alone, the horror of finding Giles Oxley, Stella's questions, Ginny's appearance at the Emporium all came rushing back with a vengeance.

So I told her.

Mum shook her head with dismay. 'What is it with you? You seem to attract death wherever you go!'

I burst into tears.

'Oh dear.' She patted my arm in an absent-minded sort of way. 'Oh well. Never mind.'

Never mind?

'Can't I come in for some tea and sympathy – actually, a brandy would be better.'

She hesitated. 'Do you mind if we chat about this tomorrow?'

'Tomorrow?' I was disappointed. 'You've got something more important than consoling your daughter who just had a dead body fall on top of her?'

But my mother was gazing across the courtyard at the converted piggery – her writing house.

'Wait,' I said. 'You're writing again!'

'Yes, I am.' Mum beamed happily. 'Harem Historicals! I spoke to my agent this afternoon and pitched the idea for the new series, and she loved it. We're meeting on Monday in London to discuss. I need to get up to the attics.'

'Attics?'

Mum rolled her eyes. 'Cassandra Mary's steamer trunk, remember? Just think of all those secrets she brought back from the desert, waiting for me to reveal!' She pulled me in for a quick hug. 'You'll be fine. You've got Mallory to console you now. You don't need your mother.'

'I'll always need you, Mum.'

'Perhaps he'll bring his saxophone to distract you.'

My cheeks burnt at the memory. I'd been surprised when Mallory admitted he played the saxophone – and even more foolish to tell my mother the romantic circumstances of how I'd found out.

'Hmm,' she said dreamily. 'I wonder if I could slip one into the Arabian desert?' She thought for a moment. 'How about this for the opening chapter . . .'

She closed her eyes and spoke in a low, sultry voice. 'The beautiful young woman lay sprawled on the silken cushions, her eyes half-lidded with expectation. The air shimmered with the languid plucking of a qanun, its delicate strings weaving through the scent of jasmine and cardamom. A ney's breathy melody drifted in the background while the soft thrum of the darbuka pulsed in time with her heartbeat. She didn't stir. Not yet. She was waiting.' Her eyes snapped open. 'Well? What do you think?'

'You don't need a saxophone,' I said drily.

She patted my arm again. 'Let's talk properly tomorrow morning over coffee and Dear Amanda. Be here at ten sharp. You can tell me about your discoveries...'

'The dead body, you mean.'

'... and what was June on about? Beard burn?'

'She's incorrigible. There's no way she'll stay.'

'And wait until you hear about Delia's new man,' Mum chattered on. 'But right now, I must away! The muse calls!'

I watched her flit off towards her writing house and decided there was no point trying to say anything else.

Tomorrow would have to do.

Chapter Twelve

Darkness had fallen by the time I pulled up to Jane's Cottage. Perched at the end of the service drive on a bluff, it offered spectacular views by day, but tonight, all was pitch black. No moon. No stars. It had started to rain again.

I thought of the bright glow of Mum's security lights and how dark and quiet it was up here. How remote.

I was a Londoner, born in Tooting, and had lived in the city all my life. Moving to the country to keep a promise to my father to look after Mum had never been part of the plan. But I'd grown to love it – the silence, the forests, the rolling hills. Tonight, though, as I headed for my front door, I found myself thinking I ought to get a dog.

Jane's Cottage had started life as a summer house in the 1800s, built on the original site of Warren Lodge, where the warrener once kept watch over the Honeychurch rabbits. Poaching had been a serious business back then, punishable by death. A few of the old warning signs still dotted the estate.

It was a small house, but it suited me. The dowager countess had let me remodel it. I'd knocked through one of the two downstairs bedrooms to make a larger living room. I'd converted the loft into a mezzanine, added a spiral staircase, upgraded the kitchen and squeezed a power shower into the tiny bathroom.

Maybe I'd been foolish to spend so much on a house that wasn't mine. It had never crossed my mind that I wouldn't stay – until that unfortunate business with Eric Pugsley.

It made me feel so . . . restless.

I'd be lying if I hadn't thought about a future with Mallory. He was renting Delia's son's barn nearby. Although we often stayed over at each other's places, living together wasn't something I wanted. But at forty, time was racing by, and if we were going to have children, my biological clock was ticking.

My phone pinged. A text from Mallory saying he wasn't sure if he could come after all. I'd half expected it. He signed off with *Love you*, and it wasn't until I read those words that I realised how much they meant to me.

Resigned to an evening alone, I pulled on the baby-blue faux-fur onesie Mum had bought me for Christmas. It was, without question, the most unflattering thing I owned – part marshmallow, part deranged Teletubby – but gloriously warm and snuggly. I made a light supper of baked salmon and roasted beets, slipping the second fillet into the freezer for another night. I'd been here before. Dating a police officer came with unpredictable schedules.

Tray in hand, the remains of a bottle of Sancerre under my arm, I settled in front of the TV.

I caught the news – and almost choked on my wine.

Stella must have taken my warning to heart. The theft of the Kaiser Adler was the lead story. Police were treating Oxley's death as suspicious and urging anyone who'd been seen eyeing up the Kaiser Adler at the Dartmouth Antique Emporium to come forward with anything, 'no matter how small'.

There was a brief mention of Oxley being investigated for 'alleged' bribery and corruption, but otherwise the focus was on his skill as a prototypical model railway builder. A short clip of his dioramas at the Emporium was followed by an interview with a specialist who explained just how rare – and valuable – the Kaiser Adler was. Most critically, he said, it would either have been earmarked for sale on the black market or stolen for a serious collector.

I thought back to the exhibition. Plenty of people had shown an interest in the Kaiser Adler, but only one person stuck in my mind. Alison Fisher. She had expensive tastes, yet she didn't strike me as the connoisseur type.

I heard a car pull up outside. My spirits lifted – and quickly dropped. I really did not want Mallory seeing me dressed as a Teletubby.

The knock at the door, rather than the sound of a key in the lock, stopped me short.

It couldn't be him. I gathered what dignity I could, conscious of my ridiculous outfit, and opened the door.

Chief Inspector Stella Greenleigh stood there, ID in hand, rain trickling off her trench coat. She gave a tight smile. 'May I?'

I stepped aside and waved her in.

Her eyes raked over my appearance with ill-disguised amusement. 'Did I wake you?'

'Would you like a cup of tea?'

'No thank you.'

Without a word, she slipped off her coat – though I hadn't asked if she wanted to – and handed it to me. For a split second I pictured tossing it into the corner and stomping on it. Instead I hung it on a peg by the front door. It was a genuine Burberry, not a knock-off – another woman with expensive tastes.

Uninvited, she took the armchair, crossing her long legs clad in perfectly tailored navy trousers and Gucci loafers. A beige cashmere polo completed the look. No jewellery, just barely-there lipstick. Her long dark hair was swept back into a low ponytail. She would have been beautiful if not for the hard edge to her presence. Mallory had once loved her, which meant there had to be some warmth there somewhere. I just couldn't see it.

Meanwhile, I was starting to sweat – the curse of man-made fibres.

'You look flushed,' Stella remarked. 'Do you want to change into something a little less . . . flammable?'

'I'm fine.'

She reached into her handbag – Prada – and took out her notebook and rollerball.

'Let's run through your movements,' she said. 'And please be specific about timing.'

So I told her again.

'And this diversion. Can you describe the road workers? What were they driving?'

'They both wore high-vis vests. It was a white transit.'

'Ages?'

I shrugged. 'One was wearing a South Devon Rangers baseball cap. The other had a handlebar moustache. Late twenties, early thirties. Did you see anything on the CCTV at the Emporium?'

Stella looked up. 'Other than you loading the case into the car?'

Which basically meant she wasn't going to tell me.

'Let's talk about the Emporium now,' she went on. 'You were there for the entirety of the exhibition, which ran' – she checked her notebook – 'for two weeks?'

'Not all the time,' I said. 'But most.'

'Was there anything unusual, anything or anyone that stuck out? Perhaps someone showing too much interest in this train?'

'There was a woman who came to the exhibition at least four times,' I said. 'As I mentioned, I wasn't there every day. Alison Fisher. She's the new manager of Sunny Hill Lodge. It's a residential nursing home on the outskirts of Totnes. Very upmarket.'

'And why did she stand out?'

I gave an apologetic smile. 'It was just a feeling.'

'A feeling,' Stella muttered, but wrote it down all the same. 'Can you describe her?'

'Fifties – I wondered if she'd had work done, maybe Botox. You can always tell.'

'Can you?'

I glanced at Stella. Her skin was flawless, and yet she too had that waxy sheen on her forehead. I looked away. If I'd felt hot before, now I was on fire.

'Go on.'

'Lots of jewellery. She carried a genuine Birkin bag.'

'A Birkin?' Stella cut in sharply, then continued in a flat tone. 'Not something I would expect to see in this part of the country.'

'I thought the same,' I said, though my eyes drifted to her Prada.

She noticed. A small smile cracked the mask. 'Was this Alison Fisher alone?'

'She was with two men,' I said. 'She referred to the older one as Uncle Tony. He was mid to late eighties. Anthony and Marcus Draycott.'

Her pen stilled for just a beat before she jotted the names down.

'I had Harry Honeychurch with me – he's eleven.' I didn't mention that he stood to inherit the Honeychurch Kaiser Adler.

'So these men – the Draycotts – were they interested in the train?'

I hesitated. 'No, not really. To be honest, I'm not sure why they were there. They left before the raffle was drawn. It was Alison Fisher who seemed most keen.'

'You mentioned Harry Honeychurch. Any connection to Honeychurch Halt?'

'Not now, no. The Halt used to be part of the estate before it was sold to the South Devon and West Moorland Railway. The ninth earl was forced to sell under a compulsory purchase sometime in the late 1800s. Is this connected to Connie Hicks?'

Stella's eyes locked with mine. 'Why would you say that?'

'Because Connie's father was Stan Holden, the signalman who was injured during the botched robbery. And the strange thing is, he's now living at Alison's nursing home. Don't you think that's odd?'

'Has Mallory discussed this with you?' Her tone was sharp.

'Of course not. As I told you, I met Connie to value her father's railway memorabilia.'

'Where is the memorabilia now?'

'In the boot of my car,' I said.

Her eyes widened. 'Here? Why?'

'I brought the boxes home with me. That was why I was at the Halt this morning. I was returning them. I've catalogued and photographed everything. If you'd like, I can email you a copy of my report.'

'Thank you,' she said. 'That would be helpful.'

'Oh.' I wasn't expecting that. 'I couldn't find anything of value.'

'People's idea of value is subjective,' Stella remarked. 'Sentimental things are often priceless. Did she give any hint as to which piece might be . . . priceless?'

'None. She had been anxious to get them valued, and then suddenly she changed her mind. I told her to pick the boxes up from my showroom on Thursday evening. I waited. She never came. Her husband called me, worried, and the rest you know.'

Stella got to her feet. 'If I have more questions, I'll be in touch.'

I followed her to the door. She slipped into her trench coat. 'I'll take those boxes with me.'

'I was going to give them to—'

'Perhaps you need a coat?'

I flung a raincoat over my shoulders, pushed my feet into my wellies – no small feat given the thickness of the faux fur – and followed her outside, where I transferred the boxes into her car. I was glad to see the back of Chief Superintendent Stella Greenleigh.

Mallory didn't reply to my texts. My call went straight to voicemail, but I left a message to tell him that Stella had just paid me a visit.

That night, I couldn't sleep. My mind kept replaying Stella's questions. Why had she been so keen to take Stan's memorabilia away? She seemed far more interested in those boxes than in the Kaiser Adler – or Oxley's death.

It was only when I heard the dawn chorus that I finally drifted off.

Chapter Thirteen

'Oh, good heavens,' Mum declared as I walked into the kitchen at ten sharp. 'Look what the cat dragged in. Very boho.'

I'd only woken twenty minutes before, thrown on some clothes and shoved my hair up into a scarf-wrapped topknot.

My mother, however, was perfectly made-up. Neat skirt and blouse, pearls at her neck. I recognised that look. It was her professional writer look. She once quoted the legendary Barbara Cartland, 'Romance is beauty, I must look beautiful to write it.'

'Sit down,' she said. 'Have a cup of coffee. Let's give the *Dipperton Deal* a quick skim – it's a good one this week – but then I must away. My typewriter calls.'

I pulled out a chair. 'I'm glad someone is cheerful.'

Mum gave an exaggerated sigh. 'What's happened now? Did you find another body?'

'Mallory's ex-girlfriend turned up on my doorstep last night asking all sorts of odd questions.'

Mum gasped. 'Chief Superintendent Barlow!'

'Greenleigh, you mean. Barlow was her married name. She's now firmly single.'

'Perhaps you'd better start from the beginning – actually, perhaps not. I don't have time for you to go on too much this morning.' She sat back. 'Off you go. Give me your elevator pitch.'

'Elevator pitch?'

'The term is used for writers who bump into an editor or an agent in an elevator and try to pitch their story between floors. You've sixty seconds or less.'

'Oh,' I said. 'I can't remember how much I told you.'

'You went to Honeychurch Halt and someone had died. You'd only seen her the day before, so it was upsetting. Yesterday you saw Oxley's parked car. You thought he'd fallen ill. You stopped to assist, but alas, he was dead. Enter Chief Superintendent Greenleigh. Did I cover it all?'

'Yes,' I said grudgingly.

She pointed to the newspaper. 'Oxley's death didn't make this week's edition, nor did the Kaiser Adler.'

'It only happened yesterday,' I pointed out. 'The *Deal* would have already gone to press, and they don't have a digitised version. But it was all over the national news.'

'Bit awkward, don't you think?' Mum said. 'Here, Oxley has the centre spread, the Kaiser Adler is the *pièce de résistance*, and there is no mention of his being suspended.'

'Or dead,' I said drily, but it was more a gallows comment – not because I didn't care. 'Let's talk about something else.'

'*Regardez!*' Mum angled the newspaper so I could read it too. 'What do you think?'

> The Icebound Gentleman
> In celebration of the Honourable Gerald
> Honeychurch (1840–1912)
> this Easter weekend
> 2.00 pm–4.30 pm, entry £4.
> Includes high tea in the Polar Tearoom &
> commemorative souvenir book.
> Step into the frosted boots of one of Britain's most
> gallant explorers!
> On display for the first time in over a century:
> his original fur-lined overcoat and snow goggles;
> Florian, the famous polar bear, brought back from
> his final voyage;
> plus a rare public appearance of the Grenville
> Standard, paraded across battlefields for generations
> and now revealed to the public for the very first time.
> Local legend whispers: according to a long-standing
> village tradition, touching the golden fringe of the
> Grenville Standard is said to bring blessings of
> health, fortune and fertility. One-touch-only policy.
> Gloves provided. Booking essential.
> Call Delia Evans on 01806 772119.
> (As seen on TV.)

Promotional photos included a grainy figure kitted out for the Arctic covered in ice crystals – it could be anyone

– and Florian standing at the entrance to the Polar Tearoom, with a three-tier cake stand, a pot of tea and a china cup and saucer set on a snowy white tablecloth with a vase of spring flowers.

I thought of the current state of the tearoom – the chaotic muddle of wiring, the sagging ceiling and the controversial bifold doors. 'Who Photoshopped this?'

'June. She's techno savvy.'

'Techno savvy?' I raised an eyebrow.

'Or whatever they call it,' Mum said dismissively. 'But this . . .' she tapped the front page, 'it's only a week away! Delia's bitten off more than she can chew, that's for sure.'

'Especially if the Grenville Standard doesn't turn up.'

'And then there's Henri and his demands.'

'Henri,' I echoed.

'Her new man.' Mum shot me a mischievous grin. 'She's asked for Amanda's advice.'

Every Saturday, Dear Amanda's problem page provided us with great entertainment, and frankly was the main reason we'd started this weekly ritual. Amanda's true identity was a mystery. Since she'd been writing for years before Mum and I moved to Little Dipperton, it was natural to assume it had to be one of the village's elderly residents. At one time, we thought it was Muriel Jarvis, the postmistress, but then she died and the problem page continued. I had my suspicions that it could be the dowager countess, only because her no-nonsense, take-no-prisoners view seemed to translate to print. But logically, given Edith's failing health, how could that work? Someone at the *Dipperton Deal* had to be in cahoots.

Mum turned to Dear Amanda and smiled. 'Enjoy.'

I took a sip of coffee and leant in.

> Dear Amanda,
> I am in love. I have met a gorgeous man online who is very generous and has bought me two pairs of Louboutins and an electric bicycle.

I snorted into my coffee.

'I do wish you wouldn't do that,' Mum grumbled. 'It's so unattractive! Read on.'

So I did.

> For several years, my husband and I have been living apart. Recently I asked for a divorce, but he refuses to sign the paperwork. My soulmate is old-fashioned and won't see me in person until I'm legally free.
> From,
> Lovestruck

I was stunned. 'I'm not sure what to make of that.'

'I told her, Delia, you've only got one life. Live it!'

'Seems like Amanda agrees with you.' I read her reply aloud. '"At your age you don't have time to linger. Force him to sign. Good luck."'

'So Delia's going to the prison and demanding Lenny sign the divorce papers.'

'I didn't even know she was visiting him. She doesn't drive.'

'FaceTime,' said Mum. 'Letters. Reminding her of their until-death-do-us-part pact.'

'That's disgusting. Poor Delia.' I was getting upset. I'd nearly ended up as one of Lenny's victims myself. 'I really don't want to talk about him. Maybe it's a good thing she's met someone. What's he like?'

'I've seen photos. He's got all his hair. Reminds me of George Clooney. Younger than her, too.'

'Oh, Mum,' I said dubiously. 'I don't know about meeting someone online. That might not even be his real picture!'

'It is,' Mum insisted. 'They've spoken on Zoom. He moved his head.'

'Filters can make people look more attractive.'

She regarded me with amusement. 'Why can't she have met the man of her dreams? You have.'

'It just feels odd. Look what happened to Eric last year.' I sighed.

'Eric met that woman on holiday, not online,' Mum reminded me.

'Well, this Henri must be after Delia's money.'

'She doesn't have any.'

'Is he in good health?'

Mum blinked. 'What do you mean?'

I shrugged. 'Without meaning to be cynical, when a man gets to a certain age – to quote Amanda – he's looking for a nurse or a purse. Since Delia doesn't have the purse, maybe he's after the nurse!'

'Henri says she doesn't need to work,' Mum said. 'He wants to take her travelling.' She took a breath. 'I'm a tiny bit worried, I admit, but maybe you can make her see sense when you take her on Monday.'

'Take her where?'

'Now before you get annoyed, hear me out,' Mum began. 'You know I have to go to London to see my agent—'

'The answer is no,' I said firmly. 'I don't want to take Delia to the prison, thank you very much.'

'Please, dear,' Mum pleaded. 'You don't have to go inside. You can wait in the car. Delia's solicitor is bringing all the documents.'

'Why can't her son drive her there?'

'First of all, he wouldn't approve. Secondly, he's been posted back to Germany. And that ghastly daughter of hers lives in Scotland.' She reached across the table and patted my hand. 'Be nice. Let's help Delia so she can spend her remaining years being adored, pampered and ravished.'

'Ugh.' I tried not to picture that. 'Where is this prison anyway?'

'Wiltshire. Near Devizes,' Mum said. 'Just a couple of hours from here.'

'That's an entire day!' I groaned. And a whole day trapped in a car with Delia was something I'd do nearly anything to avoid.

'Please, darling. Just this once. For me.'

'For you?' I was resigned. 'I suppose I could visit some antique shops in the area.' I didn't know Devizes well, but

I was aware of a handful – Saddlers Antiques, Old Bell Antiques, Henry Aldridge & Son, to name a few.

Mum's phone rang.

'I'll leave you to it,' I said, getting up.

'Calm down, Delia. Take a deep breath.' Her eyes narrowed, then her expression turned incredulous. 'Don't be silly.' She caught my eye and gestured for me to sit. I couldn't hear what was being said on the other end, but it was definitely hysterical. 'You're both imagining it.' More frantic chatter. 'What do you mean? . . . I can't . . . What are you . . . Fine! I'm on my way.'

She ended the call with an eye-roll and stood.

'What was that about?'

'I've got to go.'

'I thought you were hell-bent on writing today,' I said. 'What's happened?'

Mum paused dramatically. 'June's collapsed. She claims the polar bear moved.'

'This I have to see.'

Chapter Fourteen

'We wanted to call an ambulance, but June wouldn't hear of it,' Delia said, clearly rattled. 'I found some old smelling salts of her ladyship's, but she knocked them clean out of my hand. Said she just needed to lie still for a minute.'

'Looks like someone felled a tree,' Mum muttered.

June was sprawled on the floor with a wad of towels under her head, eyes shut, arms flung wide, feet neatly together. On her way down, she'd taken the tablecloth and everything on it with her. Broken plates and glasses had already been swept into the corner.

'I heard screams first.' Delia's voice cracked. 'And then she staggered into the kitchen and just keeled over. When she hit the floor, it was like an earthquake. I thought I'd lose all the china on that dresser.'

'She should see a doctor,' I said. 'She might have a concussion.'

'She doesn't want to,' Delia replied.

'She's alive,' Mum said briskly. 'I can hear her breathing.'

So could I – steady and heavy.

'Well,' Mum declared, 'if you're considering her as your replacement, she can't be fainting all over the place. What about the ninth earl's *Fur, Feather and Folly* collection? Not to mention the polar bear. She's neither use nor ornament. If you ask me, she's a liability.'

'I can hear you.' June's eyes stayed closed, but her voice was strong. 'And that bear moved. Delia saw it too.'

'Not literally.' Delia faltered. 'But . . .'

'Show us,' Mum ordered.

'You can leave me here,' June said, still not opening her eyes. 'I'm fine.'

We trailed after Delia through the warren of dim corridors. As we neared the Polar Tearoom, she stopped short, visibly uneasy. 'Go on then, Iris. Have a look.'

Mum and I exchanged an amused glance.

At first, nothing seemed out of place. Florian was no longer blocking the end of the passage. But then Mum gave a startled little cry and grabbed my hand.

'There!' she whispered.

In the gloom of the dimly lit passage, the bear's blurry outline was visible behind the polythene sheeting in the makeshift doorway. Huge. Menacing. Sinister. As if he was ready to spring out and attack. I admit it, my heart skipped a beat.

'Oh, for heaven's sake,' Mum said, recovering quickly. 'Eric must have moved it. June's been nagging him for ages. You said he had to. You said he had a dolly.'

Delia bit her lip. 'I saw Eric first thing this morning, and he apologised that he wouldn't be able to move the bear today.'

'He's just teasing you,' Mum scoffed. 'Probably planning to surprise you.'

My mind jumped straight to Harry. Several Christmases ago – coincidentally during that dreadful business with Lenny – Harry and his little friend Fleur had tampered with the mummified hawk from the Crimea and managed to terrify half the village. That, too, had been part of the ninth earl's illustrious taxidermy collection. But if Harry was responsible this time, I just couldn't see how he'd have managed to move the bear alone. It had to weigh at least half a tonne – probably more.

In one fell swoop, my mother swept the sheeting aside and strode into the Polar Tearoom. 'We're perfectly safe. Florian doesn't have a weapon.'

Delia and I followed her in.

'Oh dear,' Mum said. 'Looks like he's broken the bifold doors.'

We both turned. Sure enough, the glass in one of the panels was cracked.

Delia's hands flew to her face. 'Oh no! How could that have happened?'

It seemed to be the final straw. She sank onto a wooden sawhorse, her face crumpling. 'I'm so stressed out. I feel the world's against me.'

'Of course it's not. You've got me. I'm on your side.' Mum's tone softened, as it often did when Delia was upset.

It was such an odd friendship, thriving when one of them was in trouble, but if either seemed happier than the other, it brought out a streak of dormant schoolgirl malice.

'I know,' Delia said, swallowing hard. 'But . . . I'm going to lose June. The tearoom still isn't finished, and now the bifolds are ruined. I've got a wait list for the Grenville Standard, but it's still missing. And when I tracked the delivery for the box of commemorative souvenir books . . .'

'*Tales from the Tundra: Adventures of an Arctic Explorer*,' Mum put in helpfully.

Delia nodded. 'They arrived yesterday, apparently, but no one has seen them.' A lone tear slid down her cheek. 'His lordship is going to be furious. I promised him I could pull this off. I got sponsors to foot most of the bill, and advance ticket sales covered the rest. I swore it wouldn't cost him a penny.'

'But the bifold doors are on him,' Mum reminded her. 'And you were on *West Country Round-Up*. All that publicity! All those people desperate to touch that fringe. Still, you're right to be worried, Delia. I know I would be.'

'Mum! Can't you see that Delia is upset?' I'd never actually felt genuinely sorry for Delia before, but over the last year, she'd put her heart into making Honeychurch Hall a success. It wasn't really her fault that things had gone pear-shaped.

She shot me a look of gratitude.

'Getting upset isn't going to solve anything,' Mum declared.

'I know that, Iris,' Delia retorted. 'You have no idea how hard it is for me to face Lenny. I haven't seen him since his sentencing.' Another tear crawled down her cheek. 'I'll never forget that look of despair. Our last conversation when he was still free. "Delia," he said. "Don't leave me. Remember our wedding vows. I don't know what I'll do if you abandon me now."'

'Well, that's bad luck on Lenny.' Mum's voice was hard. 'It'll all be over by Monday evening. We can celebrate your freedom. Maybe Henri will buy you another pair of shoes.'

Delia brightened. 'He promised me a new handbag.' This thought seemed to cheer her up. She threw back her shoulders. 'I suppose I'd better get on. Shall we see if June has recovered?'

June had. So we left them to it.

Mum dropped me back at the Carriage House to pick up my own car.

'Harry moved that bear,' she declared.

'Maybe.' But I was only half listening, distracted by a text from Mallory to say he'd be stopping by late afternoon.

Then my phone rang.

'Kat Stanford?' came a woman's voice. 'Alison Fisher here. I know we're set for Tuesday, but I wondered if you could do me a favour and squeeze in an extra valuation this afternoon. It's for one of the residents – her daughter's only here for the weekend and says she wants to take the painting back with her.'

I hesitated. Truth was, I didn't want to risk missing Mallory. But then I thought of Stella's questions. Oxley's death and the theft were public knowledge by now. Maybe Alison had a theory of her own about the Kaiser Adler.

And then there was the matter of Stan Holden.

Even though the police had taken his memorabilia, part of me wanted to see him. But what good would it do? How far along was his dementia? Did he know Connie was dead?

'Of course,' I heard myself say. 'I can be there within the hour.'

I dashed home to have a shower, hoping at least to make myself presentable for whatever lay ahead.

Chapter Fifteen

'Let's go to my office first.' Alison greeted me in reception, which looked exactly as I remembered it – pleasant enough furniture, bland carpet. All easy on the eye.

'I so appreciate you coming at such short notice,' she gushed. 'Do come this way.'

Today she was encased in a tight-fitting pencil skirt, Louboutins – was everyone wearing them in Devon these days? – and a flimsy leopard-print top with a plunging V neck.

She led me to a pair of double doors, stopping to tap a code into a small keypad mounted on the wall. Designed, of course, to keep the more vulnerable residents safe.

Once we were through, I saw that the place was very different now. Under Margery, classical music had drifted through the corridors, along with a pleasing scent of botanical air freshener. Most telling of all, any signs of disability – walkers, commodes, hoists – had been discreetly tucked away.

Not any more. Now, Radio 1 played louder than necessary. Mobility equipment cluttered the passages, and lingering in the air was the sharp, medicinal tang of disinfectant.

As I trailed after Alison, I noticed how few doors even had plaques – just the odd small nameplate here and there, breaking up long stretches of identical closed doors.

I peered into the residents' lounge as we passed. Wingback chairs sat in a circle, perfectly arranged – and completely empty.

'We're at full capacity, and two carers are out sick this afternoon,' Alison said, neatly contradicting my suspicion that no one was actually here. 'It always seems to happen at the weekend. Fortunately I live on the premises, so I can step in whenever needed.'

I managed a non-committal grunt.

'Our residents nap in the afternoons, unless there's a planned activity – flower arranging, small-animal visits, bingo, that sort of thing,' Alison went on. 'They're offered a three-course luncheon with three options. Supper is two courses with two options. We're privately funded, of course, and perhaps' – she paused to give me an indulgent smile – 'more expensive than most in the area, but I always say that you get what you pay for. Don't you agree?'

'It sounds like Stan Holden was very fortunate to be moved here,' I said. 'Connie mentioned you were the one who found him wandering along the main road.'

'Oh? She told you.' Alison seemed surprised. 'I'm just glad I was in the area. Who knows what would have happened to him.'

'Is his room on this floor?'

'No.' Alison's reply was brisk.

'How is he coping?' I asked. 'Does he know that his daughter is . . . well . . .'

'Dead?' Alison said bluntly. 'His son-in-law – Ian, Connie's husband – broke the news but I don't think he understood.'

I knew that Ian Hicks had come down from Shropshire. 'Is he staying here?'

'No, at the Seven Stars in Totnes,' said Alison. 'Naturally, we have a guest room for out-of-town visitors, but he declined the invitation. To be honest, Ian had never met Stan. It seems Connie hadn't been close to her father at all.'

I remembered Connie saying as much. Stan must have led a lonely life.

'I wondered,' I said in a rash moment, 'could I visit Stan?'

'Visit?' Alison seemed surprised. 'I'm afraid you'll be disappointed. He rarely makes any sense.'

'I'll take my chances,' I said.

Her eyes narrowed. 'Ah . . . is this about those boxes you were putting in your car on Thursday?'

Of course, Alison had been there when I'd transferred them from Connie's boot.

'Have you brought them with you? I'm sure Stan would love to have something familiar in his room.'

This was awkward. The police had taken them – though I still didn't understand why. So I told her.

Alison stiffened. 'The police? Whatever for?'

'Your guess is as good as mine.'

'Goodness, Stan's claims must have been right all along!' She gave a little laugh. 'Was there anything of value?'

'Not that I could see,' I said.

'Did Connie mention someone called Jacob to you?'

I shook my head. 'No. Why?'

'An old friend of Stan's, apparently. He speaks of him often.'

An awkward silence fell between us.

'Are your parents still alive?' Alison swiftly changed the subject.

'Just my mother,' I said.

'Well, when she's ready, do think of us.'

'I'll be sure to mention it,' I said, knowing my mother would rather throw herself under a train.

Alison opened the door to her office and stepped aside for me to pass.

I tried to hide my surprise. Her office looked more like a Regency drawing room than part of a care home. The walls were papered in a delicate damask, set off by painted panels in soft sage green. A graceful rosewood writing desk stood near the window, paired with a buttoned leather chair. Antiques – and expensive, too.

There was no computer in sight, only a stack of ivory writing paper and a cut-glass paperweight etched with the Sunny Hill Lodge logo. A gilt-framed oil painting – possibly a French original – hung above a silk-upholstered love seat. A silver tray stood on a side table, holding a cut-glass decanter and two crystal tumblers. Surely this couldn't be where she ran the business. I thought of her predecessor, whose office had always looked as if a bomb had just gone off.

Alison gestured for me to join her on the love seat.

'As you know, many residents have to downsize when they're no longer able to manage at home,' she began. 'One of our services at Sunny Hill Lodge is helping the families dispose of their possessions – valuations and so forth. As I mentioned at the Emporium, we could perhaps come to an arrangement with Kat's Collectibles? A generous retainer, maybe?'

'I'm quite busy with my own valuations and working my booth.'

'Of course you are.' Alison laughed lightly. 'We don't have people dropping dead every day. Perhaps once or twice a month. You could name your percentage – that's how you work, isn't it? A cut of the final sale?'

I gave a polite smile. 'Let's talk about the painting you mentioned on the phone first.'

Alison stood up and picked up a painting that had been leaning against the wall.

I recognised it immediately. *Summer Light Over Bramble Down* by Edward Hartley. It had once hung behind Margery's desk.

'Edward Hartley,' I said. 'An early-twentieth-century English painter known for his idyllic rural scenes. Margery loved it. She said it reminded her of childhood visits to her grandparents' farm.'

A pink flush flooded Alison's décolletage. She looked down at her hands as if to regain composure. 'Yes, when we bought the home, we bought many of the paintings and antiques too.'

'Oh?' I frowned. 'I thought this was for the daughter of one of the residents?'

'Yes, that's right.' Her eyes flickered before she met my gaze. 'It is.'

I let it go, wondering if I had misheard.

'Let me take it over to the light.' I already knew the value of this artist. Just a few hundred pounds, nothing more, but I prided myself on my professionalism, and as my mother would say, if a job's worth doing, it's worth doing well.

I carried the painting to the window. 'Do you have a cloth? Something I can put on the writing table so as not to scratch it?'

'Of course.' Alison disappeared through a door – I caught a glimpse of a washbasin and loo. She returned with a white hand towel. 'Will this do?'

For someone who said she was used to handling antiques for residents, I wasn't impressed.

I carefully laid the painting down. The frame was nothing remarkable – a standard gilt surround from a provincial workshop, most likely mid 1960s. The back confirmed it – machine-cut mitres, panel pins instead of hand-forged nails, and a backing board freckled with the telltale brown spots of age.

I took out my loupe and leant in to study the brushwork and the distinctive looping signature. Everything about it was perfectly genuine, just not especially valuable. Margery had loved it for sentimental reasons.

I straightened up. 'Probably around five hundred pounds.'

'I thought as much. I'm sure she thought it was worth thousands!'

'I'll write up the valuation this evening and email you a copy for the daughter to take with her. If she'd prefer a hard copy, just let me know.'

'Perfect.' Alison smiled. 'How much do I owe you for your time?'

'That won't be necessary,' I said. 'Consider it a freebie.'

'I'll see you out.'

'Would it be possible to see Stan now, before I go?' I said.

Alison shrugged. 'Of course. Let me find someone to take you.' She picked up the phone and dialled. 'Elena? Stan has a visitor. Could you take her up?' She listened for a moment, then nodded. 'That's fine, thank you.' Replacing the receiver, she turned back to me. 'We'll meet her by the lift. As I mentioned, we're a little short-staffed today, but it's no trouble.'

'Oh.' I felt uncomfortable – I didn't want to put anyone out – but I was determined to see him. 'I appreciate it.'

Alison ushered me into the corridor. We headed for the lift.

'Did you hear about Giles Oxley?' she asked, suddenly changing the subject.

I nodded.

'I couldn't believe it. We'd only spoken to him a few hours before,' she said. 'And the Kaiser Adler! Stolen! I heard it on the news. I'm surprised, but not really surprised. It was worth thousands!'

'I know. Terrible,' I agreed, careful not to offer anything more but secretly glad she'd brought it up. I hadn't found a way to raise the subject without sounding obvious.

'Do you think he was murdered for the train?'

I studied her face for any hint of meaning behind the question, but all I saw was curiosity. 'It could have been a heart attack,' I said. 'My boyfriend's a police officer. He's always telling me not to jump to conclusions.'

'Oh! How exciting,' Alison exclaimed. 'So you must have the inside scoop on all the latest scandals.'

'I wish.' I smiled. 'His favourite phrase is "I'm not at liberty to say."'

We both laughed.

'What will happen to Oxley's magnificent dioramas?'

The thought had crossed my mind, too. 'Maybe they'll be donated to a museum.'

'We never know when our number's up,' Alison mused. 'I see it every day, being here surrounded by the elderly. Some people don't understand why I do this, but I love it. It matters to me.'

'Have you been doing it for long?'

'This is actually my first nursing home.' She seemed proud. 'I own it! Of course, I have sleeping partners – investors – that I answer to.' She gave a small laugh. 'Aren't we all beholden to someone?'

I thought of my own situation at Honeychurch Hall and how easily Edith could turn me out if she chose. In a different way, Stan was beholden to Alison for taking him in.

A young woman in her early thirties, dressed in a pale blue tunic, was waiting by the lift.

'Ah, there's Elena,' said Alison. 'She'll take you to Stan's room.'

She made the introductions and then left us.

'You come,' Elena said with a gentle smile.

We took the lift to the first floor. Elena answered my questions in broken English. Yes, she was freelance – all the carers were. No, there were only a handful of residents at the moment and – with a smile – yes, they were always short-staffed and busy.

Alison had mentioned they were at full capacity. I was about to ask Elena just how many residents there were when she stopped outside a door.

'We here.' She knocked and ushered me inside.

Chapter Sixteen

The room was clean, but sparse, with just a free-standing wardrobe and a chest of drawers. A TV was mounted on the wall along with a mirror and a framed print of a landscape that could be anywhere. An unmade hospital bed and an overbed table, with a jug of water and a couple of paper cups, completed the picture.

There was nothing personal – no photographs, trinkets or books. I thought of Stan's boxes of memorabilia and thought Alison was right. He would have liked to have had something familiar here.

Stan sat in a wingback chair angled towards the window, looking out over the grounds. He seemed diminished, almost swallowed by the chair. Unshaven, with wisps of hair clinging to his bald head, he wore thick-framed glasses patched with tape, a striped dressing gown over pyjamas, and slippers. A walker stood within easy reach.

'Stan?' Elena called out cheerfully. 'Look! You have visitor.'

But Stan kept his gaze on the window.

'Stan. You have lady visitor.' Elena raised her voice, then dropped it conspiratorially. 'You talk trains. He like.'

'Thank you.' I stepped forward just as Stan seemed to register my presence.

His eyes widened. 'Valerie!' The word burst out of him, urgent, almost desperate.

Startled, I glanced at Elena.

'I think his wife,' she explained quickly. 'Connie his daughter. Jacob maybe son. Maybe friend.' She nudged me forward. 'Go. I stay.'

I wished I hadn't come. This was a mistake. It was obvious Stan's dementia was more advanced than I'd thought.

But I was here now. I dragged the walker closer and sat on the seat in front of him. Taking his hand, I tried a smile.

'Valerie?' He frowned, searching my face.

'I'm Kat,' I said gently.

His expression darkened. He snatched his hand away. 'You're not Valerie! Where is Valerie?'

Elena hurried to his side, nodding for me to leave.

'We try,' she said ruefully.

I backed towards the door, where Alison was waiting, watching me closely. She must have followed to see how I was getting on – and of course, she'd been right. I felt wretched. Behind me, Stan was mumbling, pushing Elena away. She had the patience of a saint, crooning to him in her own language until at last he began to settle.

I slipped into the corridor. Alison closed the door.

'As I said,' she murmured, 'dementia is a cruel disease.'

'I didn't mean to upset him,' I said. 'He thought I was Valerie.'

'Ian told me Valerie was Connie's mother – Stan's wife,' Alison said as we headed back to reception. 'He speaks of Jacob, too, but Ian said that wasn't Connie's brother's name. I'm afraid Ian wasn't very forthcoming. I got the impression that father and daughter rarely saw each other.'

I felt depressed.

She hesitated, then added casually, 'Does the phrase "Grid 17B" mean anything to you?'

I shook my head. 'No. Why?'

'Oh . . . no reason. He's mentioned it once or twice. It seemed to worry him. I wondered what it was.'

A shadow crossed her face. 'My mother was diagnosed with early dementia. I was twenty-five. I cared for her myself. It was just the two of us. My father was . . . never in the picture. And Queenie, my grandmother – no one in the family dared call her anything else – used to say Dad couldn't organise a piss-up in a brewery . . . excuse my language. She lived to ninety-five and I was terrified of her.' Her expression softened. 'My uncle stepped in – more of a father to me than my own ever was. He put me through nursing school, and I'll always be grateful for that. I suppose it's why I chose this path. I wanted to make some kind of difference.'

'That says a lot about you,' I said.

She gave a rueful laugh, colouring as if she'd gone further than she meant to. 'Families, eh? Were you close to your grandparents?'

I shook my head. 'Both sets had died before I was born.'

I felt myself soften towards her. It sounded like she'd not had an easy time of it. Maybe she was like the rest of us – just muddling along, doing what she could to get through life. I almost felt the inclination to share something of my own, but just then we reached the double doors and I was relieved to be let off the hook. Mum always said that trading confidences was never a good idea.

Alison tapped in the code. 'Perhaps you can find out when the police will be done with Stan's memorabilia. I think he'd like it here.'

I nodded. 'Yes. It might bring him some comfort.'

We parted with a handshake. I was surprised to find I actually liked her.

Chapter Seventeen

Mallory was early. Even though he had a house key, he was sitting out front in his car. As I pulled up alongside, he was glued to his mobile.

I went to unlock the door. Moments later, he came to join me. He looked exhausted – bloodshot eyes, five o'clock stubble in the early afternoon.

I launched myself into his arms. 'I'm so happy to see you! I've been desperate to talk to you. What on earth is going on?'

He gave me that smile that always made me melt, then kissed me gently on the forehead. 'Too much to go into. I can't stay long. I just needed to see you – make sure you're OK.'

'I'll live,' I said. 'But it's been brutal. And finding Oxley . . .'

'I know.'

'I've got so much to tell you,' I rushed on as we entered the house. 'Have you eaten? I can rustle up some scrambled eggs.'

'I just ate with Stella.'

Stella. I turned away so he wouldn't see my face, which I was pretty sure had turned a shade of green.

'How long have you got?' I asked, sounding just a little too cheerful. 'An hour? Two?'

'I wish,' he said ruefully. 'Maybe ten, fifteen minutes.'

'Of course,' I said. 'Time for a quick cup of tea?'

Inside, he kept his coat on and seemed preoccupied, distracted.

I set the tea down on the counter. 'Since you only have a few minutes,' I began, 'I'll get straight to the point. Why is Stella working two cases on your patch?'

'She's my superior officer.' He removed the tea bag, added milk. He didn't look at me.

'So you're working together again.' I tried to keep it light, but I could hear the edge in my voice.

Mallory looked up. 'Yes, Kat. We're working together again. I can't tell you why, so please don't ask.'

I nodded. 'I assume she shared our conversation from last night.'

'She did,' he said mildly.

'Well, let me tell you what she didn't ask me,' I said. 'Connie Hicks. There's no way she could have ended up in the camping coach by accident. She could hardly walk. I think someone turned up between the time she called me and when her husband rang, worried that he'd not heard from her.'

He didn't comment.

'Why would the Major Crime Unit be involved in two—'

'This isn't someone cheating at the harvest festival or stealing from the church honesty box,' Mallory warned. 'Please, Kat. Stay out of it.'

'I can't. I'm already in it,' I shot back. 'Connie. Oxley. I've been thinking. The one thing they had in common is Honeychurch Halt. Trains. You do know her father was the signalman who got shot in that heist, right?'

'There is no connection between the two.' Mallory's voice was firm. 'Oxley was robbed. Connie was . . . unfortunate.'

I felt a flicker of disappointment. 'You really think I'm going to believe that?'

He didn't answer.

'So why did Stella take Stan Holden's train memorabilia with her?' I demanded.

'What are you talking about?' Mallory's tone sharpened. 'What memorabilia?'

So Stella hadn't told him everything.

'She took the boxes when she came here last night,' I said.

Mallory looked shocked. 'You didn't tell me Stella came here. I thought you spoke on the phone.'

'Don't you think it odd that suddenly Connie wants her father's memorabilia valued, she dies, and then Stella turns up and takes it away?'

He set his tea on the counter and walked over to the window, standing with his back to me.

'There was nothing of any value in those boxes, Mallory,' I went on. 'That's what's so strange. Yes, the Kaiser Adler is worth thousands – I can see why someone would want to steal that – but what can possibly be of interest in Stan Holden's stuff?'

No answer.

I thought of something Connie's mother had said. 'Connie mentioned diamonds—'

'They were never on the train,' Mallory said, not realising that he'd just let something slip. I seized the moment.

'According to the waybill at the Emporium, they were.' Alison had joked that maybe the historical inaccuracy by omission had been the answer to the challenge. Perhaps she'd been right. 'Is this the cold case you're working on?'

He finally turned. His face gave nothing away. It took me straight back to when we'd first met – that police officer mask, blank and unreadable. Rather like Stella's.

I knew I'd pushed too hard.

'You valued Stan's stuff, so you made an inventory?' he said, neatly changing the subject.

'Yes,' I said. 'It's on my laptop at the showroom. I told Stella I'd email it, but actually, I forgot. I meant to do it this morning, but June collapsed, so—'

'Tell me exactly what was in the box.' His voice cut me short.

'Mismatched locomotives, rolling stock, old track. Some photos of the Halt before it closed down. A vintage poster . . .' Then a jolt of dismay. *Damn*. 'And Findlay's book on railway management.'

I hadn't told Stella about that.

Mallory raised an eyebrow. 'Findlay's book?'

'I bought it from Connie Hicks for thirty pounds and gave it to Harry for his birthday.'

Mallory sighed. 'I'm sorry, Kat, but you'll have to get it back.'

Harry had been thrilled with the gift. 'That's going to be awkward,' I said. 'He needs it for a school project.'

'I understand. All the same, we need to take a look at it.'

'We?' I said tightly. 'Meaning you and Stella?'

He hesitated, then looked away. 'Just get it back, please.'

Something in his tone made my stomach drop. He seemed different. Distant.

'How was I supposed to know it was important?' I blurted out. 'Have you any idea what it was like finding Oxley? I feel like you don't even care. You're shutting me out because of Stella, aren't you? She's cold, Mallory. Completely unfeeling. I honestly don't know what you ever saw in her.'

The words were out before I could stop them – thoughts I'd suppressed ever since Stella turned up on the scene.

He ran a hand through his hair, exasperated. 'Please – just get that book back. It could be important.'

I stared at him. No response to my outburst about Stella. Nothing about how it felt to stumble across Oxley's body. Just the book.

His mobile rang. He glanced at the caller ID, then stepped into the living room.

'Yes. I can be there in half an hour,' I heard him say. 'I'll meet you in the hotel bar.'

When he returned to the kitchen, he looked almost nervous. 'She's staying at the Seven Stars in Totnes.'

'I see.' My stomach felt like lead. 'She might run into Ian Hicks. That's where he's staying, too.'

Mallory took me gently by the shoulders. Our eyes met. He looked utterly spent. 'All I can tell you is that this is a big case. You've got to trust me – oh, and don't forget to email that inventory.'

And then he left. No goodbye kiss. Just a widening gap between us. I had never felt so alone.

My time with Shawn had been full of 'I'm not at liberty to say', but this was different – this time I was caught up in it too. So why the silence? I hadn't even told Mallory about Alison Fisher's offer of a retainer, or the polar bear hoax – things I'd imagined we'd laugh over together, maybe give Harry a gentle scold and move on.

I felt utterly miserable. The rest of the afternoon stretched ahead, but it wasn't as if I didn't have things to do. I had the Hartley valuation to write up for Alison. I'd take another look at the inventory before sending it to Stella and Mallory – who knew, maybe I was slipping and there was something I'd missed. Then I wanted to download and print off the photos I'd taken of the heist diorama for Harry's project. I'd zip those up to the Hall and ask if I could borrow the Findlay book for a few days.

As I left home and sped down the service drive, it suddenly hit me that Mallory hadn't once mentioned the Kaiser Adler.

And somehow that seemed the strangest thing of all.

Chapter Eighteen

As it turned out, I was kept busy. I was spot on with my estimate for the Hartley painting and zipped that off to Alison. I had a slew of emails to answer, most of them about the Oxley Challenge and – unbelievably – what would happen now the Flying Scotsman prize was off the table. One enterprising soul even offered me money for the tickets – at a discount, naturally – as if the trip were still floating out there, waiting to be claimed. Stan's inventory turned up absolutely nothing suspicious, and my scanner left an annoying vertical line through the middle of every photo I printed off for Harry. I spent what felt like hours fiddling with the wretched machine.

I left the laptop open with a livestream running in the background – an arts programme I liked to tune into when I could. And that was when the news cut in.

Oxley's death and the stolen train were still the lead story. Then the bulletin switched live to Giles Oxley's house – a grand Edwardian pile – where Ginny Riley, true to form, was on the doorstep badgering his widow. The poor woman stood frozen.

It was in appallingly bad taste. Ginny really was the limit. A large man – Felicity Oxley's father, according to the caption on screen – shoved Ginny off the step, sent Troy's camera flying and shouted a string of obscenities that were hastily bleeped out.

West Country Round-Up ended with yet another plug for Honeychurch Hall's Easter weekend extravaganza – this time spliced with dramatic footage of a live polar bear from a David Attenborough documentary, complete with breathless commentary on how dangerous they were. It ended with a flourish about the bravery of the Honourable Gerald Honeychurch. Tickets, we were told, had sold out, and there was a waiting list to 'touch the fringe' of the legendary Grenville Standard.

I wondered if my mother had watched the news, but before I could reach for my phone, it rang.

'Did I interrupt anything?' came a deep, familiar voice.

David Wynn, my former fiancé.

Unexpectedly, my spirits lifted. I broke into a smile. 'You only call me when you want something.'

'I could say the same of you,' he said warmly.

After the initial awkwardness that follows broken love affairs, David and I had settled into an easy friendship. Not one where we would socialise, but given his line of work as an art investigator, our paths often crossed.

'It's gone six, so I'll wait while you pour yourself a glass of wine.' After a decade together, he knew most of my habits.

'I'm not at home,' I said. 'Wine will have to wait. So . . . to what do I owe this honour?'

'The Kaiser Adler,' he said.

'That was quick.'

'When I heard it was last seen at the Dartmouth Antique Emporium, it was the perfect excuse to call you.'

'Did the police notify you?'

'After his widow did,' said David. 'Felicity Oxley moved fast.'

It had taken her less than twenty-four hours. 'I'm surprised.'

'I'm not,' he said. 'What's more, this particular model was only insured three months ago.'

'So Giles Oxley acquired it recently,' I mused. 'Interesting.'

'All the more interesting is that his widow has no documentation to support his purchase, or where he got it. As you know, without provenance . . .'

'She won't be able to make a claim.'

'I can tell you, she was not happy,' David said with a chuckle. 'She assumed that filing a claim meant instant payment, no questions asked. We need a crime reference number. We need a copy of her insurance policy, which at the moment she is unable to provide.'

'I want to sympathise, but . . .' I grinned. 'This is exactly the kind of case I know you love.'

'Guilty as charged.' David laughed. 'Anyway, since the insurance policy was only taken out recently, and Oxley lives in your area, I wondered if you'd done the valuation.'

'Unfortunately, no,' I said. 'I saw the Kaiser Adler for the first time at the *Crime on the Line* exhibition. A real masterpiece. Security wasn't exactly tight – although there were CCTV cameras.'

'Hopefully they were working.'

'Honestly, I'm not surprised it was stolen – there was immense publicity. It's just awful how it happened. I . . . I found him.'

'Good grief!' David sounded appalled and his concern was immediate. 'Tell me what happened.'

I told him everything – the diversion, finding Oxley's car, the horror of his body collapsing on top of me.

'Are you OK? Do you want me to come down? I hate the thought of you being there on your own. Unless . . . well, unless your boyfriend's with you?'

'I've got Mum close by,' I said, though his kindness touched me. It was alarmingly easy to remember the good bits of a relationship – to look back through rose-tinted spectacles. Ours had ended for good reason. I mustn't forget that.

'Mallory's not around then?' he asked.

'No,' I said.

'Ah.'

Just that – one small syllable that smacked of judgement.

'He can't be,' I said. 'He's working the case.'

A silence fell between us.

'Let's talk about this model of train,' David said, suddenly all business. 'Each one has a single stripe painted on the undercarriage – a barely noticeable line of colour along the bottom edge of the engine cab. You can only see it if you tilt the cab. The stripe colour matches the serial number from the twelve built.'

'I know that, David,' I said.

'Ah, but you don't know which stripe this one has.' His voice held an irritating note of triumph. 'Felicity Oxley told me theirs was the second in the series, marked with a teal stripe.'

'There was something else.' I remembered what Harry had spotted. 'The front buffer beam was studded with miniature rivets, but on the left-hand side there was a gap. One was missing.'

'Good.' I could hear David smiling down the phone.

'Interesting that Felicity knows these details,' I said. 'She must have paid close attention to the train.'

'She told me her husband spent hours in his workshop building his layouts and dioramas. She said it was his obsession and that the only way she could spend time with him was by offering to hold the glue pot.'

I wondered if the rumours about their marriage being rocky was true.

We spent a few minutes catching up. I told him about Alison Fisher's offer of a retainer.

'It's a private nursing home,' I said. 'I liked her, but there's something . . .'

'Ghoulish?'

'Yes.' I hadn't been able to put my finger on it before. 'You do have a way with words.'

'You want my advice?'

'Do I have to take it?'

'Since when did you ever?' He laughed. 'Ad hoc is fine, but be careful about agreeing to a retainer. You could get dragged into all sorts of nastiness – contested wills, family feuds, probate disputes.'

'That's what I thought, too.'

We ended our call. I was glad that we'd stayed friends. Our romantic relationship might have finished, but when it came to our professions, it felt good to be able to talk to someone who understood the business – and who understood me. I had already decided to turn down Alison Fisher's offer, but having someone validate my concerns helped.

I closed the showroom, jumped back into my car and whizzed up to the Hall to leave the photos for Harry. As always, the rear entrance was left unlocked. The place felt still, which suited me fine. I wasn't in the mood to see anyone. I left the envelope addressed to him on the kitchen table and headed for home.

Findlay's book could wait until tomorrow.

I was just about to change into the dreaded onesie when I heard a car pull up outside and a door slam.

There was a sharp rap at the door. My stomach flipped. For one awful moment I thought Stella had returned. But it wasn't Stella.

It was Ginny Riley.

Chapter Nineteen

'I come in peace!' Ginny raised her hands. 'I left my mobile in my car. You can search my pockets if you like. Please let me come in – just for a moment.'

'What do you want, Ginny?'

'Um. I'm getting really wet,' she said, glancing at her coat. 'This is only showerproof. No idea why they bother labelling it at all.'

'Fine,' I said. 'But make it quick.'

She swept past me into the living room.

'Wow,' she said, looking around. 'You've done a great job. What a transformation. Do you remember when we used to drink wine here and you—'

'Yes, I do. But that was before—'

'I was immature,' Ginny protested. 'How many times does a girl have to say she's sorry?'

'You can say sorry until the cows come home,' I said. 'You abused our friendship and I just don't trust you any more.'

'Oh.' She seemed taken aback at my bluntness, but it had to be said. I'd felt betrayed and exploited.

Back then, my loyalty to the Honeychurch family was non-existent. If I was honest, I'd felt much like Ginny did in the beginning – slightly scornful of how the villagers revered them where decades ago a hundred per cent of the locals had worked on the estate.

I had laughed about it, never imagining she'd actually write about it. The article – mercifully watered down by an editor who happened to know the dowager countess – changed everything between us.

I hadn't realised just how much Ginny resented the family and everything they stood for – a two-tier justice system where those who 'knew the right people' often walked away with lighter sentences, or none at all. She had written that exposé using stories I'd foolishly shared over wine.

It had only been in the last decade that newcomers – or blow-ins, as the locals liked to call us – had arrived here. But old values held firm. We would always be outsiders.

She pointed to the spiral staircase. 'Ah, so you did convert it to a bedroom up there. Can I have a look?'

'No,' I said.

She shrugged out of her coat. 'Where shall I put this?'

'You're not staying.'

Ignoring me, she hung it on a peg. She'd been in a suit earlier at the Emporium to corner Giles Oxley, but now, in skinny jeans and a fitted top, I was startled by how thin she'd become.

'No cameraman tonight?'

'I told you, I come in peace.' She dropped into the armchair. Besides, Troy's with his wife. They're separated, but still living together – it's a mess. I don't want to talk about it, and I certainly don't need your judgement.'

'So why are you here?'

She sat back in the chair, her eyes meeting mine. 'Oxley was suspended on full pay. He kept a list of names. Your Rupert, along with a handful of other high-flyers, was bribing him to push through planning permissions. On listed buildings. On bad land like that old railway station, Honeychurch Halt. You can't build there. There's protected wildlife, plus soil contamination from years of track maintenance and diesel, not to mention the old fuel tanks and drainage systems.'

'Rupert doesn't own the Halt,' I said.

Ginny sprang to her feet and began pacing. 'It's not right, Kat, and you know it. Do you have any idea how much money these bastards have been slipping Oxley?'

I didn't know what to say, but it didn't matter – Ginny was on a roll. 'Even just four or six houses is maybe thirty grand in bribes. For a development of ten or twenty homes, you're talking fifty to a hundred thousand. Rupert clearly has money to burn.'

'I told you, he doesn't own the old Halt.'

She stopped and turned to me. 'I'm not talking about the Halt. I'm talking about here.'

I felt the colour drain from my face. 'Here? You mean Jane's Cottage?'

'You asked me why I came, so this is why. As your friend...' she took a breath, 'Rupert's been granted planning permission to build ten' – she lifted her hands for air quotes – '"executive" homes on the north-west boundary. And five more here, at Jane's Cottage.'

I was too stunned to speak. So this was why he'd been refusing all my offers to buy the cottage.

He was up to his old tricks again.

In my early days of living with Mum at the Carriage House, Rupert had tried to get planning permission to turn Eric's scrapyard into a theme park, until the dowager countess stopped him. Did she know about this? Was that why she'd asked me to ride the north-west boundary in the morning?

'And you know what else? I'd bet anything that he's already flogged the land to developers! I spotted him in the Emporium car park yesterday. Nice new Range Rover. What do those start at? Basic model a hundred grand, minimum?'

I didn't know what to say. I was still trying to take it all in.

'Of course, with Oxley dead, all those permissions – especially the dodgy ones – will be revoked,' Ginny went on. 'Rupert will have to pay the developer back every penny. Offering a bribe is a criminal offence. Once that list comes out, there'll be a full investigation into his finances, and he'll be prosecuted.'

'How do you know all this?' I thought of the feisty little woman who'd rushed from the Hall just days before. 'The new planning officer, Gloria Weaver, told you, didn't she?'

Ginny mimed a dramatic little zip across her lips, neither confirming nor denying. 'There's no cap on the fines – it could run into hundreds of thousands. Maybe even a prison sentence. It's serious, Kat. Let's see if he can wriggle out of that!'

I was still reeling.

'The theft of the train was just a diversion,' she raced on. 'I know I'm right. Oxley was murdered by someone on that list, I'm sure of it.'

'There's no proof he was murdered,' I began. 'I found him, Ginny.'

'I know.' For the first time, her voice softened. 'That must have been awful. But yes – I do have proof.' She took a deep breath. 'What I'm about to tell you is strictly between us. You cannot breathe a word to Mallory. If you do, she'll lose her job.'

'Then I don't want to know.'

'Troy's sister works at the morgue,' Ginny blurted out. 'Oxley's cause of death was hypoglycaemia due to exogenous insulin administration – bit of a mouthful, isn't it?'

'A diabetic episode.' I frowned. Just like Connie Hicks. 'Was he diabetic? So how can that be murder?'

She cocked her head, clearly relishing the moment. 'Because he *wasn't* diabetic. Never had been. Someone jabbed him with a needle.'

I thought of the strange little cap I'd found in the footwell while searching for Oxley's mobile.

'You know something,' Ginny said sharply. 'I can tell by your face!'

I shook my head. If the cap was significant, I certainly wasn't going to tell her.

'Off the record . . .'

'There's never an off the record with you,' I said.

'Somehow Oxley was persuaded to stop at Ashcombe Barton and was bumped off,' Ginny mused. 'Let's take Rupert out of the picture for the moment. It could've been a bitter landowner who felt hard done by. Or some fanatical environmentalist. But it was deliberate. And d'you know what else is weird?'

I waited.

'That same morning, the morgue had another case of hypoglycaemia due to exogenous insulin administration – a Connie Hicks.'

My stomach turned over.

'But here's the difference – Oxley was injected with insulin despite not being diabetic. Connie, on the other hand, *was* diabetic. She died from an overdose – way too much insulin, more than she'd ever administer herself.'

I tried to keep my expression neutral, but my heart was hammering in my chest. I was right. There *was* a connection between Connie and Oxley. Mallory had lied to me.

'What's more,' Ginny continued, 'Caitlin – oops, forget I said that – only mentioned it because in both cases there was mild bruising on the abdomen. Whoever did this got up close and personal.'

'Connie could have accidentally administered it herself,' I pointed out.

Ginny raised an eyebrow. 'Unlikely. The thigh was her usual choice.' She checked her watch. 'Got to go – I'm meeting a source.'

'Be careful, Ginny,' I said.

'And you should be too.'

'Me? Why?'

'Because you found Oxley's body. That makes you involved whether you realise it or not.'

I nodded, but a jolt of anxiety shot through me. Did that mean I was *involved* – through Stan's memorabilia – in Connie's death too?

'Remember your promise,' Ginny said. 'Not a word to anyone.'

'Where are you meeting this person?' I asked.

'Seriously? You think I'd tell you?' She grinned. 'I'm glad you still care.'

Ginny's visit had unsettled me in more ways than I could count.

Something Mallory always said drifted through my mind: people were usually killed for one of four reasons – they heard something, they had something, they knew something or they saw something.

Surely there had to be a fifth.

Revenge.

Chapter Twenty

'Did I wake you?' was the first thing I heard as the phone dragged me out of a deep sleep.

'No, Mum. I was already awake,' I lied, reaching for my clock – then I remembered I'd had a rough night after Ginny's unsettling revelations and turned the alarm off in the early hours.

'Well, it's happened again. The paramedics are on their way.'

I shot upright. 'What?'

'The polar bear. Only this time Delia's completely freaked out. I was going to pop up there and wondered if you'd like to—'

'I'm on my way.'

For the second time in as many days, I skipped my shower and pulled on old clothes – though I did at least brush my teeth.

Mum was already waiting for me on the drive. She jumped into my car and we sped up to the Hall.

'You look like something the cat dragged in,' she remarked.

'Haven't we had this conversation before?' I grumbled.

'You don't want to let yourself go,' she said. 'That's the kiss of death on any blossoming romance.'

Ignoring the dig I said, 'OK. Fill me in.'

'They were on their way to work – Delia was on her bicycle, with June loping alongside, ready to catch her if she toppled off. While Delia padlocked her bike in the courtyard – don't ask me why she bothers – June went on ahead into the kitchen. That's when Delia heard a bloodcurdling scream – her words, not mine. June had fainted, but on her way down she caught the side of her head on the farmhouse table. Delia couldn't revive her. So she called the paramedics.'

'June will be all right, won't she?'

'Who knows. Delia said there was blood everywhere. They're taking her to hospital now.'

'Where was Florian this time?'

Mum cast a sidelong look, eyes twinkling with mischief. 'In the kitchen, holding one of those spiked ball things on a chain.'

I gasped. 'A flail?'

'Must have pinched it from the armoury in the Great Hall.'

'The polar bear was holding a flail?' I repeated. 'Are you having me on?'

'No,' Mum said. 'But I'll tell you this – Harry's gone too far this time. Ah, here's the ambulance now. That was fast.'

She pulled onto the grass verge to let it pass, blue lights flashing as it weaved around the usual potholes. The Cruickshank twins waved and flipped on the siren. Through the rear window I caught a glimpse of June on the gurney.

Delia was waiting for us in the cobbled courtyard behind the service wing. She picked her way towards us on her Louboutins – never the best choice on uneven ground.

The moment Mum got out of the car, Delia crumpled into her arms.

'Oh, Iris. I . . . I just can't go back into that kitchen,' she stammered, her voice shaking with emotion. 'Not with that bear in there. I had to lock him in.'

Mum gave me an eye-roll. 'Kat will sort it out, don't you worry, love. We'll stay out here.'

Delia shot me a grateful look and whispered, 'Thank you.'

For some inexplicable reason, my pulse began to race as I marched down the dark flagstone passage towards the kitchen. The door was shut, and Delia had even shoved a chair under the handle for good measure. I set the chair aside, then gingerly pushed the door open. I immediately spotted a pool of blood around the base of the table leg.

Instinctively I called out, 'Hello?'

Naturally there was no reply. *It's a stuffed bear, Kat. Don't be ridiculous!*

Bracing myself, I flung the door wide and stepped in, scanning the room. There was no sign of Florian. Perhaps he'd wandered off? For a wild moment I thought I was losing my mind. Then I turned and let out a sharp cry.

The polar bear had been stationed right behind the door. And yes, he was holding a flail. The wooden shaft was wedged against his chest, the chain looped around one giant paw, with the spiked ball dangling mere inches above the floorboards.

No wonder June had fainted. I nearly did myself.

But as the adrenaline wore off, the practical part of my brain kicked in. This was just a childish prank. There had to be a logical explanation, and I was going to find it.

I crouched to examine the plinth beneath the bear. The edge of the baseboard seemed unusually thick, and when I ran my fingers along it, I felt a tiny ridge. I pressed it. A faint click. Then, with a soft whirr, the plinth rose half an inch, revealing four discreet wheels underneath.

A portable polar bear.

I almost laughed. Mystery solved.

'Well?' Mum strolled in with Delia trailing nervously behind. 'We gave up waiting.'

'The bear is on wheels.' But when I tried to demonstrate, I realised it was even heavier than I thought. Not something an eleven-year-old boy would be able to manage alone.

'You'll have to tell her ladyship,' Mum said. 'It's very naughty of Harry to do that. Doesn't he realise June's terrified of stuffed animals?'

'Of course he doesn't,' said Delia. 'We wouldn't dream of troubling Lady Lavinia – and certainly not the dowager countess – over something so silly.' She stared at the bear. 'You know, I never realised until now just how creepy they are. June's right. What if the guests in the Polar Tearoom react in the same way? What if . . . what if everybody faints!'

'You're getting hysterical,' Mum said firmly. 'Now then. Sit down and—'

'What if June doesn't recover?' Delia dragged a chair over and sank into it. 'What if she dies? How am I supposed to cope?'

'I'm sure you'll manage.'

'I asked his lordship if we could move the *Fur, Feather and Folly* collection out of the Museum Room. He said no. So now we'll have to issue a disclaimer. Is that a health and safety requirement? Will we need an inspection? Oh, it's all too much!' She buried her face in her hands.

'We'll sort it out. Now calm down,' Mum crooned.

'The Grenville Standard is still missing,' Delia wailed. 'And *Tales from the Tundra* – gone. Vanished. What on earth is happening here?'

'You've just got too much going on,' said Mum. 'But frankly, things aren't looking good. The Polar Tearoom is a disaster. Then there's the waiting list for the Grenville Standard, and all those people who've already ordered copies of *Tales from the Tundra* . . . It sounds like you'll be handing out a lot of refunds.'

Delia sat up, stricken. 'Yes. Oh, God. What will his lordship think?'

Just then, Lavinia strolled into the kitchen, dressed in her usual jodhpurs and another moth-eaten jumper.

'Ah, there you are.' She seemed agitated. 'Rupert wants his newspaper. You know how he likes it brought to him at nine sharp.'

Delia scrambled to her feet, grabbing the table for balance – she really needed to change those shoes. 'I . . . I haven't had a chance to collect it from the front mat, milady.'

'There was an incident,' Mum put in helpfully, but Lavinia didn't appear to hear.

She glanced around the room – completely ignoring the polar bear clutching the flail – and zeroed in on the stained floor. 'Good grief! Is that blood?'

'June fainted, milady,' said Delia. 'I was just about to—'

'Rupert thought he saw an ambulance.' Lavinia paused. 'You'd better clean up that mess before he comes looking for his newspaper.'

'I'll go and get it.' Mum nodded to Delia and hurried out of the kitchen.

'And what's this I hear about the Grenville Standard?' Lavinia twisted her wedding ring, visibly uncomfortable. 'I understand it's missing.'

'It's only mislaid, milady,' Delia said, her voice tight. 'Who told you?'

'Well you'd better un-mislay it before Rupert finds out.'

Delia pressed her lips together, struggling to keep her expression neutral.

'And . . . there's something else.' Lavinia swallowed. 'The souvenir books. It seems they've been *mislaid* too.'

'Did June tell you that?' Delia asked quickly.

'It doesn't matter who told me. It's . . . Rupert mustn't . . . Edith wants to see them. She didn't know anything about it. She's *frightfully* upset.'

'But . . . but . . .' Delia stammered. 'His lordship—'

Lavinia's raised hand cut her off. She was trembling. A flush crept into Delia's cheeks.

'And the Polar Tearoom,' Lavinia rushed on. 'Still unfinished. You promised it would be ready. Rupert says there are wires hanging out of the wall.'

'But—'

'Let me speak!' Her voice was shrill. 'And now I hear you want to move the *Fur, Feather and Folly* collection out of the Museum Room? Rupert says those exhibits have been there since Queen Mary was on the throne.'

'But June—'

'Edith is very upset about all the hoopla on television.'

'I thought it would help bring in funding,' Delia protested. 'Ticket sales—'

'Rupert says you are not the *custodian* of a National Trust property. He says this is a private estate and you are simply the housekeeper.'

'Head of house, milady,' Delia muttered.

'All this publicity.' Lavinia shook her head. 'It's made Edith deeply upset. Which has upset the earl and which automatically comes down on me since I manage below stairs. Surely you must see that?'

Delia nodded miserably. 'What would you like me to do? Cancel everything? Refund the tickets? I'll do whatever your ladyship asks.'

'No. We'll go ahead. That's all. There.' Lavinia let out a breath and smiled with relief as though she'd been merely passing on instructions – which I had a sneaking suspicion she had. 'Now if you'll excuse me – oh, and move Florian back where he belongs.'

And with that, she swept out of the kitchen.

My mother reappeared brandishing the *Sunday Times*. 'What did I miss?'

Delia filled her in.

Mum was indignant. 'I'd have told her to stuff it. Honestly, no wonder you're thinking of leaving.'

'It's not Lavinia,' I said. 'It's coming from Rupert. He's too much of a coward to say it himself and she's too weak to stand up to him.'

'I *am* leaving, Iris.' Delia sounded determined. 'Henri is begging me to give it up. Says I never have to work again.'

A loud, jangling bell echoed from deep within the house.

'Is that . . . the service bell?' Mum looked startled.

Delia jumped. 'The newspaper!' She snatched it from my mother's grasp, kicked off her heels and dashed off in her stockinged feet.

'Mind you don't fall over!' Mum called after her.

'Looks like it's down to us to move the polar bear,' I said.

And that's exactly what we did.

'He'll stay there for now,' Mum said as we left him in his original spot in the reception hall. 'Are you going to tell her ladyship Harry did it?'

'And risk her wrath? I don't think so. Besides, I'm not exactly sure he did.'

Mum snorted. 'Well, if not Harry, who? Hardly June.'

'I have no idea,' I said. 'I'm riding with Harry later. I'll talk to him then. Let's go home.'

'Attics,' Mum reminded me. 'Remember? And we came in your car.'

'Mum . . .'

'Aren't you the least bit curious about that steamer trunk?' she said. 'We won't be long. I have to get back to my writing. My meeting's tomorrow.'

So to the attics we went.

Chapter Twenty-One

We climbed the narrow back stairs, the walls painted a dull, oppressive green. Mum went ahead, passing through a door and stepping onto the landing that overlooked the reception hall.

Light from the domed atriums spilled across faded picture lights and left ghost marks where paintings once hung. Imprints of long-gone furniture showed on the threadbare carpet. Only the dowager countess's walnut credenzas remained, containing her precious porcelain snuff boxes.

We carried on up an even tighter flight of stairs until we reached the servants' floor. The air turned colder, the walls mottled with damp and flaking paint. Fine trails of sawdust weaved along the skirting boards – death-watch beetle, I was sure of it. The voracious pests hollowed the beams and cost a fortune to eradicate.

Rupert had chosen to buy a new car instead.

At the top, a final flight led us into a corridor tucked beneath the eaves, lit only by dusty dormer windows.

Mum stopped. 'I'm glad you're up here with me,' she whispered.

'You don't have to whisper,' I said, louder than I needed to.

'I know, but . . .' she gave a little shiver, 'attics and basements always give me the creeps.'

I knew exactly what she meant. Honeychurch Hall had its share of ghost stories, one of which I knew to be true. I'd seen something once, something that defied logic but that had without question saved my life. I never spoke of it again. Not even to my mother.

'You go first,' she said.

'I can promise there won't be a polar bear behind this door,' I joked, then stepped inside.

I flipped the switch. A single bare bulb flickered to life, casting a weak glow across the eaves.

At the far end, an octagonal window let in a slant of grey light. The attic seemed to stretch into infinity, vanishing into the shadows. It was a hoarder's paradise.

'I'll never find that trunk up here,' Mum muttered.

'I don't even know where to start,' I agreed.

Tennis racquets and golf clubs poked out of cracked leather bags. Large mirrors stood propped against an oak chest. Moth-eaten curtains were piled over sofas with torn cushions and chairs with broken arms. A brass bedstead leant against the wall. In one corner, there was an old Hotpoint twin-tub washing machine from the 1950s.

'Over there!' Mum pointed to a pair of steamer trunks, half hidden beneath a haphazard pile of lampshades, dusty books and bundles of documents tied with string. 'Her ladyship said it had travel stickers. Something about Egypt.' She pushed up her sleeves. 'It's got to be one of those.'

Between the two of us, we dragged out the first trunk. It was heavy, and the leather was badly scuffed. Brass initials – H.R.H. – were engraved above the lock plate. Mum unlatched it, releasing a waft of must and camphor. Inside were bits of old army kit: rolled canvas, a leather belt with a rusted buckle, and a pair of worn riding boots. Underneath lay several leather-bound photo albums with spines worn through.

'This isn't it,' she declared, but leant in all the same. She tapped the initials. 'Ah, H.R.H. – Harold Rupert Honeychurch, the tenth earl. Born in 1865 and died on the *Titanic*. Poor man. I wonder if he left a diary . . .' She thought for a moment. 'Do you think I could write a steamy romance set in the Barrack Hospital? I could call it *Florence Nightingale's Floozies*.'

I burst out laughing. 'First of all, the tenth earl wasn't born until several years after the Crimean War ended. And second, let's stick to the Harem Historicals or we'll be up here all day.'

We wrestled the second trunk out. It was much larger than the first.

'This is it!' Mum shrieked. 'This is the one!'

It was nearly four feet long and clad in weathered oxblood leather. Brass dome rivets lined the edge and brass fittings reinforced the corners. A heavy iron lock plate was engraved with the monogram C.M.H. – Cassandra Mary

Honeychurch. A half-torn Cunard Line shipping label with a faded Cairo stamp joined other shipping tags from Port Said, Alexandria, Brindisi and Southampton. It looked like she was just like her father – an adventuress, defying the conventions of her time.

'There's no key!' Mum cried with dismay.

I tried the lock, but it was stuck fast. 'It's jammed.'

'We need Alfred up here,' she declared. 'He'd be able to open it in a flash.'

She was right about that. As stable manager, Mum's stepbrother kept his past hidden, but breaking and entering had once been one of his many accomplishments, earning him a few stints behind bars at the pleasure of an earlier HM.

Mum cast around and found an iron. She brought it down hard on the catch. 'Done it!'

We lifted the lid together, and a sharp scent of jasmine and tobacco rose up. For a moment, it was as if the desert was right there with us.

Inside, the trunk was lined in quilted ivory silk, now yellowed with age. The upper compartment held a series of tiered removable trays, made of cedarwood and lined with velvet. Each tray – fitted with delicate brass pulls – slotted into the next.

The top tray contained various small items: a hand mirror with a tortoiseshell back, a brush set, several dried rose petals pressed into the folds of a lace handkerchief.

We lifted the trays out and set them aside. Beneath them lay the trunk's main cavity. There were kid gloves in tissue paper, Egyptian cotton undergarments yellowed by time and exquisitely made.

'Who would choose a thong over these things?' Mum marvelled. 'Who wants to wear dental floss on one's nether regions? Oh, look at this!' She picked up a roll of fabric and shook it out.

'That's a burnoose,' I said.

Mum delved deeper. She withdrew a small wooden box inlaid with mother-of-pearl and slid out the lid. 'Look,' she gushed. 'What have we here?'

Inside lay a smattering of tarnished coins – silver sixpences, a few shillings stamped with the profile of King George V. There were Egyptian piastres, francs and centimes, and Indian rupees.

I was impressed. 'Gosh, Cassandra was quite the traveller.'

Mum sat back suddenly with a wail of despair. 'No letters! There have to be letters. And photographs.'

I reached for the second tray. It looked shallow, yet from the side it seemed deeper than it should be.

I had a hunch.

Carefully I ran my fingers along the seams. There, just beneath the fabric, a small bump. I pressed. There was a soft click, and the false bottom popped open, revealing a hidden compartment stuffed with letters.

'Well!' Mum clapped her hands with delight. 'Aren't you clever! First the bear, now this!'

There were bundles of envelopes tied with ribbon. And photographs too. One, a sepia-toned *carte de visite*, showed a woman I assumed was Cassandra in desert dress, standing beside a man in tribal robes.

'I bet that's her sheikh,' I said.

Mum squealed and snatched up a leather-bound journal tied with a length of faded red silk. She clutched it to her chest. 'It's her diary! I don't believe it.'

Our eyes met. Hers were brimming with tears.

'You're not crying, are you?' I teased.

She gave a wobbly smile. 'You've no idea what this means – to me, to my writing. Cassandra may just have saved my career.' Then, briskly, 'Right. Help me find a box. I'm taking this lot home.'

I found one holding nothing but a single bell-shaped Victorian lampshade of faded pleated silk. It would do for Mum's purposes. I lifted the lampshade out and set it on top of a mid-century gramophone cabinet.

That was when I spotted something half hidden under a dusty length of curtain. I pulled it aside, and there it was, nestled in its case – the Honeychurch Kaiser Adler!

So much for being 'somewhere' in the attic!

The light was poor. I pulled my mobile out of my back pocket and hit the flashlight. The beam caught a long gouge crossing the eagle's wing – the same mark I'd noticed when I helped Oxley load the case into the back of his Bentley.

I made a space on the floor, shifting the case to the ground to ease the lid off. Carefully I removed the engine from its pillows and made my way to the octagonal window.

Each one has a single stripe painted on the undercarriage. David's words echoed. *A barely noticeable line of colour along the bottom edge of the engine cab. You can only see it if you tilt the cab. The stripe colour matches the serial number from the twelve built.*

Oxley's Kaiser Adler was teal, number two in the limited series.

I tilted the undercarriage. And there it was. A teal stripe. Not only that, the front buffer beam was missing a rivet.

I stared at it in confusion. This was unmistakably Oxley's prized Kaiser Adler from the exhibition. But what was it doing here, hidden away in the attic?

And then I knew.

Of course it wasn't *his* at all. It was the Honeychurch Kaiser Adler – and it always had been.

Chapter Twenty-Two

To begin with, I just stared at the train in horror. The only possible explanation hit me so hard I could barely take it in.

Rupert had killed Oxley to get the Kaiser Adler back. Or maybe he'd got Eric to do it – Eric, who'd do anything for his lord and master.

Rupert had bribed Oxley in kind, and Oxley was exactly the sort of collector who wouldn't have dreamt of selling the engine on.

Rupert must have panicked when the subject came up with the dowager countess on Harry's birthday. He knew he'd have to get the train back before he was found out.

But then the more rational part of my brain took over.

Oxley had taken the Kaiser Adler from the exhibition early. Perhaps he'd agreed to meet Rupert – or Eric – to hand it back, especially if the planning permission he'd got for Rupert was going to be revoked. The deal was off. It made sense for Rupert to demand the train's return.

But that theory fell apart. Ashcombe Barton could be reached by any number of narrow lanes from Honeychurch Hall. Why stage a diversion if Oxley had agreed to meet and simply hand it back?

And then the obvious flaw. Oxley had been injected with insulin. The idea of Rupert even thinking of doing something like that was laughable. Besides, where would he get it?

But now I was faced with a dilemma.

Oxley was dead. Murdered.

If I didn't report finding the engine, I would be concealing a crime – perverting the course of justice, becoming an accessory after the fact. Yet the Kaiser Adler clearly belonged to the Honeychurch family. No wonder Oxley's widow couldn't produce any documents. There weren't any.

I'd have to tell David, too. And the police.

Ginny's gripes about the Honeychurch clan always getting away with . . . well, murder hit me afresh. For the first time, I almost wished I could talk to Shawn, who had dealt with enough Honeychurch scandals in his time . . . and hushed them up.

It put me in an impossible position. A man was dead. His death was already under investigation by the Major Crime Unit. Like it or not, I was part of this now.

I placed the train back into the case and covered it with the curtain.

'What are you doing over there? Did you find me a box?' Mum called out. 'I'm itching to get home and look through this lot.'

I wasn't ready to share what I'd found. Not yet.

I helped her carry the box out, barely registering her excited chatter. All I could think about was confronting Rupert. I needed to be sure of my facts before I went to the police.

'I'll run you home,' I said, 'but I won't come in.'

'I don't want you to,' Mum said, launching straight into whether she should show Cassandra's diary to her agent in London. She didn't even notice my silence.

Twenty minutes later, I was back at the Hall.

I slipped through the bifold doors. Bumping into Delia was not part of the plan. This had to be done in secret.

I took the passage Florian had been blocking earlier and made my way to the library. It was a Sunday morning, and according to Lavinia, Rupert was a creature of habit. With any luck, he'd be there reading his newspaper.

I braced myself. Rupert always made me nervous, but this time I held all the cards. If anyone should be afraid, it was him.

Outside the library door, I tried to still my racing heart. Then I tapped – three quick knocks – and without waiting for a reply slipped in and closed the door behind me.

Rupert looked up from his *Sunday Times*, startled. He scrambled to his feet, ever the gentleman. 'What the devil . . .?'

'I know what you did to Oxley,' I blurted out.

The colour drained from his face. 'I don't know what—'

'Oh, spare me, please! The Kaiser Adler that was on display in the Emporium is the same one I just found in the attic.'

'You have no right to—'

'Edith gave us permission.'

'Did you tell her? Does she know?'

'I haven't said anything. Yet.'

'She mustn't find out,' he ordered. 'Do you hear?'

'You need to call the police and tell them what happened,' I said, ignoring his question. 'I know you were bribing Oxley. I know about the planning permissions at Ivy Cottage, and at Jane's.'

Rupert blinked. He didn't even try to deny it.

'A man died because of you,' I pressed on.

'I need to speak to Shawn.'

'Shawn can't help you this time,' I said coldly. 'You can't even speak to Mallory. This is with the Major Crime Unit in Plymouth now.'

I didn't think Rupert could go any paler, but he did.

He pulled open a drawer, took out a packet of cigarettes and a Bic lighter. The packet was already open. His hands fumbled as he lit up. He didn't offer me one – not that I would have accepted.

I'd never seen him smoke before.

'Open a window.'

I did as he said, then sat down opposite him and waited.

He drew in a shaky breath. 'Eric had nothing to do with Oxley's death.'

'So Eric was involved?' I was disgusted.

'He said Oxley was already dead when he got there.' Rupert's eyes met mine, and instead of defiance, I saw alarm.

'It was stupid. He should have . . . Well, no use thinking about that now.'

'You have to go to the police,' I said again, more urgent this time.

'You don't understand.' His hands shook. 'Oxley is just a cog in a bigger wheel. I can't . . .' He sprang up and went to the window.

Much as I didn't want to believe him, I did. 'How did you arrange to meet Oxley?'

'Text,' he muttered, still staring outside.

My heart sank. 'Eric took his mobile, didn't he?'

Rupert spun around, eyes wide. 'How d'you know?'

'Because I found Oxley's body!' I snapped. 'And his mobile was missing.' Frustration boiled over. 'You need to hand that in. Now.'

He waved me off. 'Eric's already dealt with it.'

'How could you be so stupid?'

Rupert flinched. The days of feeling intimidated by him were over.

'The second that phone connected to a tower, it left a footprint,' I went on. 'It doesn't matter if he physically made a call or not – just being active is enough. The network logs it automatically.'

Rupert sank back into his chair, raking a hand through his hair.

'And even if Eric switched it off, the last mast it pinged before going dark will still show the time and location.'

Silence. Then a muttered string of curses.

'He turned the phone off here, didn't he?'

Rupert shot to his feet again and started pacing. 'The train has been found. End of story.'

'But it's not,' I said. 'Don't you see what's happening here?'

'And I told you, Katherine,' his voice turned icy, 'neither Eric nor I had anything to do with Oxley's death.'

Our eyes locked. That old arrogance was there, and it made my hackles rise.

'Felicity Oxley filed an insurance claim,' I said. 'She didn't know the train was a bribe. You're going to need proof before you can reclaim it.'

'What!' Rupert spluttered. 'That's absurd.'

'You'll have to prove it's yours.'

'But . . . we've had it for decades.'

'Maybe Edith can confirm—'

'I told you. Under no circumstances must my mother find out.'

'And there's something else,' I said. 'If you say Oxley was just a cog in a bigger wheel, the police will want to keep the train as evidence.'

Rupert fell silent. Frowning. Thinking.

'You do know that every planning permission Oxley granted will be investigated, and probably revoked?'

Still no answer, but his jaw clenched tight.

'Just tell the truth,' I said quietly. 'It's always the best way.'

His eyes met mine. 'I can't. It's too late.'

Too late – because Ginny was right and he'd already sold the land.

'Who did you sell the land to?' I said. 'The police will want to know.'

Rupert drew himself up. 'Thank you for the information, Katherine,' he said stiffly. 'I'm asking you to give me time to sort this out.'

'Sort it out?' I said. 'How?'

'That's none of your concern. Now, please leave.'

I hesitated, but realised there was nothing more to say. I'd done my part.

I moved to the door, but then I remembered the Findlay book.

'Is Harry here?' I said.

'He's out with friends,' Rupert replied. 'Another birthday treat. Why do you ask?'

'Oh.' This threw me. 'We were supposed to ride today.'

Rupert lifted his paper, pretending to read. 'He won't be back until this evening.'

I left the Hall the same way I came in, grateful to reach the sanctuary of my car, only to spot Lavinia hurrying over, waving.

'Tinkerbell's gone lame,' she said. 'Harry's free Tuesday. Ride out at ten. Must dash. Meeting a chum.' She gave a curt nod and strode off without waiting for an answer.

'I need to check my diary,' I muttered under my breath. The Findlay book would have to wait until then, which I knew wouldn't make Mallory happy.

Truthfully, I was relieved. A ride to the north-west boundary could wait. I didn't think I could handle any more shocks today.

I headed home.

Rupert had asked for time – well, it wasn't his to demand. He was right about one thing, though: it wasn't my business. Yet I was morally bound to tell David – and Mallory too.

Even so, something bothered me. If Rupert and Eric hadn't killed Oxley – and I was inclined to believe they hadn't – and if the Kaiser Adler wasn't the real motive, then who had murdered Oxley, and why?

Chapter Twenty-Three

As I approached Honeychurch Cottages, Keith's flatbed truck was blocking the drive. I gave the horn a quick tap.

Nothing.

I tried again. Still nothing.

Annoyed, I got out and headed to number 2 just as the door opened. A man stepped out, arms full of magazines and what looked suspiciously like a knock-off Birkin. For a second, I didn't recognise him. Without the heavy beard, Keith looked years younger. June's complaint about 'beard burn' came back to me – he must have shaved it off just for her. Clean-shaven, he had a deep cleft in his chin I wouldn't have noticed before, giving him a bit of a Kirk Douglas look.

'Sorry,' he said, jerking his head at the awkward load in his arms. 'Just grabbing these for June.'

'Is she all right?'

'No.' His voice was flat. 'Stable now, but they've got her on oxygen and monitors. They're fitting a pacemaker.'

'Oh gosh, I'm sorry.'

'Arrhythmia. Sudden onset of ventricular tachy . . . tachy . . .'

'Tachycardia.'

'Yeah. That's it. Triggered by shock.' His eyes welled up with tears. 'I didn't even know about that stuffed lion at the museum. We never talked about things like that. If she doesn't make it, I'll never forgive myself.'

His anguish was so raw, I reached out and squeezed his shoulder. 'How can it be your fault? Plenty of people are creeped out by taxidermy.'

'Jesus. I thought I'd lost her.' He stopped, colour rising in his cheeks. 'When I said lost, I didn't mean it like that.'

'Didn't you?'

'I don't actually . . . Look, it was just a bit of fun. A bit of banter.'

'But you shaved off your beard.' I raised an eyebrow. 'And we all know June doesn't like beards.'

'Eh?' Keith's flush deepened. 'It was a dare.'

'A dare,' I repeated. 'And what was the forfeit?'

He licked his lips. 'Look, maybe she wants more, but' – he shook his head firmly – 'that's never going to happen. My wife would kill me.'

'Then why are you taking June's things to the hospital?' I pressed.

'Because . . . because I feel responsible.'

'How? Why?' I demanded.

Keith froze. I could almost hear the cogs grinding in his head. Then, quickly, 'Someone needs to talk to that kid.'

'Harry?'

'He shouldn't go around scaring people like that.' He tossed June's things onto the passenger seat and climbed into the cab.

Unfortunately, I knew exactly who that someone was likely to be.

Me.

By the time I got home, I was desperate for a shower. I washed my hair – no easy chore given the amount I had to deal with. There was a reason why I'd garnered the nickname Rapunzel. There was something oddly calming about the water pounding in my power shower. It always cleared my head.

Even if I'd been tempted, granting Rupert's request for more time was out of the question. I could already picture Mallory's face at that suggestion. No, my plan was simple: report that the Kaiser Adler had turned up and let the chips fall where they may.

And then there was David. Of course he had to be told. If he found out through the police that I'd kept quiet, whatever fragile relationship we'd managed to preserve would be finished.

I'd start with Mallory, then call David.

But when I picked up my phone, I noticed a missed call and a voicemail from an unfamiliar number.

It was Troy, asking if Ginny had stayed at my house last night.

A ripple of unease ran through me as I called him back. It went to voicemail.

Seconds later, he rang again and I answered.

'Sorry,' he said. 'I had to find somewhere private. I'm worried.'

'I'm sure she's fine.' I didn't want to get sucked into someone else's drama – I had enough of my own.

There was a pause.

'Did she tell you,' he began, 'that things between us are a bit ... er ... delicate?'

'That you're married, Troy? Yes,' I said bluntly. 'If you're that concerned, report her missing.'

'I can't! It's ... complicated,' he said. 'But you can. I don't care what people say about waiting twenty-four hours. Something's wrong. It's not like Ginny to just vanish. She was meant to meet me early this morning.' His voice cracked. 'When I walk the dog.'

So, a full-blown affair then.

'But she didn't turn up. Please, Kat.'

This was déjà vu. Ian Hicks had called me when he couldn't reach Connie. That hadn't ended well.

'Did she say where she was going?'

'Dartmoor. Tinner's Rest, near Holne Ridge.'

'Holne Ridge? By Venford Reservoir?'

'That's it.'

It was maybe a thirty-minute drive away.

'Presumably you rang the pub?' I asked.

'No answer. And I couldn't exactly leave a message, for obvious reasons. It doesn't open until noon.'

'She should never have gone alone,' I said, stating the obvious. 'You think she would have learnt her lesson.'

I thought of the last time she'd been chasing a story and ended up being abducted and abandoned on Dartmoor.

'She did,' said Troy. 'She's certified in Krav Maga. She knows how to defend herself.'

Krav Maga. The brutal military-grade training the Israelis used would have taught her exactly how to fight back. 'I suppose that's something.'

'No, it's the opposite.' Troy's voice was edged with fear. 'If she could defend herself and didn't, then something bad must have happened.'

'You're overreacting,' I said, mostly to reassure myself. 'What exactly did this person she was meeting offer her? She must have told you.'

'He said he had Oxley's mobile – a list of names of those he was dealing with . . . sorry, had been dealing with.'

My stomach lurched. Rupert had told me that Eric had Oxley's phone. I just couldn't wrap my head around it. Eric was fiercely loyal. Why would he ever agree to meet with a journalist? It made no sense.

'What about Ginny's mobile?' I said. 'Have you tried tracking it?'

'Of course I have.' His voice rose. 'She once logged into her account on my laptop. I didn't clear the history – but there's barely any signal on the moors. You know that.'

If I hadn't heard the panic behind his frustration, I might have wished him luck and left it at that.

But a cold sense of dread had begun to take hold.

'The only other possibility,' Troy said, 'is that she had an asthma attack.'

'She had asthma?'

'Always carried an inhaler,' he said. 'She didn't want anyone to know. Thought it made her look weak... Oh hell, I've got to go. We're at Paignton Zoo. It's my eldest's birthday. If you find anything, don't text or call me. I have to be the one to call you.'

And with that, he hung up.

I sat there staring at my phone. What was I supposed to do?

I waited until noon, then called the Tinner's Rest.

Chapter Twenty-Four

'Yes, she was in here last night,' said a cheerful man with a broad Devonshire accent. He'd introduced himself as Graham. 'Her date didn't show up. I remember her because this is a local pub and, well, she stuck out like a sore thumb.'

'What made you think it was a date?' I asked.

'There's no phone signal up here,' he said. 'She kept coming to the bar and asking if someone had called and left a message for her.'

'And had they?'

There was a pause. 'Who is this?'

'I'm a friend. She didn't come home last night.'

'Hang on.' A clunk. Presumably Graham had put the phone down somewhere. He came back on the line faster than I expected. 'There's a white Volvo SUV outside. We've only just opened, so it's got to be one of those dog walkers, and they know they're not supposed to park here.'

I hesitated. 'Does it have a press placard on the windscreen?' Though even as I asked, I realised how unlikely that was – Ginny wouldn't exactly advertise a meeting with a source.

A beep cut in. Another call. 'I have to take this,' I said. 'I'll ring back.'

It was Troy, calling from the reptile house – how apt, I thought – to see if I had any news.

'The landlord says there's a white Volvo—'

'That's Ginny's car!' he cried. 'Kat, please . . .'

'I can't just drop everything!' I exclaimed.

But even as I said it, I knew I would.

The Kaiser Adler calls would have to wait.

I gathered a few things – wellies, my raincoat, and a change of clothes just in case. I made a thermos of coffee and some sandwiches, and filled up the hip flask with cherry brandy.

According to Google Maps, the Tinner's Rest was several miles beyond the village of Holne, but I wasn't taking any chances. I grabbed my Ordnance Survey map – no one sensible relied on satnav on Dartmoor – and headed out.

In just over half an hour, I'd crossed the cattle grid and was out on the moor.

The twisting road rose and dipped, following the natural contours of the rugged terrain. There were no formal verges or hard shoulders. Instead, the edges dropped off abruptly into shallow gullies or grassy ditches.

Due to the recent rain, the passing places were rutted and boggy. Further hazards came from grazing cattle, jaywalking sheep and the legendary wild ponies that wandered at will. Granite tors ranged along the skyline: Hound Tor, Vixen

Tor, Yes Tor, Brat Tor – dozens of them, each steeped in folklore; each very different from the others. If I hadn't been on a mission, I would have stopped to breathe in the scent of gorse and peat and take in the view. With most of the central moorland standing at over one thousand feet, on a clear day you could see the sea.

Storm clouds were building on the horizon, but that didn't seem to stop the tourists – or the large excursion coach that crawled along in front of me at 5 mph. Finally it turned off.

Holne was a quiet village with deep tin-mining roots, mostly frequented by hikers, dog walkers and the occasional wild swimmers who swam in the River Dart below Holne Bridge. The Tinner's Rest was several miles on, down another narrow lane. Google stated that it had been built in 1625, at the height of the tin-mining boom. It was once a rough-hewn shelter where local tinners gathered to be paid after a long day's streaming on Holne Ridge. Apparently the current publican's ancestors had run the books and weighed the ore in what was now the saloon.

The pub was clearly signposted, offering a traditional Sunday lunch. The car park was already packed. Ginny's Volvo was parked in the far corner under a bank of hawthorn.

I took the last space and hurried over to her car. Cupping my hands against the driver's window, I saw – just like with Oxley – a magnetic phone holder, but no phone. She probably had it with her. A crumpled OS map lay in the passenger footwell. On the back seat was her coat. My stomach tightened. She'd left the night before. Troy had been right to be alarmed, and now so was I.

I tried the door handles. Locked, of course.

I stepped back, eyes raking the horizon. Open moorland spilled onto the car park. Trails went off in all directions, leading towards various tors on the skyline. And that was when I glanced down and saw it.

Under the wheel arch.

A blue inhaler.

I knew it was Ginny's.

Chapter Twenty-Five

I hurried into the pub. I needed to find Graham.

The contrast between the silence, damp and cold of outside with the stuffy bar buzzing with patrons was jarring. People were wedged into every corner, chattering noisily above the clinking of cutlery. A log fire roared in an inglenook. Windows were fogged up with condensation. Damp coats steamed on walkers and dogs, and the smell of roast beef and overcooked cabbage made my stomach turn.

I threaded my way to the bar, anxious to attract the attention of anyone serving behind it.

A man in his sixties with close-cropped grey hair and an ancient zip-up fleece gave me a nod. He finished serving two white wine spritzers to a couple of tourists – easy to spot in their pristine Barbours that had never seen a speck of mud. They seemed to be asking him a question. He pointed to a sign on the wall that said *No Wi-Fi here. Pretend it's 1990*. They laughed and bore their drinks away.

'We're sold out for lunch today,' he began, but then something in my expression stopped him short. 'Are you all right, me lover?'

'I'm looking for Graham.'

'That's me.'

'I called earlier about my friend ...'

'Ginny?' His face clouded with concern. 'Step this way.'

I followed him to the end of the bar, where he guided me into a passage that led to the toilets. 'Still no sign of her?'

'She has asthma.' My voice began to wobble. 'I found her inhaler. Her coat is still in her car.'

'Right,' he said briskly. 'Let's get on to the Dartmoor South Rescue.'

'We should call the police.'

'If anyone can find her, it'll be the DSR.' Graham gave a reassuring smile. 'The police will be looped in automatically.'

I was almost taken aback by how calmly and seriously he accepted my concern. No questions like *Are you sure? When did you see her last? Have you called all her friends?* It was different here on the moors, and that difference scared me all the more.

He led me through a door marked *Office* and gestured to a chair. 'Draco's partial to that spot.' An old Vizsla with a snowy-white face sprawled across a battered two-seater sofa.

Graham picked up the phone and dialled. I barely heard what he was saying, my mind racing through a gazillion scenarios.

'They'll be here shortly,' he said. 'My brother-in-law leads one of the hill parties. If she's been out all night . . .'

The door swung open and a woman with frizzy grey hair and a lumpy hand-knitted cardigan peered in.

'This is my wife, Justine.' Graham quickly brought her up to speed.

She looked worried. 'Can't take any chances. The weather can be unpredictable – mild one minute, freezing cold the next. She could've wandered anywhere.' Justine paused, thinking. 'Graham said she was waiting for someone?'

I nodded.

She hesitated. 'Is it possible that her friend met her in the car park after we closed up?'

'Maybe,' I said. 'But why leave her coat behind?'

Justine licked her lips and cast a nervous glance at her husband.

'What?' I said sharply. 'You've remembered something?'

'Only that I heard a motorbike outside around twelve thirty, maybe one,' she said. 'Made a hell of a racket. I looked out, and it was parked next to the white car. The interior light was on – someone was in the driver's seat.'

So Ginny's contact had shown up after all. 'And then what happened?'

'The biker saw me watching from the window,' she said. 'I pulled back pretty quick. Didn't want any trouble.'

'Did you see his face?'

'It was dark, and besides, he was wearing a helmet. He left soon after.'

I was confused. 'But Ginny stayed in the car? She didn't leave too?'

'That's all I know,' said Justine. 'But I can tell you that motorbike had a big engine. I know the sound of a big engine. Our boy used to ride one back in the day.'

A cold dread settled over me. Whatever feud I'd had with Ginny didn't matter any more. Something was badly wrong.

The door opened again, and this time a woman, late thirties, stepped inside. 'Dad, Uncle Colin's here,' she said. 'They're all waiting outside.'

'Right then,' said Justine, reaching out her hand to me. 'Come on, love. Don't you worry – we'll find her.'

There was something surreal about the scene outside. The car park had turned into an impromptu base camp. Two Dartmoor Rescue Land Rovers sat with their back doors open, equipment already being handed out – high-vis packs, radios, waterproof charts. Their paintwork was white with broad orange and yellow Battenberg markings and *Mountain Rescue* in bold blue across the side. Red-jacketed volunteers arrived in their own 4x4s – mostly mud-splattered Defenders, some with orange flashing lights duct-taped to the roof.

I kept out of the way as the team formed a semicircle, checking maps and dividing up the grid. A search dog – a lean black Labrador with a neon harness – barked once and was silenced by a sharp whistle from her handler. I heard a distinctive whirr as someone launched a drone, and it disappeared into the mist that was beginning to roll in.

The teams moved fast, heading for the open moor, where they began to fan out.

The first hour seemed to go fast, but the second dragged, and when four o'clock came and went and there was still no sign of Ginny, I was beginning to give up hope.

A black Escalade rolled into the car park. It was Troy, frantic with worry. 'You weren't answering my calls.'

'There's no phone signal here.' I filled him in on what I knew. I took out the inhaler. 'Is this Ginny's?'

Troy's face fell. 'Where's the person in charge? Who's leading the search?'

I pointed to an older, weathered man who seemed to be ex-army from the way he was directing operations. Troy strolled over. I just waited, getting cold and feeling numb. Ginny hadn't taken her coat. She'd been out all night.

Don't think of it, Kat!

When the Labrador returned with her handler, followed by the man carrying the drone, the very real possibility that Ginny could die made my stomach turn. I walked across to Troy.

The radio barked to life. 'Control, message from member of the public. Dog walker's found a woman – thirties, cold but coherent. Sheltering in ruins near Graddon Mire. What3words incoming.'

The ex-army man, whose name I hadn't caught, muttered expletives under his breath and began relaying the message to the various teams. He turned to us. 'Graddon Mire is three miles from here. We've been searching in the wrong place. You'd better follow me.'

Within moments, the coordinates pinged through. Engines started and doors slammed.

I ran with Troy to his Escalade, in hot pursuit of the convoy.

All he did was mutter *thank God, thank God*, over and over again. All I could think about was how Ginny had ended up three miles from her car.

The track to Graddon Mire was brutal – rutted, slick with rain, and bog on either side.

Ahead, I saw several vehicles clustered on the drier ground: a couple of cars, a Dartmoor Rescue Land Rover, and further back, an ambulance.

A group of searchers stood around the ruin, a tumbledown shell of mossy stones and a collapsed lintel. The remnants of two walls still formed a rough corner – enough to give some kind of shelter from the elements.

Troy pulled up alongside the ambulance. I was out of the car before he'd turned off the engine. Ginny was already being lifted onto a stretcher, wrapped in a foil blanket. She looked impossibly small and frail, her eyes shut.

'Ginny!' I rushed forward, then turned to the paramedic. 'Will she be OK?'

He didn't answer.

Troy clung to the side of the stretcher as the paramedics picked their way over the uneven ground. I tried to keep up. Within minutes, they had her in the back of the ambulance. The rear doors slammed shut before I had a chance to catch my breath.

I turned to Troy, but he was already getting into the Escalade, clearly not intending to wait for me!

I'd been abandoned.

'I can drop you back at the pub,' said Justine, who had been hovering nearby. 'Hop in. Sorry about the smell of dog.'

I clambered into her Kia Soul. I suddenly felt incredibly tired.

'Your friend was lucky,' Justine said as we jolted over the bumps that Troy's Escalade had managed with ease.

'I know,' I said.

'Graddon Mire's no place to go wandering. Unless you know the way through, it's easy to disappear.'

'I just don't understand how she ended up there,' I said.

'Maybe you need to find the fella on that motorbike,' said Justine. 'She must have known him, otherwise she'd never have let him in her car.'

'Yes, that must be it.' I nodded. 'Of course.'

Justine had no idea Ginny was working on a story, and I wasn't about to enlighten her. This man had tricked her into driving to meet whoever had Oxley's mobile phone. He must have left his motorbike back at the pub, abandoned Ginny, then returned her car, which made sure a local search would be useless.

It had been a calculating plan that made my stomach heave. Ginny was meant to die.

'The main thing is that she's safe.' Justine broke into my thoughts. 'And that's all that matters.'

If only that were true.

We pulled into the car park, which had emptied out of customers. It was almost six in the evening now. Graham came out to greet us. He already knew Ginny had been found. I explained that we would have to leave her car overnight again.

Back in my own, I turned the key. The radio crackled to life with a news bulletin that filled me with dismay.

'The hunt continues to recover the Kaiser Adler, a model train worth in excess of eighty thousand pounds. The owner, Giles Oxley, was recently found unresponsive in his car by another motorist. His recent exhibition at the Dartmouth Emporium, *Crime on the Line*, was widely regarded as his best work. Oxley, a controversial figure, was under investigation at the time of his death for bribery and corruption. Police are treating his death as suspicious. And now tonight's weather . . .'

I stabbed the off button. I felt sick. I should have called Mallory and David before tearing off to Dartmoor. Things were getting out of control.

I was certain that Oxley's death and Ginny's abduction were connected. Two mobile phones at the centre of things. Eric had taken Oxley's in the hope a trail wouldn't lead back to Rupert. Ginny's phone was her life. Her research, her interviews, her contact list.

Ginny's pursuit of Oxley had been plastered all over the evening news. She'd been seen by enough people at the Emporium the day Oxley died.

But this was where everything fell apart. Ginny had been abducted and dumped on Dartmoor. Had someone ambushed her in the empty car park? Was that why her inhaler had been left on the ground?

And if it was the same person who'd injected Oxley with insulin and overdosed Connie Hicks, wouldn't they have done the same to Ginny? Why let her live?

By the time I got home, I had a full-blown stress headache. I was emotionally exhausted. I wanted nothing more than to hear Mallory's voice, but my phone battery was dead. I had to call David – I couldn't put that off any longer.

I put my phone on charge, then headed for the kitchen to pour myself a stiff gin and tonic. That was when I spotted the note on the counter scrawled in Mallory's unmistakable hand. *Tried calling. No answer. Sorry I missed you. Won't be able to call tonight. Hope to see you tomorrow. Love you.*

When my phone finally had enough charge, three missed calls lit up the screen – all from Mallory, all while we'd been combing Dartmoor for Ginny. He'd left three voicemails too, saying he'd be stopping by at four.

Armed with my drink, I sat down and rang David. It all came spilling out in a breathless, hysterical rush. When I finally stopped, there was a long silence.

Then, 'Take a breath, babe.' David hadn't called me that in years. 'This isn't your problem. But yep, the earl is in serious trouble unless he can prove provenance – and even then, he's committed an offence by not reclaiming the Kaiser Adler through the proper channels. Technically that locomotive becomes proceeds of crime, liable to seizure by the police or the Crown.'

My heart sank. 'Oh.'

'Technically,' he repeated – which reminded me that that word had driven me mad when we were together – 'the earl could still be charged. Not for theft, but for how he took the engine back. Unlawful retrieval.'

'Oh,' I said again.

'Wait a moment . . .' David's voice cut off abruptly. I heard the faint murmur of a news bulletin in the background.

I waited.

'I didn't . . . Oh, this puts a totally different spin on things.' His tone had hardened. 'You didn't mention that Oxley's death is linked to the theft of the train.'

'Rupert didn't do it.'

'You don't know that.'

'I can't . . . I don't want to . . . There's someone here. I've got to go.'

And there really was. I heard a car door slam, footsteps crunching on gravel.

'Let's hope it's your policeman,' David said.

I hung up.

It was a policeman. But not Mallory.

'Can I come in?' It was Shawn.

'It's really not a good time,' I said, because I knew exactly what he wanted. He'd spoken to Rupert.

But he just gave me a steady look and stepped past me, gentle but firm.

'We need to talk.'

Chapter Twenty-Six

'If this is about Rupert or Eric, I have nothing to say.' I followed him to the kitchen. He went straight to the fridge, as if he was still in my life.

'Nice collection,' he said, peering inside. 'Devon Rock, Salcombe Gold . . . Mallory's got good taste. But no Peroni.' He turned and smiled. 'Do you remember?'

Yes, I remembered, but if Shawn thought he was softening me up by reminding me of our past, he was wrong.

'That disastrous Airbnb in Florence with the tiny balcony.' Our eyes met, but I looked quickly away. It had been one of our first weekend city breaks together. Everything that could go wrong went wrong – flight delays, lost luggage, a taxi that had a puncture. And then a mix-up with the Airbnb. The host had left a six-pack of Peroni as an apology.

But that was another lifetime, and I didn't want to go there. Shawn had ended our relationship so abruptly that it still stung. What with just having had an argument with David, the last thing I wanted was to deal with another ex.

Shawn closed the fridge empty-handed. He must have sensed my mood.

Even though our break-up had been over a year ago, it felt odd to be in such close proximity. I knew he had a girlfriend. He knew I was with Mallory. Superficially we were always polite and friendly but this was the first time that the two of us had been alone.

'I don't want anything to do with this,' I said quickly.

'Eric gave me Oxley's mobile,' Shawn said. 'Surprised?'

I was. Very surprised. I'd half expected him to toss it into the ornamental lake.

'Unfortunately, this train – if you pardon the pun – has already left the station,' he went on. 'Like it or not, Eric and his lordship are on the list of potential suspects.'

'Sounds like you know more than I do.'

Shawn hesitated. 'It would be helpful for his lordship to have an idea how the investigation's going. If you take my meaning.'

'I don't,' I said coolly, though I knew exactly what he was angling for.

'It's important, Kat,' he said. 'Eric's role in reclaiming the Kaiser Adler . . .'

'You mean following Rupert's orders.'

'. . . is something that needs to stay quiet. You need to make Mallory see how absurd it is to think they were involved in Oxley's death.'

'It's not Mallory's case, Shawn.' A thrill shot through me. 'It's been handed over to Major Crime in Plymouth – Chief Superintendent Stella Greenleigh.'

Shawn's jaw actually dropped. The genuine shock on his face thrilled me all the more. 'Major Crime? Why?'

'I have no idea.'

'But Mallory would know,' Shawn insisted. 'Given their history.'

'Just like ours?' I hadn't intended to sound so bitter. 'You expect pillow talk to include confidential information? Because ours certainly didn't.'

He stiffened. 'That's hardly fair.'

'Let things run their course,' I said. 'Why shouldn't Eric and that wretched earl not answer for what they've done? Why are you so desperate to protect them? Why?'

Shawn didn't reply, though I could see he wanted to.

'Why?' I asked again.

Still no answer.

'You do know it's not just about the train?' I said. 'Did Rupert tell you he gave it as a bribe to Oxley for planning permission? Ten executive homes on the north-west boundary at Ivy Cottage and five more here at Jane's?'

Shawn's expression stayed neutral. If he knew, he wasn't about to admit it.

'So what are you going to do? Turn in Oxley's phone? You can't hold onto it. It's evidence, and you know it.'

'I'd better go,' he said quietly.

'You have to hand it in,' I repeated. 'Or—'

'Or what? You'll run to Mallory?' He gave a grunt of disgust. 'I came here tonight in good faith, to work out how to help his lordship through a very sticky situation.'

'Sticky situation!' I squeaked.

'You know he didn't kill Oxley! All you're doing is letting the real killer get away.' He spun on his heel and stormed to the door.

I followed, barely able to contain my fury. 'All I'm doing is letting justice run its course! Turn in that phone.'

Shawn wrenched the door open and swung back to me, eyes hard. 'Let me be the one to decide, Katherine. And remember, this stays between us.'

'And if it doesn't?'

'Then you'll have to pick a side.'

I slammed the door behind him, more shaken than I wanted to admit. This was the Shawn I remembered. Not the man on the balcony in Florence.

Two ex-boyfriends, two unpleasant confrontations. It was hard not to see a pattern. There had to be a lesson in there somewhere.

Thank God for Mallory. If I had to choose a side, it was an easy choice. The side of truth.

That night I tormented myself with the events of the day. I called the hospital but was told that because I wasn't family, they wouldn't tell me how Ginny was. I didn't want to phone Troy in case he was home with his.

To be honest, I was getting fed up with all the subterfuge that seemed to be swirling around. Ginny and Troy. June and Keith. Shawn mentioning our past, which I would hate for Mallory to do with Stella. Though why wouldn't he? They were together for a long time, as Shawn liked to remind me.

I tried my mother, but didn't expect her to answer. When she was writing, she went to ground. Leaving a message was futile. Her voicemail greeting said, 'Don't bother to leave a message, because I won't be listening to it.'

Around ten, a text pinged onto my phone. It was Delia, reminding me to pick her up for our trip to Devizes in the morning.

I sighed. *No good deed goes unpunished.*

Chapter Twenty-Seven

HMP Erlestoke was a Category C men's prison for those serving long-term sentences for serious offences, including murder, GBH, armed robbery and gang-related violence. It was a two-hour drive from Little Dipperton.

I decided to make the most of my day out and planned to visit the Henry Aldridge & Son auction house, world famous for *Titanic* memorabilia. In fact, in 2013, they had authenticated the violin played by bandmaster Wallace Hartley during the final moments of the doomed ship, and sold it for more than £900,000!

Delia seemed on edge. She wore her navy Marks & Spencer wool coat with her Louboutins and carried a new mid-tone blue Birkin. It *had* to be a knock-off.

I complimented her on her appearance.

'I put make-up on my bruise. Can you tell?'

'No, you can't,' I said, and meant it. 'I see you got your new handbag.'

'It arrived this morning. Special delivery.' She hugged it to her chest. 'A bit bigger than I'd like, but I'll get used to it.'

'Did you know that Jane Birkin's actual handbag sold at Sotheby's for over eight million pounds?'

'Good lord!' Delia gasped. 'Eight million? For a handbag?'

'It's the most expensive ever sold at auction. Before that it was a white crocodile Birkin with diamonds. But Jane's was battered, scribbled on, stuffed with personal bits and pieces – exactly why people wanted it.'

'So how much do you think this bag's worth?'

'I'd have to look when I'm not driving,' I said. 'It depends if it's a knock-off or the real thing.'

'Knock-off?' Delia scoffed. 'Henri would never send me a knock-off. Look at these shoes! They're the real thing. He keeps sending me gifts! Yodel know where I live now and say, "Another gift from your admirer. Lucky you!"'

'That's very generous of him,' I said. 'Remind me what he does for a living.'

'He's a hedge fund manager.'

'And he lives in London?'

'He travels a lot. London. Paris. New York.'

I tried to ignore the burst of alarm bells pealing in my head. Delia didn't have any money, so if this Henri was some kind of scam artist, he was going to be seriously disappointed. I was worried for her.

'You met him online, didn't you?'

'We've talked online, but no,' Delia shook her head, 'a flyer came in the post.'

A flyer in the post? In today's world of internet dating?

'You mean an insert in a newspaper?' I asked.

'It was just posted through my letter box,' she said. 'June saw it. She goes on dates all the time. Said it would be a laugh and that you only live once.'

I supposed that was true, though in my experience, you could waste an awful lot of 'once' on men who weren't worth the effort.

'I'm sure you can't wait to meet him in person,' I said. 'Let's hope you still like him when you do.'

'Iris said the same, but she's only jealous,' said Delia. 'She mentioned filters. I'm not sure what she meant.'

'If you've only spoken to him on Zoom, there are ways to, er . . . enhance one's appearance. Iron out wrinkles, that sort of thing.'

'Oh,' said Delia. 'I did ask him to stand next to a door last time we spoke, just to check how tall he is. I'm not attracted to short men.'

I didn't comment.

'I feel confused,' Delia said suddenly. 'Lenny was furious that I wanted a divorce, and now suddenly he wants it too.'

She swallowed. 'Do you think he's met someone?'

'In prison?'

'Maybe some woman is writing to him. You hear about that sort of thing all the time.'

I thought of Delia's letter to Dear Amanda claiming that Lenny was refusing to sign the paperwork. It did seem odd that he'd changed his mind.

'You do realise that with the new divorce laws, you can do everything online – no blame, no confrontation – and

Lenny wouldn't be able to contest it.' Not that he had a leg to stand on.

'No,' Delia said firmly. 'He put me through so much grief. I want him to see the new me.'

Oddly enough, I understood. Even when you were content – maybe in love with someone new – there was still that sting of wanting the person who once rejected you to wish they hadn't. To want you back, even if you didn't want them any more.

'Are you meeting your solicitor there?' I said, deftly steering her away from dangerous ground.

'Yes,' she said. 'He's got all the papers. It'll be supervised, of course.'

'It'll soon be over,' I told her. 'And then, just think, you'll finally meet Henri in the flesh.'

Delia nodded. 'When you reach a certain age, you start to feel time's running out. He's already talking about marriage.'

I shot her a sideways glance. Her eyes were fixed on me, almost as if she needed my blessing.

'I want to live!' she burst out. 'Besides, I'm fed up with her ladyship and his lordship giving me such a hard time.'

'I think it's more Rupert than Lavinia,' I said, because I believed that was true. 'He's under a lot of pressure.'

'Why are you defending them?' Delia cried. 'It's as if they're forcing me to hand in my notice.' She went on, her voice harder now, 'I've worked tirelessly to raise the Hall's profile on social media. It was me who got on *West Country Round-Up*, and all they've done is complain. They say they want privacy, but how do they expect Honeychurch Hall to be put on the map if no one knows about it!'

It was a good point.

'And the whole incident with Florian.' Her voice rose. 'Harry is such a naughty boy. June practically died!'

June's brush with death made me think of Ginny. I hadn't heard a squeak from Troy, and I still didn't know if Ginny's car was being recovered or what exactly had happened to her. You'd think she might have called me by now.

I cleared my throat. 'Shall we put the radio on?' We still had another hour on the road, and I wasn't sure how much more I could take.

Delia flicked the switch, and the soothing hum of Radio 2 filled the car. Something mellow from the seventies drifted out, followed by a cheery presenter announcing a listener's birthday. It felt bizarrely normal.

Finally we saw the sign for HMP Erlestoke. Turning off the B3098, we wound our way along a narrow lane flanked by hedgerows and open fields. It was hard to believe a prison was tucked away out here, hidden in the folds of the Wiltshire countryside.

We pulled up at the main gate and stopped beside a security hut.

'We'll need our ID,' I said, already fishing out my driver's licence and wondering what Delia was planning to use. She'd lost her own licence years ago – a sore subject no one dared bring up.

She rummaged in her Birkin. 'Senior railcard.'

'And you'll have to go through a metal detector,' I warned. 'So I hope you're not hiding weapons in that bag!'

It was a feeble attempt to lighten the mood. Delia was visibly shaking with nerves.

I pulled into the visitors' car park. Near the front entrance, a man in a dark suit was already waiting.

'I think that's my solicitor, Mr Williams,' Delia said. 'Oh God, I don't think I can go through with this.'

'You'll be fine. Just remember why you're doing it. Think of Henri.'

'Yes,' she whispered. 'Henri.'

'Call me when you're ready to be picked up.'

Hopefully I'd get an hour or two to myself. I hadn't driven all this way to sit in a car park.

I headed into Devizes, determined to track down the auction house. After being funnelled down Long Street by *No Entry* signs, circling Market Place twice and inching through roadworks on New Park Street, I finally spotted Henry Aldridge & Son on Bath Road on the outskirts of town. But before I could even pull in, my phone rang.

Delia was ready to go home.

Exasperated but resigned, I turned around.

As I approached the prison entrance again, a chalk-grey Porsche Cayenne slipped past the barrier. I caught a fleeting glimpse of the driver, and our eyes met for the briefest moment. For one wild second, I could have sworn it was Alison Fisher.

Delia slid into the passenger seat. She seemed subdued.

'How did it go?'

A tear trickled down her cheek. 'He said he'd always love me. He cried.'

I reached over and squeezed her arm. 'Well it's done now. No looking back.'

We set off again.

'He was so nice, Kat.' Delia's voice began to crack. 'He was the Lenny I remembered before that woman destroyed our marriage.'

No mention, of course, that he was inside for murder.

'He's happy now. He's made friends,' she said. 'He's got a lovely cellmate called Don.'

'Did you tell him you'd met someone?'

'He guessed. He said I'd never looked more beautiful and he hoped he was a good man who would take care of me. Why couldn't he have said all those things when we were together?'

I stared at her. She couldn't honestly be buying this.

'And then he said he was sorry that I had been forced to work,' she went on. 'That a real man would be able to support his wife. So I'm going to do it.'

'Do what?'

'Hand my notice in after Easter.'

'But . . . that's this weekend.' I was dismayed. 'I thought you were going to wait until the end of the summer. Don't you think you should see how you feel after you've met Henri?'

'No,' Delia declared. 'I told Lenny how they've been treating me, and he said to tell them to stuff it. June can take over . . .'

'If she makes a full recovery.'

'. . . she doesn't care how they talk to her. It's like water off a duck's back. I suppose it's because she's so tall.'

'What about the taxidermy stuff?' I pointed out. 'You heard Lavinia. They won't get rid of it, and if June doesn't like it, that'll be a problem.'

'She'll have my dailies coming up from the village. They can deal with Florian and the *Fur, Feather and Folly* collection.'

'Delia,' I began, 'I honestly don't think you can rely on June long-term. Mum was right – you should interview some other people.'

'If she leaves, she leaves,' Delia cut in. 'That's no longer my problem.'

I had absolutely no response to that, so I did the only sensible thing and sought refuge, yet again, in Radio 2.

It was only as we finally reached Little Dipperton and were passing the community shop and post office that Delia yelped, 'Stop! I need to post this letter.'

To my astonishment, she unbuttoned her coat, loosened the pussycat bow at her throat and reached inside her blouse to pull out a brown envelope.

'Did Lenny give you that?' I said sharply.

'Why?' She thrust out her jaw. 'It's just a letter.'

'And the security guard said you could take it out?'

'The security guard didn't see it,' she said with a tinge of mischief.

I was shocked. 'You mean you smuggled it out?'

'In my bra.'

'That's illegal,' I gasped. 'Honestly, Delia, don't you realise that if you'd been caught, Lenny would be in all kinds of trouble. Prison mail is monitored.'

Delia looked startled. 'Well, it's not Lenny's, although he gave it to me. It's from his cellmate.'

'But that's even worse!'

She held the letter in her hand as if it was on fire. 'What should I do?'

'You should turn it in to the police.'

She gasped. 'I couldn't! I promised!'

'But it's not even your letter!' I snatched it out of her hand, glancing at the name – a Philip Greenleigh, with an address in Tavistock. I blinked. Greenleigh. Stella Greenleigh. Surely a coincidence – or was it?

Delia snatched it back, and before I could react, she was out of the car and had popped it into the postbox.

I knew the last collection had already gone. The minute I dropped Delia home, I'd call Mallory.

'And you have to promise not to say anything,' she whined as she slid back into the car.

In this instance, I wasn't promising anything.

A hearse appeared in the opposite direction, forcing me to pull tightly to the side to let it pass. One of the two young men in the front gave me a cheerful thumbs-up. It was the same hearse I'd seen at Sunny Hill Lodge.

But I didn't need to call Mallory after all. Having dropped Delia home, I crested the brow of the hill to see his black Peugeot already parked outside my front door.

Chapter Twenty-Eight

Feeling Mallory's arms around me, holding me close, was all the reassurance I needed. For now, at least, everything between us was fine.

'You OK?' he asked, stepping back to brush the hair from my face, his gaze steady and searching.

'I have lots to tell,' I said. 'How long have you got? I seem to ask you that question every time I see you lately!'

'About an hour,' he said. 'I'm still on duty, but I wouldn't say no to a cup of tea.'

He followed me into the kitchen, taking off his raincoat. 'Did you get the railway management book?'

'Oh gosh,' I said. 'I'm so sorry.'

'Kat, it's important.' He sounded annoyed.

'I know,' I said quickly. 'But Harry wasn't home yesterday, and then Ginny went missing, so . . .'

'Can you get it now?'

I stared at him. 'Didn't you hear what I said? Ginny was abducted – or that's what I think happened.'

'Ginny?' His jaw dropped. 'The investigative reporter. What's that got to do with you?'

'Because I was helping with the search party,' I said. 'She'd been meeting someone at the Tinner's Rest.'

'I don't want you tangled up in anything to do with Ginny Riley.' His voice was harsh. 'I mean it, Kat.'

I felt my face grow hot. 'What was I supposed to do? Pretend I hadn't heard she was missing?'

But even as I said it, I realised I couldn't tell him it was Troy who had called without betraying their relationship.

Mallory frowned. 'What was she doing on Dartmoor?'

Too late, I realised my second mistake. Mentioning Oxley's mobile would make things even worse.

I floundered. Every explanation seemed to circle back to Mallory telling me to stay out of it.

But I had to know. 'Is Stella connected to – or does she know – a Philip Greenleigh?'

Mallory went very still. 'Why?'

'Lives in Tavistock,' I said, suddenly unnerved by the odd look that crossed his face. 'Isn't . . . isn't that where she lives too?' It was a wild guess.

'Why are you asking?' His tone had gone flat, almost guarded.

'I told you, I need to talk to you.' I turned away, fussing at the counter, lining up the teapot, cups, chocolate digestives, anything to keep my hands busy.

For what felt like an eternity, Mallory didn't speak.

Then, at last, 'What do you know about Philip Greenleigh?'

So I told him about driving Delia to HMP Erlestoke to sign her divorce papers, and how her ex's cellmate had asked her to post a letter.

'I looked at the name and address,' I admitted. 'I told her it was illegal.'

Mallory's tea sat untouched. 'Did she say who the cellmate was?' He tried to sound casual, but I knew him too well by now.

'Just that his name was Don.'

His jaw dropped. 'Are you certain? Not Jacob?'

'Jacob? No.'

'We met Ian Hicks at the Seven Stars. He mentioned that name.'

'I think Jacob's an old friend of Stan's.'

Mallory started pacing. 'Did Delia say how she smuggled the letter out?'

'In her bra,' I said, trying to make light of it, but his expression stopped me cold. He seemed angry, as well he might.

He pulled out his police notebook and pen. 'What's Delia's ex-husband's name?'

I hesitated. This was exactly what I'd warned Delia about, and now here I was throwing Lenny under the bus. 'It wasn't Lenny's letter.'

'Doesn't matter.' Mallory's voice was curt. 'It still has to be reported. Where exactly was this letter posted?'

'In the village.' I was getting nervous. Mallory was beginning to scare me. 'It missed the last pick-up, so it won't go tonight.'

'Bethany runs the post office, right? Lives above the community shop with Simon?'

'Yes,' I said. 'You're going to intercept it, aren't you? Please leave Delia out of this.'

'I can't promise anything,' he said flatly.

I felt wretched. Why had I thought he would do anything different? He always played by the book.

He strode to the front door, grabbed his coat from the hook.

'You're leaving already?' I asked, disappointed. 'I thought you had an hour.' I trailed after him. 'At least tell me who this man Greenleigh is. Is he related to Stella? A brother?'

Mallory stopped and turned. 'He was her father,' he said quietly. 'He died a few weeks ago.'

'You knew him?' I said, feeling a sudden rush of jealousy I hadn't expected. 'From when you were with Stella?'

'Yes, I knew him,' he said. 'I was fond of him.'

Fond of him. Had he gone to the funeral? Had he gone with her? I felt sick. 'Mallory, I need to know—'

'You need to leave this alone, Kat.' His voice was firm. 'Promise me. I mean it.'

'I promise . . . but I have to talk to you,' I said, trying to hold on. 'I don't know what to do—'

'This is not the time.'

'You haven't heard what I'm about to say!' I protested. 'The Kaiser Adler – the one reported stolen – it's a family heirloom. Rupert took it back.'

'Leave it!' Mallory barked. 'I don't have time for all this petty village stuff.'

I reeled, stung. There it was – my worst fear spoken aloud. That Mallory was already bored of this place. Bored of me. He'd come from a world of real crime.

But then another feeling surged. Anger.

Connie Hicks had died barely a day after I'd met her. Oxley's body had collapsed on top of me. I'd helped search for Ginny on Dartmoor. And not once – not once – had he asked how I was!

I needed his support. I needed him to see me, hear me. Instead, all his energy seemed focused on this cold case and his wretched ex-girlfriend.

'If you walk out that door right now, then maybe we need to take a break.' I couldn't stop the words; they just came tumbling out.

Mallory's expression changed – first incredulity, then fury, and finally something else. Sadness.

Regret hit instantly. He wouldn't look at me. I'd gone too far. I scrambled for something to say, wishing with all my heart I'd kept my mouth shut.

'All right,' he said at last, quietly, lifting his eyes to meet mine. 'You're right I've been holding things back, because—'

'Because of Stella?' A sick feeling churned in my stomach. 'You still love her.'

'No!' His voice was sharp. 'I told you – I would never lie to you or play games. Yes, Stella's involved, but this is much bigger than you can imagine. It's a cold case, Kat. There's too much at stake.' He gave a heavy sigh. 'But if that's what you want. I'm too old to argue. I want someone in my corner who trusts me.'

'But so do I!' I was panicking now.

'We'll talk more tomorrow,' he said. 'I'm sorry, but I have to go.'

And I let him.

I heard his car pull away, then sank onto the sofa, stunned by what had just happened. Yes, I'd been overwrought. Yes, I felt abandoned – he hadn't been there for me in days. And yes, I believed him when he said it was a big case. But I'd wanted something else. Reassurance? I felt I was unravelling. Had I just ruined everything?

Then I heard a car return.

My heart leapt. He was coming back.

I ran to the door and wrenched it open.

But it wasn't Mallory.

It was Ginny Riley, holding a bottle of bubbly and an enormous bunch of daffodils. 'I've come to thank you for saving my life.'

Chapter Twenty-Nine

Ginny was the last person I wanted to see. Of course, I was relieved she was OK and surprised at how quickly she'd recovered, but I was still reeling. Mallory and I had just had our first fight, and I wasn't in the mood to celebrate anything.

'Are you OK? You look . . . Aren't you pleased to see me?'

'Don't be silly,' I said, more sharply than I intended. 'When were you discharged?'

'A few hours ago.' She waved the bottle and flowers. 'For you!'

For a moment I glimpsed the old Ginny, her warmth and impulsiveness, and felt a flicker of affection. But I couldn't face small talk. Not now.

'That's very sweet of you. I'll save it, if you don't mind.'

'Please do,' said Ginny. 'I'm not drinking. Doctor's orders. But a cup of tea wouldn't go amiss.'

Resigned, I waved her inside. 'I'll pop the flowers in water.'

Ginny followed me into the kitchen. 'Did I just pass Mallory? He nearly ran me off the road.'

I nodded.

She cocked her head. 'Don't you want to know what happened to me?'

'I . . . Of course.'

'Jeez, Kat! I got whacked on the back of the head and shoved into the boot of my own car.'

'You were – *what*?' That did it. Mallory was forgotten – at least for now.

We settled on the sofa with cups of tea and the packet of digestives. Ginny kicked off her shoes and curled her feet under her. 'Bit like old times, isn't it?'

I sipped my tea. 'Well I'm glad you're OK.'

'Oh, trust me, I'm more than OK.' She gave a secretive smile and nibbled a biscuit. 'You know, women are amazing. Aren't we amazing? Oh, Kat, I owe you big time for saving my life!'

'Troy called me—'

'You can't rely on a man, can you?' she cut in. 'Or maybe it's just me – I always pick the wrong ones.'

I took another sip. Her comment had hit a nerve. Had I picked the wrong man too? Mallory wasn't unreliable; he just wasn't always . . . available. Could I live like that long-term?

'Paignton Zoo or me.' Ginny broke into my thoughts. 'And the meerkats won.'

'He was worried,' I said. 'But what else could he do? He was with his family.'

'No, I'm an idiot,' she said. 'Men never leave their wives. It's OK. Really. Being on Dartmoor – again – made me think about what matters.'

I'd heard that before. She'd been much younger the last time ambition trumped common sense.

'Which is why I'm here really.'

She stood and rifled in her handbag, pulling out her reporter's notebook. The window of vulnerability had just snapped shut.

She rejoined me on the sofa. 'I took precautions. Troy knew where I was going. I arranged to meet the guy in a public place. I waited until closing time. The car park was empty except for my vehicle, but they jumped me when I opened the door.

'They?' I repeated, startled.

Ginny nodded. 'Trust me, one I could handle. But two? I fought back, but they cheated.' She touched the side of her head. 'It's still tender.'

'You don't look like someone who was in a fight.'

'I was knocked out, but I think I heard a motorbike.'

'Justine – the landlady – mentioned hearing one too. That would explain how the assailants got away.'

'Assailants?' Ginny grinned. 'You watch too much crime TV. Obviously they were after my phone.'

I frowned. 'So why not just steal it and leave you there? Why go to all the trouble of abducting you?'

'A warning? A threat to back off?' Her eyes were bright with excitement. 'That's what I thought at first. No, they meant to kill me. Look.' She lifted her sweater. Against her pale skin, the bruise on her abdomen stood out – small, round.

'A needle mark,' I whispered. 'But how are you still . . .?'

'Asthma meds,' she said. 'I'm on corticosteroids. The doctor reckons that – and the steak and kidney pie and huge apple crumble that I ate in the pub – slowed everything down. Just as well I didn't have an attack when I was in the middle of nowhere.'

'I found your inhaler,' I said.

'Yeah. I guess it dropped out of my pocket. I don't remember much else.'

I sat back, struck by the obvious. 'It was the same person who killed Connie and Oxley.'

'Exactly!' Ginny was ecstatic. 'And the fact that they wanted my phone? Someone knew I had recordings. It's about Oxley's list, I know it. And since Oxley is dead, I bet it's the person who was pulling the strings.'

'Ginny, be careful.' I was worried.

'I need to talk to Rupert. You have to make it happen.'

'Absolutely not.'

'But he's the link! Please. Just get me into the Hall and I'll do the rest.'

'Rupert had nothing to do with what happened to you on Saturday night.'

She shrugged. 'OK. Fine. I'll find another way. But you know the craziest thing of all?'

I waited.

'Since it was an obvious assault, the hospital had to report it. And guess who showed up to talk to me?'

'Greenleigh.'

Ginny's eyes widened. 'How do you know? Did Mallory tell you?'

'No,' I said.

'Imagine! Chief Superintendent Greenleigh from Major Crime at Torbay Hospital. And get this – they've impounded my car for forensic inspection. Come on, Kat, you must know something!'

'I don't!' I protested, but the pieces were slowly slotting into place. Maybe Oxley's corruption extended further. Maybe this was connected to that mysterious cold case.

'Kat, you have to help me here. This is a huge story. I kept thinking it was about the list, but it's who's behind it. Who's pulling the strings. Follow the money, right?'

Which – annoyingly – was exactly the conclusion I had come to.

'What about your source?' I asked. 'The one who leaked the information in the first place.'

Ginny blinked, then gave me a long look, as if I'd just asked her whether she liked to kick puppies. Of course she wasn't going to answer. Instead, she yawned and got to her feet. 'I'm suddenly tired . . .'

'You're probably still in shock. Will you be all right driving home?'

'I'll be fine. They gave me a' – she made air quotes – '"courtesy" car.' She wrinkled her nose. 'God knows who was driving it last, but it smells like fish.'

I watched as she slid into a red Vauxhall Corsa and gave a cheerful beep on the horn before disappearing into the darkness.

The silence she left behind was a relief, but it didn't settle anything. My mind was still spinning. Delia's visit to the prison, the letter she'd insisted on posting to Stella's father – of all people – from Lenny's cellmate, who didn't know that Philip had died. And now Ginny turning up with the news that Stella herself had visited Torbay Hospital.

I was desperate to talk to someone.

I reached for the phone and hoped my mother would answer. She did.

'Hello, it's your daughter,' I said lightly. 'Remember me?'

'I can't talk now, I'm busy,' came the abrupt reply.

'Oh. I was hoping to come over and—'

'No. Not tonight.' Mum's voice was curt. 'I'm in the middle of something.'

'Oh,' I said again. 'Don't you want to know how Delia got on at the prison? How was the meeting with your agent?'

'Katherine, not tonight.' And she hung up.

I stared at my phone. Clearly things with her agent had not gone well. Experience told me to leave her alone.

I made a mug of cocoa, carried it upstairs and sipped it in bed while trying not to think too much. Sleep – thankfully – came quickly.

I was rudely awakened by my mother. Again. She sounded hysterical.

'You've got to come at once!'

I sat bolt upright, head throbbing slightly. 'Don't tell me the polar bear's moved again.'

'No! Much, much worse.' Her voice trembled. 'The Honourable Gerald Honeychurch was a fraud!'

Chapter Thirty

I seemed to be making a habit of leaving the house in the morning before showering.

Mum was in her writing house, surrounded by a sea of paperwork and photographs.

'Coffee in the corner,' she said. 'Milk somewhere. Oh, Kat!'

Coffee was exactly what I needed. I joined her on the sofa.

'You'd better start at the beginning,' I said, suppressing a yawn.

'As you know, Gerald was father to Cassandra and James. It was all in Cassandra's letters to her brother – you know, the one who ran a Turkish harem and moved in Edward VII's circle.'

'OK.' I took a sip of coffee.

'You don't seem to understand how terrible this is,' Mum said, her voice tight. 'There were no glaciers. No expeditions. Only locked doors and straitjackets.'

'What do you mean, straitjackets?'

'Gerald Honeychurch was no more a daring Victorian explorer, polar bear hunter and adventurer than I am the Pope!'

I stared at her. 'And you know this how?'

So she told me. And I listened – stunned – as she revealed that poor Gerald had been diagnosed with acute melancholia and quietly committed, more than once, to a sanatorium in Switzerland.

'Oh, Mum,' I exclaimed. 'That's so sad.'

'Reading these letters, it sounds like bipolar disorder.' She seemed genuinely upset. 'The family would pack him off for months on end and fabricate a story that he had gone to the Arctic, or into deep uncharted territory.'

'Which I suppose it was,' I put in.

'You don't seem sympathetic!' Mum exclaimed. 'It was all a sham! All of it!'

I picked up a pamphlet from the pile. It was made of thick matt card and printed in faded lithographic ink. The snowy peaks of the Alps provided the perfect backdrop for a picturesque Swiss chalet decked in flowers.

Hotel des Cimes
Vaud, Switzerland
A Restorative Retreat for Exhausted Gentlemen
The mind, like the mountain, finds peace in solitude.
Est. 1885

Fascinated, I read on.

> For Whom We Care:
> Gentlemen of good breeding, reputation, or accomplishment who suffer from Nervous exhaustion, Melancholia, Delirious or excitable episodes, Unsettled ambitions, Hallucinations, spiritual crises, or other delicate disturbances of the mind.

The facility boasted private Alpine suites with writing desks, balconies and warm mineral baths. Daily walks were encouraged, but reading and other stimulating pastimes were not. Optional treatments included calming draughts prepared with laudanum or tincture of opium, 'administered under close supervision to ease agitation and restore restful sleep'.

I looked up in amazement. 'This sounds awful.'

'Fortunately, electric shock treatment wasn't widely used until the 1930s,' said Mum. 'Be thankful for small mercies.'

She gestured to a muddle of open letters and discarded envelopes. 'They tried to keep it secret.'

'Do you think Edith knows the truth about her great-great-uncle?'

Mum shrugged. 'I have no idea.'

'What happened to Cassandra and James's mother? Gerald's wife?'

'I don't know.' She pointed to the family tree that spanned one wall. 'Gerald married an American heiress – so many of them did. She's not mentioned in any of the correspondence between Cassandra and James. It's as if she just vanished.'

I thought for a moment. 'Did Gerald die in the Arctic, or is that an urban legend?'

'What do you think?' Mum produced a telegram on its distinctive buff-coloured paper.

I read:

> STOP PRESS: C. Regret to inform, Hon. Gerald Honeychurch deceased. Official record heart failure during private expedition. STOP. Better remain lost in snow. J.

'He didn't,' I said flatly. I handed the telegram back. 'You're going to have to tell Delia. The entire Easter weekend is in honour of Gerald and his expeditions.'

Mum shook her head. 'I can't.'

'You must!' I exclaimed. 'And honestly, she's so loved up with Henri, if there was ever a time to break the news, it's now.'

'There's more,' Mum said.

I raised an eyebrow.

'That,' she said.

'That' turned out to be a slim sheaf of freight documents printed in ornate German script with red ink stamps and decorative borders. It bore a faint watermark and the words *Mitteleuropäische Eisenbahn-Gesellschaft. Shipping origin, Kairo. Modellokomotive, vergoldet-Kaiseradler.*

'The Kaiser Adler!' I was incredulous. 'But this is proof of provenance . . . or is it? What on earth . . . ? Why was it shipped from Cairo?'

'No idea.' Mum had turned her attention to a stack of black-and-white photographs, muttering to herself, 'I know it's here somewhere.'

As I rifled through the freight documents, a note dropped out. I could feel my eyebrows disappear under my hairline.

'I don't believe it!'

---

17 March 1906
Hotel Continental, Cairo
Received from the Hon. James Rupert Honeychurch: two pearl cufflinks with gold backs (monogrammed J.R.H.), as stake in the game of baccarat held on the evening of 16 March 1906.

In settlement of the wager, I hereby transfer to Mr Honeychurch full possession of one model steam engine, Kaiser Adler.
Signed: A. Mahfouz

I was gobsmacked. 'The Kaiser Adler was won in a card game.'

'Hmm? Wait. It's one of these photographs.' Mum was still muttering.

'Do you think the Museum Room is full of gambling debt trophies?'

'It's possible,' Mum said, continuing to rifle. 'Taxidermy animals were very fashionable in Victorian times. Quite cheap too . . . Ta-dah! Found it.'

She passed me a photograph.

A woman in Bedouin dress rested her hand on an enormous wooden crate. On the back, written in ink: *Cass, Alexandria 1902*.

I leant in and did a double-take.

Inside the crate was a white polar bear.

Florian.

'Well?' Mum said. 'Where do you think they found that? Not at the Arctic, that's for sure.'

I had no words.

She handed me another slip of paper.

I read:

Sold to Miss Cassandra Honeychurch. One Arctic bear (stuffed, standing), origin unknown. From the estate of the late Lord Duncliffe via Mr Abedel Karim's Bazaar of Curiosities, Khan el-Kahlili, Cairo. Paid in full: 320 gold piastres, 9 October 1902.

I stared at it, stunned. 'But what about all the framed photographs of Gerald in the Polar Tearoom?'

'It's impossible to identify anyone behind those wool balaclavas and fur-trimmed caps.' Mum bit her lip. 'You're right. I've got to tell Delia. All that hoopla and expense.' She gave me a look of anguish. 'What if the real story gets out?'

'I don't know what to say.' And I really didn't.

'The event should be cancelled,' Mum declared. 'That's what's got to happen.'

'I'm staying out of it,' I said. 'There are some other things I wanted to talk to you about—'

'Can we do it another day?' Mum cut in, her eyes bright. 'I was thinking about James Honeychurch – you know, the harem chap. Naturally he'll feature in Harem

Historicals. I never did tell you how well my meeting with my agent went.'

'I'm glad.'

'He's pitching the idea to my editor today. I shall be staying by the phone, waiting for the call.'

'No you won't. You'll be talking to Delia,' I said sternly. 'Do it now. Get it over and done with.'

Mum gave a theatrical sigh. 'Very well,' she said. 'We'll do it together.'

'We won't. I'm riding with Harry' – I checked my watch – 'in about half an hour. I need to go home and change.'

As I left, I glanced at the mound of letters and photographs and thought about the elaborate lies spun to preserve a family's reputation. It was so sad. These days, mental health was approached with more understanding – with compassion, support and the chance to speak openly. No Victorian stigma. No secrecy. And no wife locked in the attic.

And really, what did it matter? No one had died. But the sheer effort that had gone into hiding the truth got me thinking about a different kind of deception.

Rupert, going behind his mother's back and selling the land to a developer. How I wished I hadn't agreed to ride the north-west boundary for Edith.

Mallory had told me to stay out of it, but this was different. Wasn't it?

One last thing. Then I was done.

Chapter Thirty-One

Just after ten, Harry and I clattered out of the yard riding Duchess and Jupiter – Tinkerbell was still lame. He'd outgrown his little black pony, who was now happily retired out at pasture. Harry was a good rider, quietly confident, and naturally balanced in the saddle.

At one time, Edith had been a keen competitor in four-in-hand carriage driving, but by her mid eighties, she'd had to give it up. She often told me she hoped Harry would one day – literally – take up the reins. I wondered if, once he got over his current obsession with trains, he might be inclined to give it a go.

After several false starts, Harry had finally found a school he loved – one focused on the creative arts – and was thriving. He was determined to win the Headmaster's Cup with his railway project, something he'd never have cared about before. When I first knew him, he was the boy who kept running away from boarding school. But now here he was, riding beside me through the Devon lanes, talking animatedly about engine numbers and headcodes.

My ignorance must have shown.

'It's easy! D6374 is the engine number,' Harry said patiently. 'And the D stands for diesel. And then say the headcode was 6B47? The first number – a six – means it was a slower freight service. The letter B indicates the region and 47 was the train's schedule.'

'Ah, interesting,' I said, enjoying his enthusiasm but frankly not having a clue what he was talking about.

'Did you know that Greenway Halt – at the home of Agatha Christie, the famous writer – wasn't built until 2012!' he went on. 'It's not original at all. It's just for visitors. Honeychurch Halt was a real halt.'

'I didn't know that,' I said.

'Most people think railway stations are all grand, with tearooms and ticket offices – but halts were nothing like that. Some only had a tiny wooden platform with a nameboard and one oil lamp! Some were request stops. You actually had to wave the train down to stop it!'

'How's your Honeychurch Halt project coming along?' I asked, knowing full well he'd chosen to copy Oxley's diorama.

'It's fun,' said Harry. 'It won't be as good as the one at the Emporium, of course.'

'Did the photos help?'

'They were brilliant!'

'Are you going to use the Kaiser Adler in your diorama?' I asked.

He gave me a scandalised look. 'No! The Kaiser Adler's completely wrong. It never ran there. You can't just throw in any old train. It has to be accurate – well, kind of. Father says that since I'm going to inherit everything, the Hornby set belongs to me, so I'm using that.'

'I'd love to see it.'

'It's not ready yet,' said Harry. 'I have to go to the Halt.'

I thought of the crime-scene tape, which was most likely still there. 'There's nothing really to see. It's all gone – and besides, I thought you were replicating Oxley's diorama.'

'I know,' said Harry. 'But I want to feel what it's like.'

'How's the essay going?' I said. 'Has the Findlay book on railway management been helpful?'

'It's epic!' He grinned. 'It's got gridirons and track maps and train timetables and a big diagram showing all the lines at Waterloo station. Oh – and drawings of engines.'

'I'd love to borrow it for a while,' I said slyly. 'Perhaps I can come by later?'

'OK. But only for a day, because I'm still using it.'

And off he went again, chattering away about sidings, branch lines, switch points and special drainage systems under old tracks.

My attention drifted to what I'd find at Ivy Cottage. Ginny had been certain. Edith had an inkling. I rarely rode this way, because it held too many emotional memories for me.

And it was where I realised I'd fallen in love with Mallory.

We turned into the green lane. It was bumpy and pitted with potholes. Green-laners – off-road motorbikes or ATVs – often used this track, but today the ruts seemed deeper, the grooves more aggressive. Slide and skid marks snaked ahead of us, and in several places the hedgerow had torn branches and bumper-shaped indentations.

Harry dropped behind as I took the lead, steering Duchess along the central raised strip where tufts of grass offered some stability. On either side, deep water-filled furrows glistened with thick mud. I didn't relish brushing off the muck or cleaning the tack when we got back – Alfred would not be pleased.

I found myself wondering whether the lane could even be granted access for heavy machinery. It was barely passable on horseback, let alone suitable for construction vehicles. As far as I knew, it was a protected right of way – possibly even a designated restricted byway, which would prohibit motorised traffic altogether.

This was another example of how reckless Oxley had been, granting planning permission without any real thought to the consequences. How were the developers meant to get in?

My spirits lifted. I could reassure Edith that her fears were groundless after all.

Up ahead, the chimneys of Ivy Cottage rose through the trees, followed by the jagged silhouette of the old chapel's bell tower.

The track opened out – and my heart sank.

A man-made clearing, raw and gouged, had already been carved into the landscape. The red Devon earth had been churned by heavy tyres. Crude outlines marked plots: wooden stakes, orange spray paint on tree trunks, bright ribbons fluttering in the breeze. Tucked beside the abandoned cottage stood a green Portaloo.

And then it struck me. Of course, they weren't planning to use the green lane. Access would come from the field beyond the boundary. The developers must have struck a deal with the neighbouring farmer, quietly securing a back route.

We drew rein and stared.

'Oh, what's happened here?' Harry cried. 'Why are there numbers on the trees?' He pointed to a group of oaks. 'There are more over there, Kat. Look!'

I swivelled in my saddle and saw them – an entire grove of mature beech trees with their smooth silvery-grey trunks, branches fanning out to form a green cathedral roof overhead. Some of the trees were two hundred years old. I couldn't bear it!

A rush of anger left me speechless. How could Rupert have allowed this? Had he even thought to apply for tree preservation orders? Did he really not care at all? I thought of Gloria Weaver and her relentless crusade for the environment. Maybe her visit hadn't just been about the bifold doors. I'd bet it was this all along.

It was a terrible thing to admit, but I was glad that Oxley was dead.

And then, just as quickly, my spirits lifted again. This development would never go ahead now. Maybe the project had already been abandoned. There was no hoarding. No company signage. No builder's name. Nothing to indicate who was behind it.

But that raised another question. As I had already suspected, Rupert had obviously been paid. Would the developers demand the money back? Would it be enough to reassure Edith that it was unlikely the development plans would go ahead now?

'Granny's going to be so upset when we tell her,' Harry said quietly.

What was I supposed to do – ask a child to lie to protect his father?

I dismounted and handed Duchess's reins to him. 'Hold her for a moment, please.'

'Where are you going?' he asked.

'Just stay there.'

I headed towards the cottage. The last time I'd been here, it had been barely habitable. Now it was on the brink of collapse – roof sagging, windows cracked, ivy pushing through the gaps in the stonework. It was beyond saving. I gave up on the idea of going inside. The door was swollen and wouldn't budge, and when I peered through the filthy window panes, I saw nothing but dust and shadows. No sign of life. No clues.

Defeated, I turned back and found that Harry had tied both horses to a low-hanging branch.

'I found this,' he said, handing me a card. 'It was squished in the dirt.'

It was a forest-green business card, embossed in gold:

Bradleigh & Sons

Crafting Tomorrow with Yesterday's Charm.
Marcus Draycott, Director

Email: MDraycott@DDGHoldings.je
Mobile: 07377 421758

I stared at the card. *Bradleigh & Sons*. They were working on the Polar Tearoom. Their name was on the planning application for Honeychurch Halt. But DDG Holdings, in the email address? A parent company, perhaps?

I'd been introduced to Marcus Draycott and his father, Tony, at the exhibition. No wonder Oxley had looked so uneasy. They were in business together. Oxley secured the planning permission, Bradleigh & Sons developed the sites.

Was that why Rupert hadn't wanted to hang around? With all the scandal surrounding Oxley, he would definitely want to keep his distance.

In a few hours, I'd be meeting Marcus's cousin Alison. Maybe I could steer the conversation to his building projects. Anything – *anything* – that might reassure Edith that Rupert's deal was dead.

It was worth a try.

Harry was quiet as we rode back across the fields.

'What are they going to build?' he asked finally. 'Houses?'

'I doubt it.'

'Does Father know they're going to build houses?' he persisted. 'It is our land, after all.'

'I don't know,' I said. 'But I tell you what, let's talk about your diorama. I've got a valuation this afternoon, but I thought I could come and see it after that. In time for tea. And I can borrow that Findlay book, too.'

Harry nodded, then frowned. 'Do you think June will be back? She promised to make me some chocolate pawprint brownies.'

Ah, June.

'You do know she was taken to hospital, don't you?'

'I know,' he said. 'But she's getting better. Mrs Evans said she nearly died of fright, but she wasn't dead yet.'

I suppressed a smile. That sounded exactly like something Delia would say.

'And you do know what scared her, don't you?'

Harry looked down at his reins and didn't answer.

'I need to ask you something,' I said gently. 'Did you move Florian?'

A faint tinge of colour rose in his cheeks.

'I promise I won't be angry. I just want to know how you managed it. He's enormous!' I added lightly. 'Did you get the flail off the wall?'

Harry looked me dead in the eye. 'No.'

I held his gaze, trying to read between the lines.

'Did you know that polar bears – *Ursus maritimus* – can stand ten feet tall?' he said suddenly. 'The males weigh up to sixteen hundred pounds, females around seven hundred. And their fur isn't actually white – it's trans . . . translucent. It just looks white because it reflects the light.'

'Is that so?' If Harry was trying to distract me, I let him. I had enough to think about.

'Underneath, their skin is black to help absorb heat,' he went on. 'They can swim for sixty miles without stopping. And they can smell seals from a mile away, even under the snow. And . . . race you back!'

He took off at a canter – a definite no-no when turning for home. It was the kind of thing that created bad habits. By the time I caught up, we'd reached the lane and he'd slowed to a walk. We had to ride in single file, and neither of us spoke again.

At the yard, we untacked our mounts, rubbed them down, scraped off the worst of the mud and handed them over to Alfred.

'Her ladyship has asked that you telephone when you have news,' Alfred said.

I nodded, heart sinking. There was no getting away from it. I'd tell her the truth.

But first I had to face Alison Fisher.

Chapter Thirty-Two

I pulled onto the forecourt at Sunny Hill Lodge and immediately noticed the black estate car with tinted windows parked by the entrance. I slid next to a silver Kia with a headlamp patched with duct tape, then started towards the door. Gold lettering on the estate's side said, *Hollis & Webb Funeral Directors*. Alison had taken my recommendation.

At that moment, the undertakers appeared. Two men in dark suits wheeling a stretcher covered in a pale grey blanket. Elena followed them out, dabbing at her eyes with a tissue. Bowing my head in respect, I stepped back into the shadows to wait for them to leave.

The rear door lifted and the men slid the stretcher inside. Job done, they exchanged a few quiet words with the carer and drove away.

Elena waited for me to join her.

'Stan gone.' Her eyes were bloodshot. She looked upset.

I gently touched her shoulder. 'I am so sorry.'

'You see Mr Hicks?' She gestured to the building. 'He inside. He clean Stan's room.'

I glanced at the silver Kia. Of course, Connie's car. I supposed Stan's memorabilia belonged to Ian now. I'd have to tell him it was with the police, which would undoubtedly lead to a few awkward questions.

'I'm actually here to see Mrs Fisher.'

'I take.' Elena led the way into reception. 'I let Mrs Fisher know. You wait.'

She keyed in the code. As the double doors opened, a dishevelled man in an ill-fitting suit, clutching a large holdall, stepped through. Elena left us.

This had to be Connie's husband, Ian.

When I introduced myself, he was suddenly alert. 'You valued his stuff for Connie, God rest her soul.'

'That's right. I'm so sorry.'

He shifted the holdall. 'The thing is,' he began, 'this is everything from Stan's room. Connie told me there were some boxes – memorabilia and the like. Valuable, she said.'

'Yes, I was going to talk to you about—'

The front door opened and Alison came in, slightly breathless.

'Kat, sorry to keep you waiting. I was outside with my husband. Mr Hicks, do you have everything you need? Your father-in-law will be greatly missed. He was such a character. Everyone here loved him.'

'I was asking the lady, Pat—'

'It's Kat,' I corrected.

'Right. Where's the rest of Stan's stuff?'

'I'm afraid the police have it,' I said.

All the colour drained from his face. 'Why? Why would they have it?'

'Still?' Alison sounded surprised.

'I don't know the full details,' I said carefully, watching panic creep into Ian's eyes. 'You'd need to speak to Chief Superintendent Greenleigh. She's leading the investigation into Connie's death.'

'Investigation?' Alison's jaw dropped. 'Mr Hicks, you told me your wife died of a medical condition. Why are the police involved?'

Ian licked his lips. 'I know how it looks,' he muttered. 'But we were skint. I saw one of those over-fifties ads in the paper – for just a few quid a month, no doctor's exam. It wasn't a big policy . . . I didn't think she'd actually . . .' He trailed off, rubbing his hand over his face, then straightened. 'I wasn't even here when she died. So why . . .?'

'Ah, life insurance.' Alison seemed relieved. 'Well, I suppose they have to check these things. Probably just a formality.'

'But why have they taken Stan's trains?' Ian whined. 'Connie hadn't even seen him in years. She said there was valuable stuff, and there's nowt in this bag or at the cottage.'

It was a valid question. Alison caught my eye and gave a small, deliberate wink. I couldn't tell if she was humouring Ian or warning me not to say more. It was most odd.

Ian thrust out his jaw, suddenly belligerent. 'I've got nothing to hide. And that's my property now. Should I call 999?'

'That's only for emergencies,' I pointed out.

'I'll tell you what,' Alison stepped in smoothly, 'leave it with me, Mr Hicks. I'll make a few calls and ring you tomorrow. We'll go from there.'

'That's kind. Very kind.' Ian brightened. He gave us both a damp handshake and shuffled off with what remained of Stan Holden's life zipped inside a canvas bag.

Alison watched the door close behind him. 'The police,' she said thoughtfully. 'Well, with all the scammers about, I suppose insurance companies have to be thorough. Speaking of which, has the Kaiser Adler been recovered?'

I froze. For a split second, I had no idea what to say. Was it common knowledge? There'd been nothing official, no mention on the news. Should I say yes? That would lead to more questions. Should I say no? That would be a lie.

'I haven't heard anything.' Officially that was true. 'Shall we look at these paintings?'

Alison nodded and ushered me into her office.

The three paintings were leaning against the side of the love seat. A Birkin in a rich forest green rested on a side chair.

'Gorgeous bag,' I said. 'You've got quite the collection!'

'It's a weakness of mine,' Alison replied with a grin. 'Some women love shoes. I'm a Birkin girl. What about you?'

'Teddy bears,' I said without hesitation. 'But I can't wear them.'

I picked up the first canvas and gave a small cry of delighted recognition. 'Oh! I know this – *Girl with the Golden Kite* by Dufresne!' I turned to Alison. 'It used to hang in the quiet lounge, with two others.' I paused, thinking. '*Interior with Oranges* by Eleanor Marris and *The Second Silence* by Vito Sarnari.'

A tide of red crept up Alison's décolletage. 'You know them?'

I did know them, because Margery Rooke had asked me to value them a couple of years earlier. I had a vague memory of some family upset at the time, though I couldn't recall the details. 'They're hard to forget.'

Conscious of Alison watching, I carried the paintings one by one over to the tall sash window. It opened onto a narrow wrought-iron balcony overlooking a line of garages.

'How much do you think they'd fetch?' Alison asked, hovering close behind me. 'Rough estimate. The family's curious.'

From what I could see, there'd been no obvious changes since the photos I'd taken two years earlier. 'About three hundred thousand.'

'Gosh! Really?'

'Around eighty-five for the Dufresne, ninety-five for *The Second Silence* and possibly one-twenty for the *Interior with Oranges*. British modernists are on the rise.' I smiled. 'Is this for insurance purposes, or are they thinking of selling?'

'I'm not entirely sure,' said Alison. 'But thank you. You'll write up a valuation?'

'Of course, but I'll need to know who it's for – is it the estate or a specific family member?'

Alison blinked. 'Just leave that part blank for now. I'll find out and let you know.'

'Full confession,' I said with a smile, 'I've actually valued these before. As I mentioned, Margery had me do some valuations a couple of years ago.'

'Ah, yes, of course.' Alison's cheeks flushed pink.

'I don't feel it's fair to charge you again – maybe just for my time. I'll still run the usual checks: recent auction results, private sales. There might have been a retrospective, or some scandal I've missed – those things can influence the market.'

'Thank you. That's very kind.' Her smile didn't quite reach her eyes. She hesitated, then added, 'Did you give any more thought to the idea of being on a retainer here? We can certainly make you an attractive offer. And let's face it, a percentage of three hundred thousand is nothing to sniff at.'

It wasn't – but I didn't need to think about it. My mind was already made up.

'I'm flattered you'd ask,' I said. 'But truthfully, I've got my hands full with mobile valuations and my booth at the Emporium.'

'But if you joined us,' Alison pressed, 'you could reduce your freelance work. I imagine most of it's worthless junk. And if you're charging a percentage of the value, it sounds like a lot of effort for very little reward.' She smiled again, resting her hand on my arm. 'Don't say no just yet. I'd love us to work together. At the very least, wait until you've seen our formal proposal.'

It was clear she wasn't used to hearing no. I gave a polite smile and turned to the window, trying to compose myself, just as the low rumble of a car drifted up from the drive below.

A chalk-grey Porsche Cayenne eased out of one of the garages and came to a stop. The driver's door opened and a man stepped out.

I did a double-take, unsure at first if I was imagining things. It was Keith.

My stomach jolted. What the hell was he doing here – and in that car? Chalk-grey wasn't exactly common, and neither was a Porsche Cayenne. I'd seen one at the prison in Devizes only days ago. Maybe there were two.

Then again . . . maybe not.

Chapter Thirty-Three

Alison joined me at the window. 'Ah, there he is.' She tapped on the glass. Keith looked up and waved. 'There's my little man.'

I shrank back, my mind spinning.

'I do wish he hadn't shaved off his beard,' Alison said with a laugh. 'I told him that until he grew it back, I was stopping his allowance. I do like a man with a beard.'

Keith was married to Alison Fisher! I hadn't even known his surname – I'd assumed it was Bradleigh.

Alison must have caught my expression, though she mistook the reason. I was still reeling.

'No, if Keith controlled the purse strings, we'd be paupers.' She grinned. 'And then Bradley shaved off his moustache too. Leigh of course couldn't grow a beard if he tried.'

'And did you stop Bradley's allowance as well?' I asked, only half joking.

'I wouldn't dare!' She laughed again. 'Are you married?'

'Not yet,' I replied.

'Nearly thirty years of marriage, two sons,' Alison said fondly.

'Are they builders too?' I asked.

She looked surprised. 'Why, yes. How did you know?'

So that was it – they'd named the company after their sons.

'Keith's doing some work at Honeychurch Hall,' I said. 'The Polar Tearoom.'

'That's right. So you must have met.'

'Just in passing.' It was the perfect segue. 'I believe Bradleigh & Sons is tied to a potential housing development on the Honeychurch estate. I'm guessing your cousin Marcus is part of that too. With Oxley's death – and talk of some planning permissions being revoked – I wondered if the project might be shelved.'

'I don't get involved in that side of things,' she said quickly. 'I run the nursing home.' She glanced at the clock. 'Goodness, is that the time? Would you mind finding your own way out. I've got a Zoom meeting at three. Just email me the report.'

And before I could say another word, she'd bundled me out of the office.

I made it as far as the secure door, then stopped. I didn't know the code. The corridor was empty. The residents' doors were all closed. There was no one in reception. I couldn't see Elena. In fact, there were no staff anywhere.

I followed the green fire exit signs, hoping for another way out.

A door with a plaque reading *Janet Ross* stood ajar. I called, 'Hello?' and nudged it open, surprised to find no evidence of life. In fact, it looked like this bedroom was now used for storage. I took in the scattered items: a silver tea service in a box at the foot of the empty bed, two Royal Worcester figurines on the night table, framed paintings stacked against the wall. On the bureau, a cluster of vintage Lalique perfume bottles – easily worth £5,000 – caught my eye. But it was the painting, *Summer Light Over Bramble Down*, propped against the wall, that brought me up short. Wasn't this the painting that the family were supposedly taking home with them last weekend? What was it still doing here?

I felt uneasy. Was this what Alison meant by keeping me on a retainer – turning a blind eye while she flogged the residents' possessions?

I needed to get out before anyone caught me snooping, however unintentionally.

At the far end of the room, a glass door led outside. I pushed, half expecting an alarm, but nothing sounded. I stepped out into the daylight and found myself beside the line of garages.

And that's when I bumped into Keith.

At first he didn't seem to recognise me. Then his eyes widened, and he spun on his heel and disappeared behind the Porsche into one of the garages.

I only hesitated for a split second. I wanted answers. I couldn't care less about his flirtation with June, but I *did* care about the dowager countess.

I paused at the threshold. It was broad daylight, but inside was gloomy and felt strangely menacing. Then I thought: why was *I* the one with the problem? I'd just found him out. Keith had a lot to lose, not least a wife who clearly adored him.

I stepped inside.

'I know you're in there,' I called out. 'I just want to talk to you.'

Silence.

Cautiously I took another step. Two hearses stood parked in the shadows. Gothic lettering on the side read: *Leighbard Funeral Services*. Leighbard? An anagram of Brad and Leigh. Of course. Keeping it all in the family. I moved closer, cupping my hand to the glass. Inside one of the hearses was a coffin, floral tributes covering the lid.

I stared. Surely there couldn't be a *body* inside! And what about the flowers? Peonies and lilacs? Those weren't in season for another month.

'What are you doing?' hissed a voice behind me.

I jumped. Keith was suddenly beside me, grabbing my elbow and hustling me outside. I could barely keep my footing.

He let go quickly. 'You need to leave.'

I didn't answer. I knew what I'd seen. 'Is it normal practice to leave a coffin overnight in a garage?'

Keith stared, panic etched on his face. 'Please . . . leave now.'

I stood my ground. 'Not until you tell me what's happening at Honeychurch Hall.'

'Eh?' He frowned, seemed confused. 'You mean the tearoom?'

'No, not the Polar Tearoom,' I snapped. 'The planned developments at Ivy Cottage and Jane's. Are they going ahead or not?'

Silence.

'Because if you don't tell me,' I said evenly, 'I might have to mention something to Alison about your flirtation with June.'

Keith's face turned beetroot. 'But nothing happened!'

'That's not what June implied,' I said, which was true. Sort of.

The red drained from his cheeks, leaving him a sickly white. For a moment I thought he might faint. He looked genuinely frighted.

'But . . . but it was just a few kisses,' he stammered. 'Yeah, June wanted more—'

'I doubt Alison would take it well,' I interrupted. 'Forget growing back your beard. She'd stop your allowance for life.'

'But I don't know anything. I swear!'

'I don't believe you. Bradleigh & Sons is all over the hoardings,' I lied. It wasn't. 'And up at Honeychurch Halt. You're quite busy for a one-man band.'

Keith seemed paralysed.

'Fine. I'll leave you to it. I'm sure Alison will be very interested.'

'No, wait.' He caught my arm. 'I just follow orders, all right? That's all I do.'

'Alison's?'

He shook his head and let me go.

I thought of the business card Harry had found at Ivy Cottage. 'Who are DDG Holdings? Draycott and Draycott Group, perhaps? So who's calling the shots – Marcus? Tony?'

The flicker of fear in his eyes told me everything.

'OK, you've given me no choice.' I turned as if to leave.

'Where are you going!'

'To talk to your wife.'

'I told you!' Keith said desperately. 'It was just a bit of harmless fun!'

'You seriously expect me to believe that? Why buy her a Birkin?'

'Eh?'

'The bag,' I said. 'I saw it. Surely your allowance wouldn't stretch to that! They retail at around ten thousand pounds. Unless it was a knock-off.'

'It fell off the back of a lorry,' he blurted out.

I laughed. 'That old line? And you gave it to June because . . .?'

'She told me it was her birthday and she never got presents. It was a surprise.'

Could it really be that simple? Keith hardly struck me as the sharpest knife in the drawer.

'I wonder what Alison would make of that?'

He gasped, panic rising. 'You can't tell her. Please don't. I swear I don't know anything. June just made me feel . . .' He swallowed hard. 'Like a real man.'

Much as I hated to admit it, I believed him.

'Don't you even want to know how she is? She nearly died.

That did it. Keith seemed to crumple. Whatever bravado he had collapsed. 'I swear I never meant to hurt anyone.'

How typical! Men always said that when they were caught.

'Well,' I said coolly. 'I suppose it's for the best.'

'Eh?'

'You ending' – I made air quotes – '"nothing happened" with June.'

He looked genuinely baffled. 'No. I'm talking about the polar bear. It was me. I moved it.'

'Wait – you moved the polar bear?' I was incredulous. 'It was *you*? But why?'

'It wasn't meant for her. I mean . . .' Panic flared in his eyes again. 'Nothing.'

'Who *was* it meant for?' I said sharply.

Silence.

'Was it *Delia*?'

He looked down at his feet.

'But whatever for?' I was flabbergasted. 'Why would you do something like that?'

A motorbike engine roared in the distance, growing louder.

'You need to go . . .'

I stood my ground. 'Not until you tell me why.'

The motorbike was almost upon us.

'I told you. I was just following orders,' he said hastily, edging away. 'Tell June I'll be in touch.'

'Not in touch,' I shot back. 'You've got a job to finish. The Polar Tearoom opens this weekend.' I grabbed his arm. 'Were you moving other things too? The Grenville Standard? The souvenir books?'

'I put them in the fish larder ... He's coming ...'

I stepped around the Porsche, noticed the green and white cross on the window indicating a first aid kit. Alison was a nurse. It had to be her car.

'Was Alison in Devizes yesterday?'

But before he could answer, the motorbike rolled to a halt behind him, a chrome-heavy Harley-Davidson CVO Road Glide with an enormous engine.

I stayed where I was as the rider dismounted with slow, deliberate movements, removing his helmet to reveal a sharp, clean-shaven face and a pronounced cleft chin – a younger version of Keith.

A prickle of unease ran through me. Something about him felt familiar, though I couldn't place it.

'What's going on, Dad?'

'Bradley, this is Kat Stanford,' Keith said quickly. 'Er ... she's ...'

'I came to value some art for Mrs Fisher and ran into Keith.'

Bradley glanced at the row of garages behind us, then back to his father. There was a loaded silence. Keith gave the faintest shake of his head.

I wasn't supposed to have seen what I'd seen. 'Well, I'd better be off. Nice to meet you, Bradley.'

As I walked away, I looked up at the window. Alison was there. Watching.

Driving home, I replayed everything. The room stuffed with personal possessions, Alison's attempts to recruit me, and strangest of all, the pair of hearses with the coffin and fake flowers inside. Hollis & Webb had collected Stan Holden's body. Something nefarious was definitely going on.

And then there was Keith, hiding the Grenville Standard and the souvenir books, and moving the polar bear. Why go to such lengths to torment Delia when he barely knew her?

Those thoughts scattered as I slowed to turn through the main entrance.

Speak of the devil – Delia was perched on the wall.

I pulled alongside and lowered my window. 'Is everything OK?'

'I'm leaving,' she declared. 'And not a moment too soon.'

Chapter Thirty-Four

'Come inside,' I said. 'Don't be hasty. Let's talk it through.'

'I suppose you knew all along about Gerald being a fraud,' Delia said bitterly. 'Nice of Iris to finally let me in on the joke.'

'Mum only just found out,' I protested. 'What about the open house this weekend? And where are you going?'

'Henri's on his way,' she said. 'I called him. He told me to tell them to take a long walk off a short pier.'

That didn't sound very French to me.

'He said, they're making a fool out of you, Delia,' she went on. 'And he's right.'

'I honestly don't think the family know the truth,' I said. 'Mum's the historian and she didn't have a clue until she stumbled on some letters up in the attic.'

'No.' Delia was adamant. 'Henri says his lordship's had it in for me for weeks.'

'Rupert's under a lot of pressure . . .'

'And he won't let me forget about the Grenville Standard!'

'Ah,' I said. 'There's something I need to tell you.'

And so I told her everything.

'It was Keith? Keith was the one moving the polar bear?' Delia's jaw dropped. 'But he knew June was terrified of stuffed animals!'

I shrugged. 'I don't think June was the target.'

'You mean . . . it was meant for me?' Delia blinked. 'I don't understand. Why would he do that to me? We barely exchanged two words, and I've kept his fling with June quiet.'

'But look, the good news is that the Grenville Standard and the souvenir books are safe.'

'I don't care. When I told Henri, he said, don't add your name to this, Delia, you'll be a laughing stock. Anyway, it's too late.'

'What do you mean?'

'I wrote my letter of resignation. I left it in the kitchen. Let's see how they manage when no one brings them breakfast in the morning – although June told me she'll be back tomorrow, so she can do it.' Delia's voice rose. 'She's been after my job from the moment she arrived.'

'That's not true,' I said, surprised to find myself defending June.

'Henri said she's been scheming.'

'Henri doesn't know her,' I snapped. 'Why does he suddenly have such a hold over you? I've never seen you like this.'

Delia's eyes filled with tears. I moved instinctively to hug her, but she was clutching her new Birkin, which made it awkward to get close.

Her jaw hardened. 'No, it's finished.'

I looked up at the sky 'Do you want to wait inside the gatehouse? It might rain.'

'Thank you, dear, but no. He'll be here very soon.'

I left her perched on the wall. To be honest, Delia was the least of my problems.

Back in my showroom, I decided to get it over with and called Edith. I told her all I knew and that unfortunately I couldn't confirm whether the building would still go ahead.

She listened without asking any questions, and at the end of my carefully rehearsed speech just thanked me and hung up the phone. I'd done what she'd asked.

I settled in front of my laptop, searching for the valuations I'd written up for Margery Rooke. I found the letter confirming the provenance from a former resident called Brenda Ellingham, dated a decade ago. She had acquired the three paintings when she lived in Paris, having bought them directly from the artists, and had receipts to prove it.

I tapped into current market trends, checking upcoming sales or exhibitions for the names of the three – Lucien Dufresne, Eleanor Marris and Vito Sarnari. There seemed to be a surge of interest, especially in Marris. This could be why the Ellingham family now wanted the paintings back.

Alison had told me to leave the line blank as to who owned them and who the valuation was for. Brenda Ellingham was long deceased and there was no other contact number.

I called Margery. After exchanging a few pleasantries, I got straight to the point.

'You mean the Ellingham paintings in the quiet room?' She sounded puzzled.

'The family have requested their return.'

'I highly doubt it,' said Margery. 'Brenda had disinherited her children years before. They never visited her. What's more, they tried to contest the will but the court threw it out. The order was clear – no further claims could be made. I was involved. It was horrible.'

'I see.' I thought for a moment. 'Perhaps they heard about the change of ownership and thought they'd try their luck.'

'Impossible!' Margery declared. 'The paintings were specifically bequeathed to the home in trust for the residents.'

'I see,' I said again. 'Presumably, when the Fishers purchased Sunny Hill Lodge, it included the artwork and—'

'I know what you're trying to say – that they could do what they liked with them – but that's not true.' Margery's voice wavered with emotion. 'I wasn't involved in the sale, I was just the manager, but I thought Brenda's bequest was a binding document. If I'd been kept on . . .'

'Oh.' I felt uncomfortable. 'Alison told me she'd hoped you would.'

'Really?' Margery's voice was laced with sarcasm. 'I used to live in the top-floor flat. I didn't just lose my job. I lost my home. I'd given thirty years of my life to that place. And they fired all my staff as well – said they wanted a fresh start. I know Alison Fisher is a qualified nurse, but she's hopeless at managing a business. Her husband may be a charmer, but he's not very bright. And don't get me started on the children – if I can call them children. Leigh's all right, but Bradley? He's a nasty piece of work.'

I wished I hadn't called her now. I honestly didn't know what to say.

'Just be careful,' Margery said. 'Although frankly, it's hardly surprising knowing who her father is.'

I didn't answer.

'Trust me, I did a lot of digging when I knew my job was on the line. I told my boss, don't get involved, you'll regret it.'

'Oh.'

'You *do* know who her father is, don't you?'

'No,' I admitted.

'Donald Draycott,' said Margery. 'Serving a life sentence for murder.'

I felt a rush of adrenaline. Lenny's cellmate was called Don! There was the link! It had been right under my nose all along. It *was* Alison I'd seen outside the prison. But if that was the case, why hadn't she posted her father's letter to Philip Greenleigh herself?

'Yes, armed robbery back in the seventies. There was an exhibition recently of . . . Oh, how silly of me. Of course you know all about that!' Margery's voice was clipped, as if she was only just holding her anger in check. 'The family are into all sorts of mischief. I told you, I went digging when I knew I'd be turned out.'

'Thank you for your help,' I said, anxious to get off the phone.

'Perhaps we can meet for lunch?' Margery's voice softened. 'I'm sorry. I'm still very upset.'

Once I'd ended the call, I stared at the wall, trying to make sense of it all. I had been thrown by Alison's interest in the Kaiser Adler but realised it had been a ruse.

I turned to Google.

It didn't take me long to find a full report of the robbery. It was dated 15 October 1974.

ARMED ROBBERY ON BRANCH LINE – TWO MEN SHOT DEAD

A daring armed raid on a goods train travelling the Honeychurch Halt branch line late Sunday night has left two men dead and another seriously injured. Railway guard Mr Edward 'Eddie' Carter, aged 46, and Police Constable Steven Cummings, aged 30, were both fatally wounded during the incident. The signalman, Mr Stan Holden, aged 35, was taken to hospital in a critical condition. Veteran driver Mr Roland Briggs, aged 58, was found tied up in his cab, gagged and blindfolded but otherwise unharmed.

Two masked men – brothers Anthony Draycott, 34, and Donald Draycott, 30 – were arrested at the scene by Detective Sergeant Harold Mercer, Police Constable Philip Greenleigh and Police Constable Dennis Collier, whose prompt actions have been commended by senior officers. The Draycott brothers have been charged with armed robbery and murder.

The train, which had been transporting bonded goods, including crates of whisky, cartons of cigarettes, several cases of transistor radios and a locked metal chest containing uncut diamonds, was diverted to an unscheduled stop, leading investigators to suspect detailed knowledge of the railway timetable and signalling system.

No firearm has yet been recovered.

I sat back, feeling a mixture of incredulity and dismay.

According to the newspaper report, Stella's father had been among the arresting officers. Was that why she had forced her way into Connie Hicks's case? Oxley's murder? Ginny's abduction? But why involve the Major Crime Unit?

Unless something new had come to light. Something Stan Holden had been hanging onto. Why else had there been so much interest in his worthless memorabilia – enough for Stella to confiscate it?

I needed to call Mallory, but as I reached for my phone, there was a knock on the door.

When I opened it, Delia was standing there in the rain, drenched and trembling, her face streaked with mascara.

'Henri's not coming,' she declared, and promptly burst into noisy tears. 'He lied.'

'Let's go and see Mum,' I said quickly. This was something I couldn't cope with on my own.

Ten minutes later, we were in the Carriage House kitchen, gin and tonics already on the table.

Between sharp expletives I'd never heard Delia use, and great gasping sobs, it all came tumbling out.

'Let me try and call him,' Mum said gently, already reaching for her phone.

'Be my guest.' Delia flung her own across the table.

I managed a glance at the screen. She'd tried to call Henri at least a dozen times.

Mum put the phone on speaker and hit redial.

The number you are trying to call is no longer in service.

'You're right,' she declared. 'He's done a runner.'

'I just don't understand why,' Delia wailed. 'I did everything he told me to do. Wait . . .' Her eyes grew hopeful. 'Do you think maybe he's dead?'

'Maybe,' Mum said warily.

'He *should* be!' Delia shrieked. 'I'd rather he was.'

Mum turned to me. 'Let's get Mallory to track this phone number. Delia's thrown her whole life away – well, what's left of it.'

'It's hardly a police matter,' I said. 'Was a crime committed? Did he steal from you? Did you give him money, Delia?'

'No,' she whispered. 'It's the other way around. I've got all those presents.'

'You should keep everything!' Mum said firmly. 'Although I'd flog that bicycle. It's a death trap on wheels.'

Delia perked up. 'How much do you think I'd get for it?'

'And we're the same shoe size,' Mum added thoughtfully. 'So if you don't want those Louboutins—'

'Excuse me!' I cut in. 'Can we focus? Delia, what exactly did you say to Henri when you spoke to him?'

'I told him Lenny had signed the divorce papers. Then I told him about Gerald being a fraud and that I'd get the blame for everything. That I'd given my blood to the Honeychurch family and no one cared. And he just said, "Leave. You've . . ."' She wiped at a fresh tear. 'He said, "You've got me." Oh!' She wailed again. 'I've given up everything! I've got no job, no money, no home . . . not even Lenny any more.'

'Delia!' Mum snapped. 'Pull yourself together. You don't want Lenny, remember?'

'I know,' she whispered. 'But we had that pact. Until death do us part.'

'Well, that was a silly promise to make,' Mum said crisply. 'Let's draw a line under Henri and sort out your future before you don't have one.'

'Agreed,' I said. 'Delia, where did you leave your letter of resignation?'

'In the kitchen,' she said. 'Next to the toaster.'

'So it's unlikely anyone will see it until the morning. Unless . . .' Mum thought for a moment. 'What about their supper this evening?'

'Tuesdays are my night off,' said Delia. 'I laid everything out in the dining room before I left. Cold beef, half a game pie, beetroot salad. A fruit tart for pudding.'

'And you addressed the letter to Lavinia?'

She nodded.

'She might not even notice it,' I said, rising from my chair. 'I promised I'd look at Harry's diorama. I'll head up there now. With any luck, we can get the letter back and no one will be any the wiser.'

As I sped to the Hall, my thoughts kept circling back to Delia. Something was off. It wasn't just that Henri had vanished the moment she'd done everything he asked. It was deeper than that. Delia might be hopelessly naïve about romance – always taking everything at face value – but that gruesome pact she'd made with the odious Lenny, the letter she'd hand-delivered for Donald Draycott, and Keith's bizarre behaviour with the polar bear told a different story. He'd said he was following orders.

Orders from who? Alison? Marcus? Tony? And why? This wasn't random. It reeked of malice and felt personal. I was more convinced than ever that Lenny was behind it.

But it wasn't just about revenge. It came back to Donald Draycott and that letter.

Lenny had been a pawn. Donald had wanted that letter to reach Philip Greenleigh.

And that changed everything.

Chapter Thirty-Five

I parked in the courtyard behind the service wing and hurried inside. Striding down the dim corridor lined with larders neatly labelled for a potential living-history museum – another of Delia's brainwaves – I stopped at the fish larder and pushed open the door.

It was colder inside than I expected. Rusted hooks jutted from a beam above a slate counter, and in the corner was a butler's sink. A high window cast a weak, gloomy light across the room. A low cupboard was set into the wall beneath the counter, I crouched and opened it. Inside, rolled into a tight bundle, was the Grenville Standard, along with the missing box of *Tales from the Tundra*.

Mission accomplished. I moved on to the next.

Entering the kitchen – immaculate, as Delia had left it – I made a beeline for the toaster. Sure enough, an envelope addressed to *Lady Lavinia Honeychurch* was propped in front of it. I grabbed it and slipped it into my coat pocket just as Harry strolled in.

His eyes lit up. 'Have you come to see my diorama!'

I smiled. 'Yes, I have.'

He went straight to the fridge and yanked open the freezer drawer. 'Do you want an ice cream? Delia doesn't work on Tuesdays, so we have to fend for ourselves. But it means I can sneak an extra one!'

I followed him through the Great Hall, noticing that the flail was back on the wall.

'You know we found out who was moving Florian,' I said.

'Oh, I know,' he called over his shoulder. 'It was the builder. I saw him do it. He gave me twenty pounds to keep quiet. It was funny.'

'Not for June it wasn't,' I scolded.

'But she's all right now,' Harry said quickly. 'You said so.'

The polar bear was soon forgotten as Harry turned into a narrow corridor. At the end stood a door marked with a brass plaque engraved with the words *Justice Room*.

I'd never been inside, but I knew Honeychurch Hall had once been one of only ten manors in the old Haytor Hundred authorised to hold court leet sessions – local hearings for petty offences and village disputes. It had even been granted its own gallows, the upright post of which still stood at Gibbet's Cross, a grim relic of another age.

The Justice Room itself was a small oak-panelled chamber. A framed parchment displaying the Charter of the Court Leet still hung on the wall. At one end, a slightly raised dais held a carved oak chair beneath the Grenville coat of arms. In the centre of the room stood the justice table – a heavy slab of oak. On top of it sat Harry's diorama.

I remembered when he used to spend hours making model aircraft. For an eleven-year-old with limited supplies, his dedication was impressive. The photos of Oxley's diorama I'd taken on my phone – close-ups, and not good ones either – were Blu-Tacked to a wall in a neat row.

'It's not finished yet,' he warned, though the level of detail was already astonishing. He'd brought down the Hornby train set from the attic and glued some track to a sheet of plywood scattered with grit. He'd fashioned a tiny platform out of cardboard. A lopsided shelter made from a cereal box stood at one end, complete with a cocktail-stick oil lamp and a painted lolly stick bearing the words *Honeychurch Halt Train Robbery*. Scraps of dyed sponge had become hedges, and a clump of moss served as a gnarled old tree. A toilet-roll tube wrapped in green felt had been turned into a small embankment.

'The gridiron yard's going here,' he said, pointing to a pencilled square where a small pile of matchsticks looked as if they could be important.

'What exactly is that?'

'It's where loads of tracks criss-cross like a grid so trains can change lines or park without bumping into each other.'

'What's the paper clip for?'

'That'll be the point lever,' he said. 'For the switch box. Grid 17B.'

I gave a start. Grid 17B. How odd. Alison had mentioned this too. Stan had been worried about it. Grid 17B had to be important.

'That's very specific.'

'It was on the map,' said Harry.

I frowned. 'Map?'

'In here!' He grinned and brandished Findlay's book.

'Can you show me?'

Harry released a fold-out diagram of gridirons at Edge Hill. 'Did you know that the Liverpool and Manchester Railway was the first railway constructed by George Stephenson, in 1826?'

The diagram was a mass of criss-crossing lines and loops, covered in labels that meant absolutely nothing to me.

'You're a smarter person than me,' I said smiling. 'What are chain drags?'

Harry laughed. 'They're for runaway wagons – heavy iron chain cables hidden just below the rails. Our old Halt didn't have those, though. This,' he added proudly, producing a loose sheet of yellowing paper, 'is what I'm working from.'

At the top, someone had pencilled *Honeychurch Halt* in block capitals. The drawing was simple, with an asterisk marking Grid 17B.

There it was again. Grid 17B.

'Where did you find it?' I asked.

'Tucked inside the book.'

Stan had sketched this for a reason.

'I'm still waiting for some stuff to arrive,' Harry went on. 'I used my pocket money – and my polar bear money – to order some epic things from Metcalfe Models. They sell kits, and if you get them unpainted, it's cheaper. This one came this morning!' He handed me a tiny figure of a boy wearing horn-rimmed glasses. 'It's a mini me!'

'Wow. That's scarily accurate.'

'I know!' He beamed happily. 'You send away a full-length photo and it's printed in 3D. Obviously I wasn't born in 1974, but I wanted to be in it. See if Father guesses that that's me.'

He carefully placed the figure on the diorama, angling it behind a shrub next to the lamp hut. 'I'm hiding.'

'Hiding?' I echoed. 'Why would you say that?'

'Because he's watching. Look – his bike's behind the hut. It's like he's spying.'

A chill ran through me. Harry had re-created – albeit in an amateurish way – Oxley's diorama. Oxley's attention to historical accuracy was legendary. The presence of a small boy brought me up short. Was it possible that Oxley had actually witnessed the robbery? He'd only been about six or seven back in 1974.

He had told me he'd always been a passionate train-spotter. I remembered asking him when the hobby had started. He'd given a shy smile and said his parents had lived just the other side of the Halt, and that he'd sneak out to watch the trains – though if he was caught, he'd 'get the slipper'. I had the distinct impression his childhood hadn't been a happy one.

'I have to do the engine number,' Harry broke in. 'And get a gun.'

The newspaper clipping said the gun had never been recovered, and yet Oxley had put it into the hand of one of the robbers. My conviction that he had been there grew deeper.

Why had Tony and Marcus shown such an interest in the diorama? Mallory had said that everything had been recovered and the diamonds – which both Connie and Alison had mentioned – had never been on the train.

An incoming text pinged in.

My spirits soared. Mallory was waiting for me at Jane's Cottage, and not a moment too soon.

I took Findlay's book from Harry, promising to return it the following day, made a quick detour to the Carriage House to return Delia's letter – relieved to find her in better spirits – and raced home.

Mallory was already waiting inside.

'I'm so happy you're here!' I said, bursting through the door. 'I have a lot to tell you—'

But one look at his face stopped me cold.

His expression was thunderous.

'You do realise what you've done, don't you?' he said quietly. 'Please sit down.'

Chapter Thirty-Six

We sat at the dining room table in silence.

Mallory seemed awkward. My heart was racing. What could I have done?

His police notebook and uncapped pen lay in front of him.

Finally he looked up. 'Why did you involve Shawn Cropper?'

I was taken aback. 'I didn't involve him. He turned up unannounced on my doorstep.'

Had Shawn told Mallory about Eric taking Oxley's phone; about Eric finding Oxley dead? I wasn't sure what to say, so I said nothing.

'And?' Mallory pressed. 'What did you talk about?'

'I'm sure you already know,' I said lightly, but he didn't smile.

'Maybe. But I'd like to hear it from you.'

It occurred to me exactly why Mallory was an excellent detective, but being on the wrong side of the table was an experience I wasn't enjoying. All I could do was tell the truth. I had nothing to hide.

'Eric had taken Oxley's mobile phone when he went to reclaim the Kaiser Adler,' I said. 'Shawn told me Eric had sought his advice. I told Shawn he needed to report it. So it sounds like he did.'

I was happy with my answer. Mallory wrote it down. 'Unfortunately, Shawn's involvement has set the village grapevine alight. Something that we had hoped could be avoided.'

'That's hardly my fault!'

Mallory rubbed a hand over his face. He looked shattered.

'And then we got a call from another ex-boyfriend of yours,' he went on. 'David Wynn.'

'David called me about the Kaiser Adler. Felicity Oxley had wasted no time in submitting an insurance claim.' I felt defensive. 'That was before I realised Eric had been the one who had taken the train — sorry, reclaimed it. It's Honeychurch property. I've got a letter that proves provenance. Mallory, please listen. I've been trying to talk to you properly for days.'

'Why did Oxley have Rupert's train in the first place if it didn't belong to him?'

'It was a bribe to grant planning permission to build houses here at Jane's Cottage and at Ivy Cottage on the north-west boundary.'

'Can you confirm this?'

'I rode to Ivy Cottage this morning,' I said. 'The land had already been mapped out — flags staked and marks sprayed on trees. The ground was cut up. As you know, Oxley had been suspended, and now, with his death, it's likely that any planning permission he granted under the table will be revoked. I don't know where that leaves Rupert. He must've already been paid for the land. Will he have to give the money back?'

'Who are the developers?'

I reached into my bag and pulled out Marcus Draycott's business card, sliding it across the table. 'This was found at the site.'

Mallory's eyes widened. The name meant something to him, I could tell. But he said nothing.

'He's Alison Fisher's cousin,' I said. 'Interesting that he's listed as a director of Bradleigh & Sons. They're working at the Hall. I saw their hoardings at Railway Cottage too, didn't you?'

His continued silence was infuriating.

'Eric will do anything for Rupert,' I went on. 'He took Oxley's phone in an effort to protect him, though of course it's futile, with all the ways digital footprints can be traced now. You know Eric had nothing to do with Oxley's death. I mean . . .' I trailed off, cursing the promise I'd made to keep Ginny's source confidential.

Mallory's eyes locked with mine. 'Do I?'

I took a deep breath. 'You know he didn't. I saw the needle cap in the footwell of Oxley's car.'

'And?'

'Which . . . which suggested he might have been injected with something.' I felt my cheeks grow hot.

Mallory raised an eyebrow. 'Really? And what makes you think that?'

Now my face was on fire. I'd always been a rotten liar. 'Because of what happened to Ginny,' I mumbled, looking down.

'And what did happen to Ginny?'

I bit back a flash of irritation. Why was he forcing me to spell out what he already knew?

'She said toxicology results showed insulin. The asthma medication saved her life. I thought maybe the same thing happened to Oxley.'

Mallory didn't respond.

'And Stella Greenleigh visited her in hospital,' I said in a rush. 'This is connected to that old robbery at the Halt. That's the cold case you're working on, isn't it?'

'Kat—'

'It is! I can see by the expression on your face!' I said, my voice rising. 'Stella's father's name was in an old newspaper report – is that why she's interested? What does she know? Why are you protecting her!'

'Do not get involved in this, Kat. Do you hear me?'

'But I already am!' I retorted.

Mallory stood, began to pace. 'Leave the past alone.'

'In case you haven't noticed, that "past" has been out there for the last few weeks. Harry is even doing a school project on Honeychurch Halt. He's copying Oxley's diorama of the heist.'

He froze. 'Then tell him to stop. Now.'

I jumped up, stepped in front of him, catching his arm. 'Mallory, what is it?'

The flicker of apprehension in his eyes was unmistakable. 'You have no idea who you're dealing with.'

I hesitated. 'There may be something I've seen – something I know without realising it.'

He cracked a small smile. 'If only.'

I pressed on. 'Oxley was a *prototypical* model railway engineer. That means—'

'I know what it means.'

'You didn't come to his *Crime on the Line* exhibition at the Emporium – five dioramas each reflecting a true crime in history. The botched robbery at Honeychurch Halt was one of them. Can we sit down?' I said suddenly. 'It's complicated.'

Mallory gave a heavy sigh. 'Fine.'

'There were five, but only two are important,' I went on. 'The 1916 exhibit of Cologne station with the Kaiser Adler train, and Honeychurch Halt – although actually, all five are important . . .'

'Kat,' groaned Mallory.

'. . . because Oxley offered a challenge. In each diorama there was a historical inaccuracy. The only one that no one could guess was Honeychurch Halt.'

'OK,' he said slowly.

'But I think I know what it is now,' I said. 'No gun was ever found at the scene, right?' I didn't wait for him to reply. 'But the diorama showed Donald Draycott holding a gun in his hand.'

'We assume it was disposed of,' said Mallory.

'Yes, I know, but that's not the point. Oxley created real-life scenarios. I think he was there. I think he witnessed the robbery. He was an avid trainspotter. He lived close by.'

'He wouldn't have been born back then.'

'But he was!' I exclaimed. 'Look at this.' I pulled out my phone and scrolled to the photos that I had printed off for Harry, settling on the critical image. 'See that figure there? Crouched behind the lamp hut?'

'A man.'

'No, it's a boy,' I said. 'Wait, let me get my loupe.'

I pulled it out and handed it to him.

He studied the image. 'OK. Yes. A boy.'

'I don't know what Oxley looked like as a boy, but I assume it would be easy to find out.' Seeing Mallory was confused, I explained how Harry had been able to create a 3D version of himself for his own diorama.

He didn't seem to hear me. He was focused on Donald and the gun. I watched his face change from confusion to surprise and then excitement.

'What is it?' I asked. 'Is it the gun? Was it recovered after all?'

'No.' He shook his head. 'Everything but the gun was accounted for. The area was thoroughly searched.'

I gasped. 'When Oxley met the two men, he seemed shocked. At first I thought it had something to do with Marcus – after all, Oxley would have been dealing with him in his capacity as a planning officer – but it wasn't. It was

Tony Draycott. He must have recognised him even after all these years. He looked as if he'd seen a ghost.'

Mallory looked thoughtful. 'Tony served thirty years for his role in the robbery. Up until a few days ago, he'd not set foot outside the Channel Islands since his release.'

'That's it!' I jumped up with excitement. 'Alison saw something in the diorama that must have spooked her uncle. For him to come to England after all this time has to be significant.'

Mallory cracked a small smile. 'You may be right. Tony has been quietly running his empire from Jersey.'

I knew all about Jersey. A tax haven for the wealthy – and maybe for those who liked to fly under the radar. After all, that was where my mother used to bank.

'Tony Draycott hasn't been under active surveillance for decades. The Channel Islands aren't within UK jurisdiction. They're Crown Dependencies, which means we can't just march in and pull records like we would here.'

'All the more reason to figure out why he's risking so much to come here!'

Mallory moved to the window, thinking.

'What was in the letter to Philip Greenleigh?' I said suddenly. 'Please tell me. You have to admit, I've been more help than hindrance.'

Seconds dragged into what felt like minutes. Finally his gaze found mine.

'Philip was young,' he began. 'He was scared. He was off-duty and on his way home from the pub.'

'Philip was local?' I was surprised. I'd assumed he'd always lived in Tavistock.

'He asked for a transfer after the incident,' said Mallory before continuing, 'It was late. He stopped to relieve himself in the undergrowth by the bridge over the cutting. He heard a gunshot, and without thinking clambered down the embankment to find Stan Holden writhing in agony.'

'Wait – Donald said this?' I needed to get the facts straight. 'Or Philip?'

'Philip told Stella before he died. Donald corroborated it in the letter he gave Delia to post.'

'Sorry. Go on.'

'Tony Draycott threatened to shoot Philip.'

'Tony? Not Donald? Oh yes, they were both wearing masks.'

Mallory nodded. 'Philip knew he was capable of it. But Donald begged him not to. Tony agreed, on the condition that Philip gave them a twenty-minute head start before raising the alarm. And that was when it got ugly.'

I waited. Mallory seemed to struggle for words.

He drew a deep breath. 'Philip slipped away, unaware that an anonymous call had already been made to the police station.'

'Oxley!' I whispered.

'The handler had mentioned it sounded like a child. It was never confirmed, but most likely.' Mallory paused. 'Moments later, PC Cummings arrived, having caught the call on his car radio. He didn't wait for backup. Donald said the guard had got free, and the two men rushed Tony, who just . . . shot them.'

For a moment I couldn't speak. 'But . . . where was Philip?'

'Hiding. Watching. He said it all happened quickly.'

'How *could* he just stand by!' I was appalled. 'How could he do *nothing*!'

'He was twenty-one, Kat. None of us know how we'd react with a gun to our head.'

I didn't answer.

'It was only when the other two officers arrived that he joined in the arrest. And when he received the commendation, it felt like a lie. But by then it had gone too far. Stella believes that guilt is what finally killed him way before his time – especially coming from a family of police officers.'

'So *this* is why Stella is involved?' I said. 'She's afraid the truth will come out and his reputation will be destroyed?'

'No,' Mallory said finally. 'She wants Tony back inside.'

'And Donald to walk free?'

We fell silent.

'If the caller *was* Oxley,' I said suddenly, 'why didn't he say anything at the time?'

Mallory shrugged. 'Perhaps he wasn't supposed to be out that night. Maybe he would have been in trouble with his parents. It's something we may never know.'

'And if Oxley saw what happened, then Tony knew he knew.' I was stunned. 'Tony pulled the trigger and let Donald take the blame. What I don't understand is why, after all these years in prison with no chance of parole, Donald would suddenly reveal who the real shooter was.' Something was niggling at the back of my mind. 'Alison visited him in prison – I know that for a fact. I wonder if she told him about the diorama.' I shook my head. 'Unless the rumour of something valuable in Stan Holden's box of memorabilia is true.'

'Go on.'

'Why else did Alison arrange for Stan to go into Sunny Hill Lodge? It does seem odd that she just happened to stumble upon him wandering on the main road. Have you any idea how expensive it is there? It must be at least fifteen hundred a week. And she paid for it out of the goodness of her heart? Somehow I don't think so.'

I marched to my tote and took out Findlay's book. 'I want to show you something.' I pulled out the diagram of gridirons and Stan's sketch of Honeychurch Halt. 'Obviously Grid 17B is significant,' I said. 'Maybe the gun was buried there?'

Mallory shook his head. 'I told you. The place was thoroughly searched.'

'The newspaper report suggested that someone helped the Draycotts from the inside . . .'

'Stan spent weeks in hospital,' said Mallory, 'although Stella was always suspicious of his role. Her father claimed he was already injured when he arrived on the scene.'

'You mean . . .' I stared at him, 'before the Draycotts even knew the police were coming?'

'Exactly,' said Mallory. 'A shot to the kneecaps. We think he was the inside man who helped divert the train onto the branch line and into the siding.'

I thought of Stan's miserable cottage, and his lonely life. It certainly didn't look like he'd been rewarded – unless he'd already spent all the money. So what was the significance of Grid 17B?

'Oh my God!' I cried. 'That's it! It was right in front of me!' I turned to Mallory, hardly able to contain my excitement. 'It's Philip. Philip is in Oxley's diorama. Look again!'

I showed him my phone, enlarging the figure facing Tony. 'Harry asked why the policeman wasn't in uniform. That's Philip. This scene is *before* the police arrived. Look, there's Stan, already slumped in the corner, injured. And Eddie, the guard, tied to an iron railing but still alive.'

Mallory went stock still. 'You may be right,' he said slowly.

'I am! I know I am! *That's* what Tony saw. *That's* why he came over. He had to see for himself.'

Mallory's shoulders sagged. 'I believe you, but it's Donald's word against Tony's now. And with Philip, Stan and Eddie Carter all dead . . .'

'What about the driver? Roland somebody?'

'Roland Briggs. Long dead too,' Mallory said. 'He was thoroughly investigated. He had no idea what was happening. Not only was he bound and gagged, he was blindfolded as well.'

'Unlike Eddie Carter,' I mused.

'Donald claimed that Tony dealt with Stan and the driver and he took care of the guard but that Philip turned up before he had a chance to put his blindfold on or double-check the bindings.'

'Which is how Eddie was able to wriggle free,' I whispered. 'What a brave man.'

Mallory gave a grunt. 'But as I said, no way to prove any of it now.'

We fell silent again.

'Well, I know something weird is going on at Sunny Hill Lodge,' I said suddenly.

'Let's go back to Stan for a moment—'

'Just hear me out,' I said. 'Alison asked me to value three paintings for a family who now wanted to sell them, paintings I'd already valued for her predecessor, Margery Rooke. It was Margery who told me that Alison was Donald Draycott's daughter – and that those paintings had been left in trust. They're not hers to sell.'

'How much are we talking about here?'

'Around three hundred thousand pounds.'

Mallory's eyes widened. 'Oh.'

'Alison offered me a retainer to help value the residents' possessions when they downsized or sold their homes.' I thought of Janet Ross's empty room. 'But I think she's selling off their things and pocketing the money.'

Mallory stiffened. 'Go on.'

I told him what I'd seen. 'No proof, obviously. But even if the Fishers bought Sunny Hill Lodge and its inventory, that wouldn't include personal effects belonging to the residents, right?'

'Probably not, but . . .' He suddenly looked alert. 'We can't touch Tony or Marcus – everything they do is squeaky clean. But Alison Fisher could be the weak link.'

'She's raking it in,' I agreed. 'How else can she afford her Birkins?'

'Birkins?' Mallory said sharply.

'She owns at least two. Real ones. Delia's got one too – and Louboutin shoes. June as well. I've seen them.'

'Wait – what!' Mallory sat bolt upright, excited. 'We were already looking into Draycott's connection to high-end luxury goods! Who is June?'

'Keith Fisher's admirer – Alison's husband. He gave June the Birkin. She worked at the Hall until she fell ill.'

Mallory's jaw dropped. 'And he gave her a *Birkin*? Just like that?'

'I know. Don't ask.' I rolled my eyes. 'And Delia. But that can't be right – surely Keith isn't Henri?' Even as I said it, I knew it was absurd. Delia had met Keith, and besides, she'd seen Henri on Zoom.

'You've lost me. Who the hell is Henri?'

So I told him everything – the moving polar bear, the missing Grenville Standard, Delia's resignation and her visit to the prison. 'I think Lenny was behind it all.'

'In what way?' Mallory asked.

'This sounds ghoulish, but Lenny and Delia agreed to an until-death-do-us-part pact. When Delia asked for a divorce, Lenny felt bitterly betrayed, and he refused. That is, until he met his new cellmate. The pair hatched a plan. In return for tormenting Delia and ruining her life, Lenny would make sure Donald's letter was smuggled out.'

'By Delia?' Mallory exclaimed. 'That was a risk. How could he know she'd do it?'

I shrugged. 'Guilt? A favour for getting her freedom, perhaps?'

He frowned. 'Why didn't he ask his daughter?'

'There's something else,' I said. 'I saw two hearses parked in the garage at Sunny Hill Lodge. One had a coffin in it, and what looked like artificial flowers. But it was Hollis & Webb, the regular undertakers, who picked up Stan Holden's body. He passed away just last night. I'm wondering if those hearses were used ...'

'... to transport the luxury goods,' Mallory finished. 'Now *that* is clever thinking. Very clever. If they're not licensed funeral vehicles, and they're being used for something else — particularly something criminal — that might be enough to support an application for a search warrant. We can request it first thing in the morning.'

He stood and drew me gently into his arms.

'You see,' I said quietly. 'I could help after all.'

He tilted my chin. Our eyes met. 'You could. You have.'

'I'm forgiven about Shawn?'

'I was just thrown by that,' he said, adding ruefully, 'I think I was jealous.'

'I know the feeling,' I muttered.

I walked him to his car, flooded with relief. I hadn't realised how upset I'd been. I now understood why he felt the need to help Stella. He wouldn't be the man I loved if he didn't.

I shut the door behind me, still thinking. There was just one thing we hadn't considered.

The inventory list that Oxley had submitted to the Emporium.

Chapter Thirty-Seven

The inventory had been compiled ahead of the exhibition. It was standard practice for serious collectors to keep detailed records – not just for insurance purposes, but for valuations or potential sales or donations.

In Oxley's case, Fiona and Reggie Reynolds had insisted he provide his own fully comprehensive insurance policy. The Emporium didn't insure individual items – only the building, basic risks and public liability. I had my own insurance at my booth there too. It was routine.

As the event coordinator, I'd been emailed a copy of Oxley's inventory. I located it in seconds on my phone. As expected, it was meticulously detailed, listing every item in each diorama, complete with photographs, descriptions and values.

My stomach turned over. The gun wasn't just listed as a gun – it was a specific model: a Webley Mk VI revolver. I typed it into the search bar.

> Standard British service weapon from 1915, used in both world wars. Six shot, .455 calibre, top-break action. Solid, no-nonsense design. Original markings highly desirable. Deactivated versions fetch around £500. Fully functional ones can reach £1,800 if they've got provenance.

A stock photo showed the classic Webley MK VI – matt-black finish, chunky barrel, standard black vulcanite grip. I turned back to my phone and pulled up the photo of the shooter.

Zooming in, my pulse began to race. The figure holding the revolver had his left hand raised, revealing a walnut grip rather than the usual black.

Oxley must have seen this gun up close.

Maybe it was discarded during the arrest. Maybe he'd picked it up.

Heart thudding, I reached for the phone.

'I'll put you on speaker,' said Mallory.

'Kat?' came a female voice. Stella. My stomach tensed. Her cool tone drained all my schoolgirl enthusiasm. I didn't want to talk to her.

I stuck to the facts. 'The shooter was left-handed.'

'Without the gun, we can't prove a thing,' she said flatly.

'I think Oxley has the gun,' I said. 'Or at the very least, he saw it. And did Mallory tell you about your father being—'

'What was that, Greg?' Stella cut in, her tone brisk. She must have covered the receiver to speak privately.

Greg? I blinked. I'd never heard anyone call him that. I thought he hated being called Greg.

'Kat?' Mallory came back on the line. 'Are all the dioramas still at the Emporium?'

'No, they were dismantled,' I said. 'Oxley has a large workshop at his home. I'd start there. You might find the model gun.'

'Thanks,' Stella said. 'We'll take it from here.'

The line went dead.

I stared at my phone, caught between anger and disbelief. There were still questions I hadn't asked. Maybe Donald had said something in that letter that might have meant something to me! And what about Alison Fisher and her wretched Birkin bags, the fake hearses, and Janet Ross's room stuffed with valuables? I'd seen them. Stella hadn't. I was also curious as to what Shawn had told her. Frankly, I knew far more than the lot of them put together.

But it was painfully clear that as far as Stella was concerned, I was surplus to requirements.

I half expected Mallory to call me later, to apologise for Stella's abruptness. But he didn't. In the end, I went to bed.

It was nearly one in the morning when the call finally came.

'First chance I've had to ring,' said Mallory. 'I spoke to Oxley's widow, Felicity. The dioramas are back in his workshop, but in crates. She's given us permission to look through everything. I'm heading over there first thing. You were right – his parents' house was only about half a mile from Honeychurch Halt.'

'They still live there?'

'He inherited the house. Look, I'll tell you something else in confidence. It was Felicity Oxley who contacted Ginny Riley about the bribes.'

'*She* was the mole! What a terrible thing to do!'

'Their marriage was rocky. She'd been threatening to leave him. He told her to go ahead, but now she's full of remorse. Blames herself for what happened. We had to eliminate her as a suspect, obviously. I just wanted you to know.'

'What about Marcus Draycott?'

'Oxley's contact list had no mention of Draycott Development Group at all. I told you – squeaky clean. The search warrant for Sunny Hill Lodge should come through in the morning too. We don't want to alert Alison. You said her husband was working on the Polar Tearoom?'

'He's finishing it this week.'

'We need to keep this quiet.'

'I understand.'

'What about Harry?' said Mallory. 'He's not likely to venture up to the Halt on his own, is he?'

'I know he wanted to,' I said. 'But it's too far to walk. Why?'

'Stella wants to make another sweep of the area, that's all.'

'I'll call him to make sure.'

We said goodnight and hung up, but sleep didn't come easily. I couldn't shake the feeling that the raid on Sunny Hill Lodge was premature. It felt rushed. Still, what did I really know about police procedures?

I awoke shortly after six. It was still dark outside.

I made coffee but couldn't face breakfast. The caffeine didn't help – I already felt jittery.

I had to wait until a decent hour before calling the Hall to speak to Harry. Expecting Delia to answer, I was caught off guard when Lavinia picked up instead.

'It's Kat. Is Delia there?'

'No, ghastly business – she's gone.' Lavinia pronounced 'gone' as 'gawn'.

My heart sank. Had Delia quit after all?

'Trouble with her daughter, apparently. Gone to Scotland for a week or two. *Frightful* timing, but . . .' There was a pause. Lavinia lowered her voice to almost a whisper. I could barely hear her. 'Rupert has been so vile recently. I thought he'd frightened her off.'

'Ah.' I didn't think for one moment that Delia's daughter was in trouble. It was just an excuse to get away.

'We don't want to lose her,' Lavinia continued. 'She's an awfully good egg.'

'What about the extravaganza?' I said cautiously.

'Pansy has stepped in,' said Lavinia.

Ah yes. Pansy of Pansy's Jamborees, her party-planning friend. I remembered her well – scatterbrained, lovable, but even more eccentric than Lavinia.

'And then we have Jane . . .'

'June.'

'. . . though frankly, I find her terrifying – but what can one do?' Lavinia gave a sigh. 'And of course, it's now going to be held in the ballroom.'

'Because of June's phobia?'

'We'll have none of that nonsense – no, the builder's cleared off. Didn't turn up! When Rupert called, the number was disconnected. I've no idea what's going on. The world's gone completely bonkers. Goodbye.'

'No, wait!' I shouted. 'I'm calling to speak to Harry.'

'He's not here.'

'Where is he?'

'Riding? Exploring? He's got Mr Chips and instructions to be back before dark.'

'But . . . but . . .' I spluttered. 'It's only nine in the morning! Does he have a mobile?'

'Good grief, Kat,' Lavinia exclaimed. 'Of course he doesn't. He's only eleven. Must fly!' And she hung up.

I stood there, speechless.

First of all, Keith not showing up – massive red flag. I knew Alison had seen me talking to him. But what if he'd got wind of the raid? I texted Mallory straight away.

And Harry. Honestly, Lavinia's idea of child-rearing had always struck me as more like horse management. She'd basically turned him out for the day and moved on.

He didn't even have a phone!

I called my mother and invited myself over. The answer was a firm no. She was far too busy writing.

That did it. My patience snapped. All my pent-up frustration came tumbling out.

'Stella? Mallory? What are you talking about?' Mum said, bewildered. 'I don't know an Alison. What gun? Ah, Delia – finally you're making some sense. Yes, I took her to the station this morning.'

'Is she coming back? Lavinia's having a meltdown.'

'She needed a break,' Mum declared. 'And I don't blame her for wanting to distance herself from the Gerald fiasco. She was an emotional wreck after all that nonsense with Henri, whoever he really is – oh, and she's decided to keep the Birkin but is putting the Louboutins on Vinted. As for the bicycle . . .'

'Mum! Stop!'

'. . . Harry's got it. I passed him on the lane with Mr Chips.'

'Where?' I said sharply.

'I had to pull over to let him squeeze by. He told me he was off to the Halt.'

My stomach lurched.

'I suppose I could spare half an hour since it's you—'

'Can't.' I cut her off, ended the call and grabbed my car keys.

Chapter Thirty-Eight

The fifteen-minute drive seemed to take for ever – no thanks to farm tractors and dithering holidaymakers reversing into hedges. By the time I turned off towards the Halt, I was starting to worry.

What if Stella was already there, accusing Harry of contaminating the area and being her usual unpleasant self? And what if – heaven forbid – Mr Chips decided to defend him? He was fiercely protective of all the family. I couldn't squash a tiny spark of glee at the thought.

I slowed as I passed Railway Cottage, where the remnants of police tape still fluttered in the breeze. Harry would have noticed that. He was bound to ask questions.

I stopped at the turning space. Delia's bicycle was propped against the hoarding.

There was no sign of Harry.

The Halt looked bleaker than ever beneath the grey sky.

That was when I spotted a flash of white and tan.

'Harry!' I called.

Mr Chips burst from the undergrowth in a volley of barks, dancing around my feet before darting back the way he'd come, urging me to follow.

Up near the camping coach I spotted a small figure in an anorak, on his knees, wielding what looked like a garden hand fork. He was jabbing it into the earth. Beside him sat a canvas rucksack, a can of Coca-Cola, a bag of crisps and a retractable measuring tape.

Mr Chips announced my arrival with another round of frantic barking.

Harry looked up, cheeks flushed with excitement. 'Grid 17B!' He pointed to the patch of gravel. 'I measured it from the sketch! This is where they buried the gun!'

The gun.

I should have known he'd seize on that. He wasn't stupid, but the thought of him finding it – touching something that could prove critical to the investigation – filled me with dread.

'The newspapers said it was never found, but I know it's here!'

'We need to leave, Harry,' I said, keeping my voice steady.

'No!' he exclaimed, redoubling his efforts.

'Harry,' I said, more firmly now, 'this is private property.'

He didn't hear me. Or he didn't care. He stabbed the fork deeper into the soil.

I heard the thud.

A dull, unnatural sound.

I grabbed his arm. 'You need to stop.'

He shook me off, determined to have his way. Mr Chips darted in and nipped at my ankle. I jumped back. No blood, but definitely a warning.

Harry wrenched something free. It was a bulky object wrapped in oilskin and caked with soil.

'Harry, give that to me,' I said urgently. 'Please – it's important.'

I lunged for it, but he spun away, flushed with excitement. 'I've got it! It's the gun!'

Mr Chips jumped in again, keeping me back.

Helpless, I watched Harry yank at the cloth, tugging and shaking until the oilskin unfurled in a series of damp folds, and the object inside dropped with a soft thud onto the earth. Mr Chips gave it a good sniff and turned away, seeming just as disappointed as Harry.

Harry stared at it. 'I *hate* cream crackers.'

I almost laughed – partly from relief – as he kicked the object aside.

A faded orange Jacob's Cream Crackers tin.

He gave it a puzzled look. 'How can you even fit a gun in there?'

Exactly. So this was Stan's 'friend' Jacob. Not a person at all – just this old tin.

I crouched down and grabbed it. It was far too narrow to hold a weapon – about ten by six inches – but then my pulse quickened.

Had Connie and Alison been right all along and the diamonds really *had* been on that train?

Harry tossed the fork aside and pulled Stan's map from his back pocket. 'It's got to be somewhere else.' He scratched his head. 'But where? This was the only grid marked!' He started to wander off.

I prised off the lid.

There were no diamonds. Just a clump of waterlogged banknotes, damp with mildew – and worthless. At the bottom lay an envelope, yellowed with time. I eased it out carefully. The ink had bled in places, but the name was still clear: *Connie*. The banknotes had shielded it for decades.

Inside was a letter.

Connie,
I'm sorry for everything. Eddie was my friend.
I couldn't take Tony's blood money. If you're reading
this, then I'm long gone. Thought maybe it might
be of use to you. Maybe help make things right.
I'm sorry for everything.
Dad

A wave of sadness swept over me. Stan might have been paid for his part in the robbery, but it sounded like *he'd* paid in another way – with his health, both physical and mental. His marriage had failed. He'd lost his family.

Yes, this confirmed everything we suspected, but it still didn't prove that Tony had pulled the trigger.

I folded the letter back into the tin and glanced at Harry, who was wandering in circles, staring at the ground, muttering to himself.

Stella would descend at any moment. Harry had dug up the tin. I didn't want him questioned – not yet. I called him over.

'Why don't you take Mr Chips and go and fetch Mallory?' I said, keeping my voice light. 'Remember the dioramas at the exhibition? He's at Oxley's house, on the other side of the embankment.'

I couldn't recall the name. I'd only been there once, when Oxley first suggested the idea.

'Tristford House,' I said suddenly. 'That's it. It's got big iron gates. Go down the track bed and cut across.'

And then I heard it – the low, unmistakable purr of a Porsche engine. My stomach dropped, and I turned, heart thumping, to see the chalk-grey car ease to a stop behind my own.

'Harry,' I said urgently. 'Go now. Please – quickly.' Something in my face must have warned him.

'But the bike . . .'

I steadied my voice. 'It's fine, honestly. Just tell Mallory what we found – say the word "Jacob" – and ask him to come here straight away.'

He hesitated, uncertain, and then bolted, leaving his rucksack and fork where they lay. Mr Chips tore after him.

I crouched to shove the tin into the rucksack and stuffed the fork into my coat pocket just as Alison sauntered over.

She waved a casual greeting, as if this was some pleasant morning ramble.

'I don't need to ask what you're doing here,' she said, sliding a Beretta from her pocket.

'Whoa! Alison! What the hell!' I jumped back in shock, hands up.

'What's in the rucksack?'

'See for yourself.' I nudged it a few inches towards her with my foot, keeping my hands raised. 'Just snacks.'

'Get it,' she said, keeping the gun trained on me. 'You know I'll use this.'

'Not really your style, though, is it?' I said, stalling for time. The police would be here any minute. 'I thought intravenous was more your thing.'

She smirked. 'Clever you – how did you know?'

'You expect me to tell you?' I kept my expression neutral, but my heart was hammering against my ribs. 'Although I am curious how Connie ended up in the camping coach. She wasn't exactly mobile, and I don't think you could have carried her.'

'Ah, Connie.' Alison pulled a face. 'I didn't realise she was actually *staying* at the cottage. Have you seen it? It's a ruin!' She smirked again. 'I suppose I frightened her. She knew there were diamonds somewhere, but she refused to tell me. I even persuaded her to come with me and look for them, but neither of us could find Grid 17B.'

'Well, it was a long time ago,' I said lightly.

'Stan was no help.' She rolled her eyes, as if amused. 'None whatsoever – even in his more lucid moments he made no sense. Kept rambling on about his friend Jacob.'

'Connie told me she'd met him,' I lied.

'She told me she'd never heard of him!' Alison's eyes narrowed. 'What else did she tell you?'

'Just that he had something valuable. And that she was relieved he was somewhere comfortable for his final days.' All lies. But I had to keep her talking.

'And you know what that was, don't you?' she said. 'That's why you're here. You've known all along – after all, you're dating a *copper*.' Her gaze flicked to the rucksack again.

She thought I'd found the diamonds. So why was she just standing there, waiting?

But then so was I.

We were both playing for time.

'Tell me – just curious,' she added. 'Where did you find Stan's junk? I looked everywhere!'

'In the pantry, under a pink candlewick bedspread,' I said. 'I just don't understand why you had to hurt Connie.'

She didn't answer.

Where was Stella? Where was Mallory?

Alison seemed agitated. She glanced over her shoulder, back to where her car blocked mine.

I eyed Delia's electric bicycle, calculating whether I could make a run for it.

'I saw you in Devizes,' I said quickly. 'Visiting your father, right? Donald?'

'I was shopping,' she said. 'Like you.'

'No, I was at the prison, Alison,' I said. 'I saw you exit the car park.'

Her face paled. The Beretta dipped. She raised it again, but her hand wobbled.

'You know your father never killed that policeman or the guard?'

She faltered. 'How do you know?'

'Because . . . I'm dating a *copper*,' I said more confidently now. 'Donald spilled the beans. He took the blame. Your lovely uncle let him rot in prison while he built a nice quiet life for himself in the Channel Islands.'

'Very funny.' She laughed, but it sounded false.

'Is your father left- or right-handed?'

'What?' she gasped. 'I don't know. I didn't know him. He . . . Mum . . .' Her face hardened.

I pressed my advantage. 'Do you know why you had to get rid of Oxley?'

A flicker of surprise. No answer. But no denial either.

'It wasn't for that list of names of people who were bribing him. It was because Oxley witnessed the robbery. Why else do you think you were told to go to the exhibition? I'm assuming you took plenty of photos of the diorama to email to your uncle. And then Tony entered the country – the first time in decades – to see it for himself.'

'I don't know what you mean.'

'Oxley *saw* Tony shoot the policeman and the guard – it's all there in the diorama for the world to see.'

Alison shook her head. 'I don't believe you. Uncle Tony has always been good to me. To Mum. Making sure we were taken care of.' She glanced over her shoulder again, but this time I heard it too.

A car.

Chapter Thirty-Nine

The Mercedes G-Wagon crept up behind the Porsche.

Alison's face flooded with relief. My mouth went dry. No one had known I'd be there at the Halt. They had shown up for a reason.

I eyed the electric bike again. It was too far away.

Tony and Marcus got out and came over. Now I saw Tony in a different light. Sinewy, lean, predatory, even in his eighties. Marcus looked nervously to his father and back at Alison, then at me.

Alison kept her gun steady, calling over her shoulder, 'I just found her here, Uncle.'

'For God's sake, Alison,' said Tony, exasperated. 'Put that thing down!' He took it from her with his left hand. Slipped it into his pocket.

'I apologise for my niece. She can be a little . . . unstable at times.'

Confusion crossed Alison's face, then hurt.

'There's no need for this. I'm a peaceful man.' Tony glanced at the rucksack and the mound of earth beside the small hole.

'Ah, you found the treasure,' he said with a smile. 'Clever.'

'It's not the gun,' I said suddenly. 'If that's what you were hoping to find.'

His eyes locked with mine. They were cold. Calculating.

He laughed. 'Really? And how did you come to that conclusion?'

'The police are just on the other side of the tracks,' I said. 'Looking through Oxley's things. You knew he witnessed everything. That's why you got Alison to do your dirty work. It was never about those names on the list. He tricked you, Alison. Just like he tricked you into believing your father was guilty.'

Tony grinned. 'You're delusional, love.'

'Does the name Philip Greenleigh mean anything to you?' I pressed.

Tony didn't flinch. 'Nope.'

'I think it does,' I said. 'He was an off-duty police officer who just happened to be in the wrong place at the wrong time.'

His expression hardened.

'You held a gun to his head, and Donald begged you to let him go.'

No response.

'And so you did,' I went on. 'But moments later, another officer arrived, just as the guard managed to free himself. The two of them tried to stop you . . .'

'Uncle, this can't be true!'

'... so you shot them dead.'

'No.' Alison shook her head. 'You're making it up.'

'Oh, come on, Alison,' I said scornfully. 'Donald saw the diorama all over the news. He knew exactly what that scene meant. He saw his chance to finally clear his name, so he wrote to Philip Greenleigh.' I didn't add that Philip was already dead. 'And *you* drove to the prison to get the letter from him. You posted it!'

'That's a lie!' Alison shrieked.

'You can check the visitors' log,' I bluffed. 'She was there on Monday.'

'I ... I didn't go inside, I swear, Uncle. I changed my mind.'

Tony stiffened. His mouth opened slightly, but no words came. He looked at Alison, not angry, just ... disappointed.

'He wrote to me,' Alison said quickly, flustered now. 'I'd not heard from him in years. He begged me to come. He's ill. Yes, I drove there, it's true. But I didn't go inside.'

'I bet she did,' Marcus sneered.

I saw it then – the chink in her armour. Right there. I pressed harder. 'Alison told me her father was right-handed.'

'I didn't!' she yelled.

'The shooter in the diorama is holding the gun – a Webley Mk VI – in his left hand. Oxley was accurate.'

Tony stared. A tic had begun above his left eye.

'You must have noticed that in the photos Alison sent you. She was at the exhibition constantly – practically lived there. Always watching. And yet not once did she ask a single question about trains. Talk about drawing attention to yourself!'

'You bitch,' Alison hissed. 'I sent you the photos, Uncle, but you didn't say anything about a gun!'

'The bullets were recovered,' I bluffed, having no idea if that was true. 'It's amazing what ballistics can do these days. Left hand, right hand . . . it all leaves a trace.'

'Alison is a good little soldier,' Tony said. 'She knows how to follow orders. Unlike some I could mention.'

Marcus shot his father a look of dislike.

There was a rift. I saw it. A rivalry between the cousins for the old man's affections.

'Yes, she is, isn't she,' I agreed. 'But I wonder if she realises that the parent company, Draycott Development Group, has been slowly distancing itself from anything tied to Bradleigh & Sons – although having Marcus's name on that business card wasn't very smart.'

Tony's eyes narrowed. 'What business card?' He turned to Marcus. 'Didn't I tell you—'

'It's no big deal,' Marcus smirked. 'The company's registered in Jersey.'

I faltered. Of course. The domain on the card was *.je*. Mallory had told me UK law had no jurisdiction in the Channel Islands. But that didn't mean Marcus was untouchable.

'Moving those luxury goods around by hearse?' I plunged on. 'Not very respectful, is it? The Birkin handbags, the high-end shoes – someone got a little complacent.' I forced an indulgent chuckle, but it came out more as a croak. 'And not only that, but giving those Birkins away as freebies – imagine! A handbag worth ten grand just handed to Keith's mistress.'

'What?' Alison turned ashen. '*My* Keith? You're lying!'

'You didn't know?' I pretended to be shocked. 'How else do you think I found out what you were up to, Alison? Let's just say beware the power of pillow talk – and gosh, this is the countryside. Who on earth carries a Birkin handbag?'

'Who is she?' Alison was distraught. 'Tell me!'

'Of course, I don't blame you for skimming a bit off the top for yourself – I know I would.'

'Kat, don't, please . . .'

'Selling off the residents' personal possessions. Trying to recruit me. Naturally I told my boyfriend,' I said, adding pointedly for Tony's benefit, 'He's a copper.'

'That's not true!' Alison shrieked. 'I didn't tell her anything, Uncle!'

I didn't dare look at Tony. But I didn't need to. The change in the air was unmistakable – sudden, heavy and filled with menace.

I'd pushed too far.

His voice cut through the silence. 'I think we'll take our friend here for a little ride. Marcus?'

My heart dropped. Mallory wasn't coming. No one was.

I took a step back. Marcus moved – slow, deliberate.

'Alison,' I said, voice shaking now, 'I'm not keeping your secret any more. The diamonds *were* on the train. Stan Holden buried them, just like he told you.'

'She's lying,' Tony snarled. 'Marcus!'

'Why else was Grid 17B important! They're in *here*!' I kicked the rucksack over. Marcus and Alison dropped to their knees, scrabbling to get to it first.

I turned and bolted for the electric bike.

A gunshot rang out, close enough to clip the air by my ear.

I didn't look back. Threw myself onto the seat, grabbed the handlebars. My hands were shaking so badly I couldn't find the power button.

Then I hit it and lurched forward, completely out of control – straight for Tony. He froze, the gun levelled at point-blank range. I couldn't have stopped even if I'd wanted to.

I struck him just as the gun went off again.

There was a sickening thud and a cry of shock as he hit the ground.

Mum's words echoed in my head – *that bicycle is a death trap on wheels* – as I careened into the track bed and flew over the handlebars, slamming into the hard dirt. A searing pain shot through my shoulder. I couldn't breathe.

Get up, Kat. Get up!

'There's nothing here!' Alison's voice was shrill. 'She lied!'

And then Marcus's shout ripped through the air. 'Dad's dead! Stop her!'

I forced myself to my feet, clutching my shoulder, and staggered towards the camping coach.

But Alison was already moving.

She took me down, arms clamped tight about my neck. I fell onto my shoulder again and the world went black for a second.

Disorientated. Dazed.

She was fumbling in her pocket.

A jolt of horror. *The syringe*. From the kit in her car. She'd come prepared.

I kicked her. She didn't even flinch. The cap came off.

I twisted left, then right, pain exploding white-hot with every desperate movement.

She was straddling me now, hunting for a way past the Barbour I'd thrown on without fastening.

My fingers found the garden fork in my pocket. I made a wild stab. Missed. Tried again. Missed. Then the tines struck bone with a sickening crack, and a jet of hot blood sprayed across my hands.

Alison let out a raw, animal scream. She reeled back, clutching her wrist, as bright crimson poured through her fingers.

The syringe slipped into the mud and vanished.

'Marcus! Help me!' Her voice broke into a sob. 'I'm ... bleeding out!'

A flash of brown and tan, and Mr Chips burst from the undergrowth, teeth sinking into Alison's ankle as she tried to pull away, screaming.

I lay there panting, bloodied and shaken.

And then suddenly the place was alive with people, shouts, boots pounding the ground.

A woman knelt beside me, her voice calm and steady. 'We found the gun, Kat. Oxley had it all the time.'

Stella.

'Is Tony dead?' My voice cracked. 'I . . . The bike . . .'

'Unfortunately, no,' she said wryly. 'But whatever life he has left will be spent in prison.'

I felt a rush of relief, then horror. 'Alison – I . . . I think I caught an artery.'

'She'll live.'

'Mallory?'

'He drew the short straw – raiding Sunny Hill Lodge,' said Stella. 'He's on his way. Hush now. Don't talk. The ambulance is coming.'

And that was when I passed out.

Chapter Forty

'So that was why it took Harry so long to raise the alarm.' Mum tut-tutted. 'Had he no idea your life was at stake?'

'He didn't recognise Stella, and she was so dismissive and rude, telling him to get out of the workshop, that he slunk away. It was only when PC Quinn found him hovering outside that he told her. And of course, hearing a gunshot made all the difference.'

Mum raised an eyebrow. 'Does this Quinn have a first name?'

'Lynne.'

'Lynne Quinn. Hmm. Very greedy with the letter n,' she said. 'But honestly, darling, you really do get yourself into such scrapes. At least you—'

'No silver-linining, please. You know how much I hate it.'

'Touché.' She laughed. 'Seriously, I'm only being flippant because . . . because . . .' Her eyes welled up. 'I was worried sick!'

The kitchen door opened and Mallory walked in.

'Is that gin, Iris?'

Mum pretended to look scandalised. 'Drinking on duty, Officer?'

'I'm now officially on leave,' he said. 'Besides, we don't have far to drive, do we, Kat?'

He pulled out a chair and sat down, glancing at my arm. 'How's the shoulder?'

Mum poured him a generous measure and slid the glass across the table.

'It'll be in a sling for a few weeks,' I said. 'Cracked bone. Nothing dramatic.'

'No swinging from the chandeliers,' Mum muttered.

I glared at her. Mallory grinned.

'Well? Are you going to tell us everything, or are you not at liberty to say?' Mum teased. 'The elevator version, please. Then you two can scuttle off to Jane's Cottage and ... well ... you know – play your saxophone.'

'Mum!' I was mortified. If Mallory caught the innuendo, he was too much of a gentleman to show it.

'The elevator version?' He sounded puzzled.

'You have sixty seconds – or less – to tell us everything,' I explained.

'Right then.' He paused, thought for a moment. 'Keith and his sons were caught red-handed as they attempted to clear out the stock from the residents—'

'Whoa! Wait,' Mum cut in. 'I've changed my mind. Forget the elevator, let's go for the stairs. Slow, with lots of stops to catch our breath. Start at the beginning, please.'

Mallory laughed. 'Stella got a tip-off that Tony Draycott was back in the country. Her father's deathbed confession—'

'What deathbed confession?' Mum demanded.

'Ignore her,' I said. 'Go on, or we'll be here all afternoon. I'll fill you in later, Mother.'

'MCU had been trying to collar the Draycotts for a very long time but never had anything on them, even though we knew exactly what they were up to,' Mallory continued. 'On paper, it looked like Alison – Bradleigh & Sons – was running the whole show. Her name was all over shipping records, bank accounts and company filings. The entire operation was tied up in her signature.'

'So this Alison was being set up to take the fall,' Mum burst out. 'I know what that feels like! You trust someone and they . . . they stab you in the back!'

I reached for her hand and gave it a squeeze. 'I know you know.'

'The betrayal hit Alison hard.'

'I bet it did!' Mum cried.

'Tony was like a father to her. Alison and her mother spent every summer – and most Christmases – together. The Draycotts were a close-knit crime family. Reputation and loyalty were everything. Tony and Donald's mother, Elizabeth, was the matriarch.'

'They called her Queenie,' I put in. 'Alison said everyone was scared of her.'

'After the brothers went to prison, Queenie moved to the Channel Islands and held the family together from there until Tony's release. She died several years afterwards.

According to Donald – who is only too happy to talk to us – Queenie wanted Alison to ultimately take over from Tony. Alison was smart, ambitious – everything Marcus wasn't.'

'And he got wind of it,' I mused. 'So it was Marcus who was setting Alison up to fail.'

'Ah, Marcus.' Mallory nodded. 'A gambler, lazy, and a disappointment to his father from the start.'

He took a sip of gin. Mum topped up my glass.

'This is really good stuff,' he said, lightening the mood.

'I know,' said Mum. 'So go on . . . I promise not to interrupt again.'

I thought back to the awful scene at the Halt. 'Alison was so sure the diamonds had been on the train.'

'Diamonds? What diamonds?' Mum exclaimed.

'They were on the original waybill,' said Mallory. 'But the security van got a puncture on the way to the station. The brothers couldn't have known at the time.'

'And yet Tony Draycott kept the story going right to the end. It was the gun that he was worried about. Oxley had listed the Webley Mk VI in the items displayed on the diorama,' I said. 'So Tony must have known he'd found it.'

'How disgusting!' Mum spluttered. 'He pulled the trigger and then blamed his brother!'

'Donald had always been in Tony's shadow,' said Mallory. 'But for once, this was his job, his lead, his chance to shine.'

'And everything went wrong,' I said quietly. 'Do you think that's why he agreed to take the blame?'

Mallory nodded. 'No one was supposed to get hurt. Queenie and Tony held Donald responsible for both deaths.'

'That's so unfair,' I said.

'Don't feel sorry for any of them.' Mallory's voice was hard. 'They're a bad lot.'

'I know, but I have to ask.' Mum leant forward. 'Where does the nursing home fit in?'

'A good question.' Mallory smiled. 'Sunny Hill was a front for money-laundering. Many of those rooms were empty. Fake invoices were generated for occupied beds, hairdressing, personal services – that sort of thing. The remaining residents who lived there were window-dressing. Half the staff didn't exist. Wages were paid into accounts controlled by the Draycotts but operated by Bradleigh & Sons. Laundry, medical supplies, consulting fees – all routed through shell companies with the money coming back clean, through dividends and offshore accounts—'

'Hence the term money-laundering – oops.' Mum promptly clapped her hand over her mouth.

'Everything seemed to be moving along until Oxley decided to hold his exhibition.'

'That lit the fuse,' I said. 'The publicity. The media circus.'

'What made it even messier was that Oxley was already in business with Bradleigh & Sons,' said Mallory. 'He had no idea of the Draycott connection.'

'True. Though Marcus was listed as a director on a Bradleigh & Sons business card.'

'Oxley wouldn't have dealt with Marcus directly,' Mallory said. 'And if you're talking about the site meeting at Ivy Cottage, Eric Pugsley admitted he attended that.'

'No surprise there,' I muttered. 'Rupert would have made sure to keep his distance – until the moment he slipped up and grabbed back his train!'

'The Kaiser Adler,' Mum declared. 'What fools!'

'I just don't understand how Alison managed to pull that off. I mean, how could she suddenly turn up at Ashcombe Barton more or less at the same time as Eric's planned rendezvous?'

Mallory smiled. 'The CCTV cameras at the Emporium showed you loading the Kaiser Adler into the Bentley. Oxley drove to the exit, then a man stepped in front of him at the junction.'

'Don't tell me,' I exclaimed. 'Alison sneaked into the car. What a risk! What if Oxley had locked all the doors? And who was the man . . . Oh, wait, don't tell me that either. One of Alison's sons.'

'They set up the diversion, unaware that was exactly where Oxley was heading anyway. When he stopped at the abandoned farm, Alison made her move.'

'And she dropped the needle cap. She must have been interrupted when Eric showed up, which was why she didn't have time to grab Oxley's phone.'

'I'm very glad we decided against the elevator version,' Mum chimed in. 'Although I'm completely lost.'

'Then she made her way home across the fields . . .'

'. . . and was picked up by her sons, the bogus road workers.' Mallory grinned. 'You really should have been a detective.'

We fell into a companionable silence.

'How much money was in the Jacob's Cream Crackers tin?' Mum said suddenly.

'Twenty-five thousand pounds. Of course it was traceable and would have been worthless to Connie.'

'Twenty-five thousand!' Mum squeaked. 'A fortune in 1974! So what happens to Honeychurch Halt now?'

'Yes. How did Bradleigh & Sons come to buy it?' I pulled a face. 'A business park! I can't think of anything worse.'

'Good question,' said Mallory. 'We traced the owner through the Land Registry. He bought the land years ago, after the railway sold it off. Stan had a lifetime lease on Railway Cottage. The owner held onto it as an investment, which he was able to sell . . .'

'. . . when he moved to Sunny Hill Lodge. Wow, Marcus didn't hang about, did he?'

'The owner of the Halt discovered the land was contaminated, unfit for development. When Bradleigh & Sons – that is, Marcus – made him an offer, he took it.'

'But they weren't intending to build,' I said. 'They wanted to tear the place apart looking for the phantom diamonds—'

'No, Kat. Looking for the gun,' Mum cut in. 'You see, I *can* keep up.'

'So when Ginny went after Oxley,' I said slowly, 'she had no idea what she was really stepping into.'

'There were a few surprises in Oxley's contacts,' Mallory admitted. 'Which, sadly, I'm not at liberty to reveal.'

'And speaking of surprises,' said Mum, 'what's this about Lenny Evans and his cellmate?'

'It was an agreement. A quid pro quo,' Mallory said. 'After months of dragging his feet over the divorce, he suddenly gave in. Persuaded Delia to visit and asked her to do him a favour.'

'Silly girl!' Mum exclaimed. 'What *possessed* her? Why couldn't Donald's own daughter do it?'

'Alison *did* go to the prison,' Mallory said, glancing at me. 'Her car was logged at the gate, but she wasn't on the visitor list.'

'How odd,' I murmured. 'Fathers and daughters. First Stella, then Alison – and let's not forget Connie.'

'Deathbed confessions can do that to people,' Mum said cheerfully. 'So what about Lenny? Please tell us they're bringing back the guillotine so I can share the good news with Delia.'

Mallory laughed. 'He'll be charged with gaslighting, coercive control and conspiracy – Donald's letter links him directly to the Draycotts. He won't be seeing daylight for a long time.'

'And Alison?' I asked.

'Charges? Two murders and two attempted – Ginny and you.' He picked up my hand and brought it to his lips. Our eyes met, and in his I saw so much love it made my heart contract.

He glanced away, back to business. 'She's looking at life, no question.'

'So she goes in and her father gets out,' I said. 'And Keith?'

'He's turned witness for the prosecution.'

'Alison will be devastated.' Even though I couldn't see the attraction, she'd obviously loved him. She'd been betrayed from every side. And yes, I felt sorry for her. Fate had dealt her a cruel hand right from the start.

'Handling stolen goods and conspiracy to commit theft,' Mallory said. 'It depends how helpful he is, but it's unlikely he'll go to prison.'

'What about their sons – Bradley and Leigh?'

'They drove the hearse, shifted stolen goods. If they knew what they were doing, that's handling stolen property. And Bradley was involved in Ginny's abduction. Two, maybe three years if the judge comes down hard. If they were following orders, they might get a suspended sentence.'

I knew I had to ask about Tony. I still kept replaying the sickening sound of the impact when the bike mowed him down.

'Let's just say there was some serious damage,' said Mallory. 'He's back inside. You die as you live. And the years he's got left won't be kind.'

I felt guilty. Mallory must have seen it. 'Don't, Kat. He would have killed you!'

'But who was the mystery man Delia spoke to on Zoom?' Mum said suddenly.

'An out-of-work actor,' said Mallory. 'Joey Chandler. We tracked him down. Lenny paid him two hundred quid to woo her.'

'Well . . . well . . . I hope he stays unemployed!' Mum exclaimed.

'Who is unemployed?' The kitchen door opened and Edith stepped inside, followed by Mr Chips.

We all jumped to our feet.

'Please, sit down, milady.' Mum darted forward to help her to a chair. 'I apologise . . . the mess, I wasn't expecting . . .'

Edith shook her off, but accepted Mallory's arm with a coquettish smile.

'We're so glad to see you up and about!' Mum was flustered. 'Can I get you some tea?'

'I'd like to try your gin, Iris,' said Edith.

She looked so much better. Seeing her back in her riding habit was reassuring – a clear sign that she was recovering.

Mum fussed, finding the right cut-crystal glass, dropping in ice and a slice of lemon, then hovered with the bottle, uncertain how much to give her.

'Oh, for heaven's sake,' Edith grumbled. 'Let me do it.' She served herself a hefty measure, added tonic water and sat back.

We were all oddly tongue-tied. Even Mallory.

'Well?' Edith said, raising her glass with a small, knowing smile. 'Chin-chin!'

'Chin-chin,' we echoed.

'You know,' she began, 'I could have told you that Gerald was a fraud if you'd asked. All this nonsense. But Mrs Evans was determined to have her fun – and who was I to spoil it?'

'Oh, milady.' Mum's relief bubbled over. 'We were so worried about telling you.'

'You should be more worried about people finding out the truth,' Edith said sharply. 'If you're going to tell a lie, Iris, you stick to it. All the way. Never admit it.'

It was such an odd thing to say. I'd long suspected Edith knew my mother was Krystalle Storm, but this felt like something more. Was she finally admitting to being Dear Amanda?

'What was it our late, wonderful Queen remarked? "Recollections may vary",' Edith said with a nod. 'The Honourable Gerald Honeychurch was a man of courage, pluck and dash. And long may he remain so.' She raised her glass in a toast. We did too.

Then, briskly, 'Now, the Polar Tearoom – yes, I'm well aware it's unfinished, but we're forging ahead regardless. It'll be in the ballroom and on the terrace. In Mrs Evans's absence, that dimwit Pansy is apparently organising the whole thing alongside the statuesque June. I'm rather looking forward to it.'

She finished her drink and stood. 'I expect to see you all there.'

Chapter Forty-One

Pansy's Jamborees had done a spectacular job of pulling the extravaganza together at the very last minute.

The ballroom had been transformed into a scene from a children's adventure story. Billowing muslin hung over cardboard icebergs, with powder-blue lights shimmering on a floor dusted with fake snow. In the centre stood a cluster of canvas tents – mock Arctic shelters – surrounded by faux ice blocks. A fireless campfire glowed with orange bulbs beneath cellophane, ringed by snowball-shaped beanbags. Children were handed activity maps to follow the expedition trail, with a badge station encouraging them to earn the title of Junior Polar Explorer.

Nearby stood a life-sized cardboard cut-out of a man in a fur coat, labelled *Gerald Honeychurch*, though it clearly was not.

And of course, pride of place went to Florian.

Out on the terrace, June served up an assortment of snow-themed Easter treats on the strict understanding that she wouldn't be expected to set foot inside the ballroom or come within twenty feet of the polar bear.

I helped myself to a pawprint brownie, while Mallory devoured a slice of Gerald's Glacier Sponge.

'It's delicious, June,' I said, adding slyly, 'Did we miss your birthday?'

June frowned.

'Keith told me he gave you a Birkin for your birthday.'

'My name's June, so my birthday is in June – and who is Keith?' She seemed genuinely baffled. Then she snorted. 'Oh, him. You'd think he'd have worked that out.'

Mum materialised at my elbow.

'He left his wife, you know,' June went on. 'I had to dump him. I'm off to the North Sea on Monday, catering for the oil boys. Terrific money.'

'Oh, will they survive?' Mum said. 'Your cooking, I mean.'

'They'll be trapped, that's for sure,' June said bluntly, and turned away to serve a customer.

'She wasn't joking, was she.' Mum grinned. 'Ah, here comes her ladyship and Harry.'

They joined us. 'I hear Mrs Evans will be home next week,' said Edith. 'I hope that frightful man signed her divorce papers.'

'He did,' I said.

'Good, because let's face it, at her age she doesn't have time to linger.'

The exact same phrase that Dear Amanda had used! Edith must have seen my reaction, because she caught my eye and winked. 'Oh – the television people have arrived.

They're filming the Grenville Standard. People can be so gullible!'

'This I must see,' I said. I dragged Mallory back inside.

Sure enough, the two presenters from *West Country Round-Up* were interviewing the queue of ticket-holders waiting to enter the specially screened-off booth where the Standard was carefully displayed on the table.

'What did she mean by gullible?' Mallory asked.

'Put it this way.' I tried to keep a straight face. 'Delia found the Standard in a cupboard in the old nursery.'

'Shh,' he said, and not a moment too soon. 'Here's Ginny.'

She waved and came over, only too eager to share her triumph – an exclusive story on the downfall of the Draycott crime family. 'It'll be in tomorrow's papers.'

And to be honest, she'd earned it.

'Just a heads-up,' she added. 'I've published the names of those who bribed Oxley too.'

I thought of Rupert, reading his newspaper in the library.

'It's nothing personal,' she added. 'You know that, right? I think we'll see a different kind of sensitivity to planning issues on Gloria Weaver's watch. And I'm all for that.'

She drew me aside, nodding to the booth. 'I take it you've been in there.'

'Of course.'

'Look,' she lowered her voice, 'I did a course in textiles at uni.'

My heart sank. 'And?'

'Come on!' She laughed. 'Seriously? Bosworth? Naseby? Flanders? The miracle of the golden fringe? It's what I do. Investigate.'

For a moment I felt panic, and then, 'Remember you owe me a favour.'

Ginny frowned and shook her head. 'I don't follow.'

So I reminded her. 'For saving your life?'

Her eyes widened. 'Seriously? You really want to use it on a piece of old curtain?'

I glanced over to where Edith was inspecting the Arctic camp with Harry. They looked happy.

'Yes,' I said. 'Yes, I do.'

She laughed and turned her attention to Florian. 'We'll focus on the polar bear in that case. At least that story's true. Extraordinary man, Gerald Honeychurch.'

I didn't say a word.

Mallory's arm slipped around my waist. 'What was all that about?'

'Later,' was all I said.

'Kat!' shouted Harry. 'I know the answer to the Honeychurch diorama!' He could hardly contain his excitement. 'Remember I told you about engine numbers and headcodes?'

'Yes,' I said slowly.

'The engine number of the train was S6374. But that's wrong. It was a diesel, so it should have been D6374! S would stand for steam!'

I was impressed. 'Well, congratulations,' I said. 'But truthfully, how on earth could anyone ever have got that?'

'You would if you knew what you were talking about.'

'He's convinced me.' Edith pointed outside to the row of ramshackle garages. 'He wants to convert those to a workshop. He said Rod Stewart has one.'

'He built a miniature New York and Chicago!' Harry beamed. 'Nine hundred yards of track!'

Edith smiled. 'Who knows how long this obsession will last.'

'For ever!' Harry exclaimed, and spotting a friend, he scampered off.

'Still, now that the estate's been made over to him in trust,' said Edith, 'he can do what he jolly well likes.'

I was stunned. Edith had finally done it, cut Rupert out of her will – and I was relieved on so many levels. The Honeychurch Hall estate would be preserved, at least for now.

Mallory leant in, lowering his voice. 'Speaking of obsessions . . . come with me.'

We made our excuses and slipped away from the terrace, through the side gate and along the flagstone path.

'Where are we going?'

'You'll see.'

I hadn't been in the sunken garden since I first came to the Hall. It was almost unrecognisable now – manicured, peaceful, transformed. Neat stone arbours opened into little secret enclaves tucked between the hedges.

Delia had done wonders. What used to be a mess of brambles and cracked flagstones was now a sanctuary. The old paths had been restored, curving in every direction, set with hundreds of tiny shells and coloured glass. Chipped statues of Greek gods and mythical creatures peeped from the bushes. A pair of stone lions flanked a miniature Parthenon, where a water fountain trickled over Neptune.

It was here that Mallory stopped. He seemed nervous. Took a deep breath. Cleared his throat. Took another one, and then:

'There never were diamonds at the Halt,' he said quietly. 'But I think I've found something better.'

He pulled a small velvet box from his pocket. His hand was shaking slightly as he snapped it open.

An elegant solitaire.

His eyes met mine.

'Marry me, Kat.'

I stared at it, lost for words.

He slipped the ring onto my finger. It was a perfect fit. 'I asked your mother.'

I was still in shock. I hadn't given my answer.

'Yes. Yes. YES!' I flung my arms around his neck and pulled him close.

He gently set me back. 'You're not supposed to cry!' he teased. 'But I'm afraid I've got some disappointing news.'

'What!'

His eyes twinkled with mischief as he withdrew an envelope. 'Take a look.'

Inside were two tickets for the Flying Scotsman for the following weekend.

'How can this be disappointing!' I squealed.

'Because there's no room for my saxophone.' He grinned. 'Though I thought perhaps, bagpipes might do.'

'They will,' I said, laughing. 'As long as you're wearing a kilt.'

Acknowledgements

It's a cliché to say it takes a village to raise a child, but creating a book is much the same – it's a shared effort from the first spark to the finished story.

The spark for *Derailment* came from my fascination with the dozens of railway branch lines that once crisscrossed the south-west of England. Most of them closed in the 1950s and '60s, leaving behind old stone bridges to nowhere, grassy embankments and the remnants of cuttings, along with stations and halts – some abandoned, others lovingly restored as homes or holiday cottages. Please note that the South Devon and Moorland Railway is a figment of my imagination.

From that spark came a lucky introduction – from my friend and fellow writer, Julian Unthank – to Paul Gregory, a railway modeller, who very graciously showed me his spectacular workshop, followed by a delicious lunch with his wife, Kate, at their local pub. Thanks to Paul, a critical clue emerged: one I would never have thought of myself.

No spoiler alert here, but I hope you'll guess what it is when you read it.

Another railway enthusiast is the incredibly talented photographer and avid trainspotter Peter Slater. It was Pete who educated me on the significance of engine numbers and headcodes – who knew? We enjoyed a spectacular day out on the West Somerset Railway, riding a steam train on the 22.75-mile heritage line from Bishops Lydeard to Minehead – a trip that even included fish and chips. A memorable experience, steeped in nostalgia and blessed with magnificent views.

Still on the subject of railways, a special thank you to my friend and neighbour Claire Smith, my go-to expert on all things auction-related. She introduced me to the fascinating world of *railwayama*: everything from vintage posters and luggage labels to station clocks and railway signs.

A note on accuracy: for narrative purposes, I've taken liberties with the official visiting hours at HMP Erlestoke. In real life, they don't allow Monday visits – something I realised far too late to fix without ruining the timeline. I like to call it creative licence, so I hope I'm forgiven.

My deepest thanks go to the amazing publishing team at Constable: my lovely editor, Jen Shannon, whose insight and suggestions shaped *Derailment* into a much stronger story; Jane Selley, my eagle-eyed copy editor, for catching everything I missed; the gifted illustrators Sarah McMenemy for the cover art and Liane Payne for the map of the Honeychurch Hall estate, and of course, Rebecca

Sheppard, our managing editor, who kept everyone on track (no pun intended).

Heartfelt thanks to my wonderful agents, Dominick Abel in the USA and David Grossman in the UK, for their guidance, enthusiasm and unwavering support. It means the world.

Thank you to Andra St Ivanyi and Dr Linda Sterry for their invaluable help with the insulin storyline.

Thank you to Mark Davis, Chairman and CEO of Davis Elen Advertising, who has championed and supported my dream from the very first draft of my first book – and his wife, Sue, who reads everything I write.

And, as always, thank you to my long-suffering family, who tolerate my unsociable, grumpy self on deadline weeks when only my old dog, Draco, will do (he doesn't ask questions).

Finally, to the readers, librarians and booksellers who continue to support my work: on behalf of all authors, we thank you!